Left Broken

Copyright © 2024 by Ashlynn Carter

All rights reserved.

No part of this publication may be reproduced, distributed, or transmitted in any form or by any means, including photocopying, recording, or other electronic or mechanical methods, without the prior written permission of the publisher, except as permitted by U.S. copyright law. For permission requests, contact Ashlynn Carter at ashlynn.carter@proton.me.

The story, all names, characters, and incidents portrayed in this production are fictitious. No identification with actual persons (living or deceased), places, buildings, and products is intended or should be inferred.

Book Cover by Ashlynn Carter

First edition 2024

*For the two biggest sassholes in my life,
you know who you are.
You were my inspiration*

German Dog Commands

English/German:
Fetch/ Bring(bring)
Let Go/ Aus (owss)
Sit/ Sitz (zit-zen)
Stay/ Bleib (blibe)
Down/ Platz (plah-tz)
Heel/ Fuss (foos)
Here/ Hier (heee-a)
Speak/ Gib Laut (gib-lout)
No/ Nien (nine)
Onwards/ Weiter (Wei-ter)
Stand Up/Vorsichtig (Vor-sich-tig)
Gentle/ Voraus (for-owss)
Go Out/ Steh auf (stay-owf)
Guard Alert/ Pass Auf (pass-owf)

Chapter 1

"Miss Addie!"

"Good morning, Mary." Addison Blackwell turned to see the maid hurrying toward her and gave her a friendly smile. "What can I do for you?"

"A letter just arrived from Lord Blackwell." Mary passed Addison a folded letter with her family's seal pressed into the wax. Addison stared at it with mixed feelings.

After a full year, her brother was finally reaching out to her. She turned the letter over to read the front. Addison huffed in frustration. It was not even addressed to her. Of course, it wasn't. Why would it be?

The letter was addressed to the housekeeper, Mrs. Brown. The problem with that was that Mrs. Brown left ten months ago. Addison had written to her brother about the situation, since he was the only one who could hire a new housekeeper. But nothing came of it.

Addison shook her head in annoyance. If he could ignore her letters for a year, she could go for her ride before seeing what he wanted. She took a deep breath to calm her rising irritation before looking back at Mary.

"Thank you, Mary. I will see to this after my ride." Addison smiled at her friend and maid before walking outside and heading for the stables.

What did Jack want? Until three years ago, both of her brothers would visit the family's country estate every few months. Then father became ill. His health would improve and then he would become ill again. Over the course of two years, her father's good days became less and less frequent until he was completely bedridden.

Jack took over father's responsibilities more and more, choosing to stay in London. Daniel was at school or visiting friends most of the time. Gradually, Jack's and Danny's visits became less frequent until a year before father finally passed away, they stopped coming altogether.

Addison took a deep breath and looked down at the letter again. He was probably wanting an update on how the household was faring. Addison tucked the unopened letter into the inside pocket of her coat as she approached the stables.

"There ya are Miss Addie. Spartan was getting restless, so I got 'em ready for ya." Joshua, the young stable hand beamed at her as she stepped into the stable. "I like the new jacket Miss."

"I altered Danny's old jacket from when he was younger." Addison did a spin to give Joshua a full look.

Years ago, Addison had taken some of Danny's old pants and altered them so that they fit her perfectly. They made riding astride a horse so much easier. She loved the feel of flying through the meadows and hills on Spartan at top speed. She would never be able to ride as fast or take the jumps she did if she were riding sidesaddle like a young lady was supposed to.

"I should only be gone a couple of hours today, Joshua. Then we can have our lesson this afternoon." Addison promised. "Have you been practicing your reading?"

"Yes, Miss." Joshua led Spartan outside for her. Normally, Addison preferred to saddle and take care of Spartan herself, but she did not say anything and followed behind, distracted by her brother's sudden letter. "You all right, Miss?" Joshua asked. For a young man of only twelve, Joshua noticed more than Addison would like sometimes.

"Yes. Thank you, Joshua. Do you know where Titan is?" She glanced around the yard but did not see her faithful companion. She let him out two hours ago after he spent the night with her.

"I don't know, Miss Addie. But I'm sure as soon as you call him, he will be here in a flash." Joshua held the reins as Addison placed her foot in the stirrup and swung up into the saddle.

Spartan was a beautiful brown stallion that stood 16 hands high. Her father purchased him for her on her birthday two years ago. Going for rides and escaping out to the stables to brush Spartan had been the only breaks she had gotten from taking care of her ailing father and her other household responsibilities. She treasured this time alone.

Addison let out a single long whistle and waited. Moments later, Titan came barreling around the side of the stables. He was a magnificent beast. James had called his breed a Rottweiler. Addison purchased him eleven months ago after...well, after the incident. She needed a companion that could also help protect her if needed.

"You ready to go boy?" Addison asked looking down at the large dog at her side. He looked up at her with his stub of a tail wagging.

"Have a safe ride Miss." Joshua called out as he went back inside the stables.

"Fuss." Addison commanded Titan in German as she touched her heels to Spartan's sides.

Spartan took off at a gentle gallop with Titan sticking close to their side. They knew the routine. Warmup for a mile or two before a bruising run across the estate lands followed by a cool down as they returned home. Spartan picked up speed and Addison leaned forward. As they flew across the land, her mind returned to her brother's letter.

Two years ago, Jack's visits had stopped completely. The only time she had seen him was when their father died, just over a year ago. Both her brothers had only stayed for three days before leaving again. Jack had returned to London while Danny went on an extended trip with a friend. Danny's constant moving around made it impossible to exchange letters with him.

Danny was only three years older than she was, so she had a much closer relationship with him than she did with Jack. Danny had gone off to school when Addison was five, but they wrote to each other often over the years. Jack was the eldest and ten years older than she was. He should have been in closer contact with her following their father's death given he was now her legal guardian, but he did not. The day after the funeral, both of her brothers left, and she was alone. This time without her father to care for. They had abandoned her when she had needed them the most.

Addison pulled Spartan to a walk and removed the letter from her coat. This letter was not even addressed to her. She had written to Jack to tell him that their steward was arrested. No response. She had sent a letter three weeks later when the housekeeper's husband passed away and she moved away to live with their daughter, asking for Jack to hire a new butler and housekeeper. No response.

Two weeks after that, two men had gotten into the house in the middle of the night. With her being the only one there, it had been terrifying. No one was around to help. The robbers had found her asleep in her bed and had nearly ruined her. Luckily, Joshua heard her scream, and she was able to make it out of her room as Joshua and his father, James the stable master, came running in.

They had saved her that night. James was the one who suggested getting Titan. He had a friend that travelled a lot and found a breed of dog that he thought would be perfect for her. Titan arrived two weeks later. She was glad for her father's insistence of her learning German. Titan had been trained in Germany and all his commands were in German.

Addison had not felt safe after the break-in, even with Titan, and had written to Jack asking for him to come home or allow her to move to London with him. Addison had asked the messenger to wait for a response. He had said that Jack had tossed the letter into the fire without even opening it.

That had been the last time she had written to him. Addison had been hurt and angry by Jack's complete disregard for her. That was the moment she decided she wanted nothing to do with men. All they ever did was abandon her. Her father had gotten sick and died, her brothers both left her completely alone to deal with their dying father, and again after he passed away.

Since Jack was no help, she took on the roles of both steward and housekeeper. With no one to tell her she needed a chaperone; she went riding every day with only Spartan and Titan as companions. And she avoided men at all costs. Well, men she did not know. After the night of the break-in, Addison would have panic attacks when around men she did not know. The doctor said it was her brain's reaction to the trauma she had sustained that night.

Looking back down at the letter, Addison tore it open in frustration. She would at least see what Jack had to say before burning it. She skimmed the letter and blinked. She reread it before looking up at the sky to gauge the time. The sun was directly overhead. The letter said Jack and Danny would be arriving that day around midday.

Addison quickly tucked the letter into her coat again before spurring Spartan back into a run, Titan right beside them. Hopefully, she could get home before they arrived. She needed to make sure their rooms were ready and that the cook knew of the additional people to feed.

Even though Jack had ignored her for two years, she still was excited to see him. And Danny, she could not wait to hear all about his trip. For the last year it had been only her and the servants. Not that she was complaining, all the servants were amazing people. They had become her family and she even helped with the daily chores when she could. With only her in residence there wasn't much to do. In the afternoons she would teach them how to read and write.

The stable yard came into view and there was a flurry of activity. Joshua was rushing out of the open stable's door. Her quick arrival startled him. "Sorry, Joshua. I did not have time to cool him down." She called over her shoulder as she ran for the front of the house.

As she rounded the corner, she saw two men standing between their horses and the front steps talking. Jack stood closest to the house with a scowl on his face. His black hair had grown a bit longer than it was at the funeral. If she still weren't so mad at him, she would run to him first. But the man with his back to her was her target. Danny's dark brown hair seemed a little lighter than she remembered and his shoulders a bit broader, but it had been a year.

"Danny!" She squealed just before reaching him. He spun around and she jumped on him. She was running so fast that she did not get to see the shocked look on his face as she wrapped her arms around his neck and her legs around his waist. His arms came around her as he took several stumbling steps backwards to keep them upright. "I've missed you so much." Addison hugged him tighter.

"Addison!" Jack's disapproving growl had her looking over at him while she continued to cling to Danny. His mouth was in a thin line and his eyes burned with anger. What was his problem?

A throat cleared behind Danny, and she turned her head to see *Danny* smiling at her with pure amusement in his eyes as he stood a few feet away. If Danny was there, then who was she hugging?

Addison slowly put her feet back on the ground and the arms around her loosened as she leaned back to look up at the man's face. Fear nearly made her heart stop. She had no idea who this man was.

She pushed off the stranger's chest as hard as she could, and she stumbled back. She needed to get away. A loud bark sounded in the distance. Titan must sense her anxiety. In her haste to put as much distance between her and the stranger as possible, Addison's boot caught on something, and she began to fall backwards. The stranger reached out and grabbed her arms as he pulled her back to him. She was able to stay on her feet, but she was back to leaning against his chest.

Danny appeared at her side and pulled her to him and squeezed her tight. "Can I get *my* hug now?" Addison gladly allowed her brother to pull her away from the stranger. "I missed you too, Addie." Addison buried her face in his chest and returned his hug. Willing herself to not shake.

"What were you thinking Addison?" Jack asked clearly irritated. "You can't just go jumping into men's arms."

"Leave her alone, Jack. Everyone within earshot could tell Addie thought Ashton was me." Danny defended her as he placed a kiss on the top of her head. Danny turned them to face Jack and the stranger while keeping one arm around her.

"And what are you wearing?" Jack's eyes widened in shock as he took in her appearance. Addison looked down at her repurposed men's clothing and felt a blush rise to her cheeks.

"Are those my clothes?" Danny asked with a laugh.

"They used to be, but they have been mine for years now. Father said I could, and they make riding Spartan easier." She gave a small shrug as she kept her eyes on the ground. No one was ever at the estate, she never had to bother with anyone seeing her in her unconventional riding clothes and starting rumors.

Titan's barking grew louder, and she heard Joshua yelling at him. Joshua sounded like he was fighting with the large dog. With Titan being 135 pounds, there was no way Joshua was going to win a battle of strength. Addison looked at the side of the house where the stables were just as Titan came around the corner pulling Joshua behind him.

Joshua was gripping Titan's thick leather collar and putting in a valiant effort to keep the dog back. Joshua was digging his feet into the ground and leaning back but Titan didn't seem to care about the extra resistance as he continued toward her.

"It is all right Joshua. Let him go." Addison called, stepping away from Danny, and heading in their direction.

Joshua fell onto his rearend as he released the canine. Titan came charging towards the group of men, teeth bared and barking. Addison stepped into his path with her hands on her hips. "Sitz." She said sternly just before he would have collided with her.

Titan skidded to a stop and sat obediently. He continued to keep his eyes on the men behind her as he growled, but he stayed in front of her. She snapped her fingers and Titan shifted his focus to her. He looked up at her with his deep brown eyes.

She knelt on the ground and wrapped her arms around him. She could feel the stares of the men on her as she buried her face in Titan's neck. He let out another low growl. Titan's presence always seemed to calm her anxiety and having him there now helped to settle her nerves about the stranger.

"What is that?" Danny said from behind her. Gravel shifted, and Titan growled again.

She placed a kiss on Titan's large blocky head. "Titan, platz." The dog laid down at her feet as she stood. "This handsome devil is Titan. He is my dog."

"When did you get a dog?" Jack asked as he glared at Titan. He was definitely not happy with her or her dog.

"I have had him for nine months now. You would have known about it if you had actually read my letter instead of throwing it into the fire." Addison snapped at him. How dare he start judging her for getting Titan.

"Don't take that tone with me Addison." Jack took a threatening step towards her. Titan stood and let out a growl as he bared his teeth. Jack stopped in his tracks and glanced down at Titan before taking a step back, returning his blazing eyes to her.

"In the first fifteen minutes of us being here, you have jumped into a man's arms, you are wearing men's clothes, and you are getting down in the dirt with a mangy mutt. Get into the house and put on some proper clothes. Your actions today have been absolutely horrendous." Jack crossed his arms over his chest.

Addison placed a hand on Titan's head. She felt her cheeks flush with anger. "What gives you the right to come into *my* home after a year of you not stepping a foot in here and think it is okay to start telling me what I should and shouldn't do?" She let out two short whistles. "No Jack. You may be my legal guardian, but I have lived on my own for *three* years. Having to look after *myself* and find solutions to *my* own problems. So no, I will not be going inside to change just because *you* deem it 'proper'." Spartan came trotting around the corner of the house. Joshua was chasing him.

"Miss Addie, I just took off his saddle." Joshua looked worried.

"It makes no difference to me, Joshua. Just make sure that he has extra oats when we return." Addison grabbed Spartan's mane and swung up onto his back. She gripped his mane tightly as she shifted into a more comfortable position. She glanced over at Danny and Ashton. They both wore matching looks of shock and disbelief. "Titan, fuss." Addison clicked her tongue and Spartan took off.

Riding bareback was always a thrill. She had spent months in the back field teaching herself the skill and now it was one of her favorite ways to ride. She was extra glad for that skill today. There was no way she would be able to stay near Jack right now. She needed a few moments to calm her anger before facing him again.

"Addie, wait!" Danny's anxious voice called after her, but she did not look back. "Ashton, I'm going after her."

Great. She wanted to be alone and now Danny was going to follow her. Addison squeezed her knees tighter to keep her seat as Spartan increased his speed. They were approaching a tall hedge. They had jumped it many times, but never bareback. There was a first time for everything. Allowing Spartan to change his gait in preparation for the jump, Addison tightened her grip on his mane and squeezed her legs. They were airborne for a few seconds before Spartan's front hooves hit the ground hard.

Addison nearly fell off, but she righted herself. She smiled at how amazing taking that jump had felt. They continued to ride through the field for several minutes. She pulled back on Spartan's reins as they approached the lake.

She was not worried about Spartan wandering off, so she slid from his back and looped his reins over his neck so he wouldn't trip on them. She found a shady spot and sat down with her back against a tree. Titan settled down next to her with his giant head in her lap.

"Sorry boys. I know we just went for a long run, but I just could not stay there right now." Addison closed her eyes. She took several deep breaths to calm herself. She knew seeing Jack again would be strained after hearing that he had burned her letters without reading them, but combining the hurt from that, Jack's demands and judgements, and literally jumping into a stranger's arms, she needed to be alone. Even if it was only for a minute. Danny was sure to arrive soon.

Chapter 2

She had really thought that man was Danny. Then when she had looked up to see those laughing ocean blue eyes looking down at her, she nearly had a heart attack. Addison's mind took her back to that terrible night.

The sounds of loud laughter and heavy footsteps reached her just before her bedroom door flew open. Two men walked in, and she screamed. She was lying on the bed as they advanced toward her with predatory smiles.

One of the men grabbed her arm and yanked her off the bed towards him. He was taller than she was by several inches with a large scar that ran down the left side of his face. He wrapped his arms tightly around her as he tried to kiss her. She fought back as she continued to scream.

The house was practically empty since she was the only member of her family living there. The only other occupants were a handful of servants, and their rooms were completely on the other side of the house. Which meant she was on her own.

The scarred man pushed her toward his friend, giving her the opportunity to grab the fire poker as she fell against the fireplace. Swinging it wildly at the men, Addison was able to make it to the door.

She had made it down the hall and to the stairs before they caught up to her. One of the men tried to grab her again causing her to lose her balance and she tumbled down the grand staircase. She was in so much pain by the time she hit the bottom that she could not move. The men were laughing as they slowly descended the stairs. One of the men sat on top of her.

Titan began to whine, and she stroked his large head. She laid down and Titan moved so that his head rested on her chest. Titan hadn't been with her long when she discovered that he could sense a panic attack coming. His weight on her chest had proven to help calm her before she could be transported back into her nightmares and helped her stay grounded in reality.

Having the flashback from that night was making it hard for her to find her breath. She was slipping back into those terror filled moments. Titan started to lick her hand as she fought her panic. She was safe. Those men were not there anymore. Thank goodness for Joshua and James. They had burst through the front door and the intruders took off. They had called for a doctor and stayed with her for days afterwards. That was when James had suggested getting Titan.

Time slowly ticked by and Titan's weight on her was slowly calming her. Her shaking hand began to run over his sleek fur just as a deep growl rumbled through his body. Danny must have arrived. She hadn't even heard him approaching because of her pounding heart. She kept her eyes closed as she continued to pet Titan. His body tensed as footsteps approached.

"Addie? Are you okay?" Danny's worried voice asked from several feet away. Titan growled as he moved to stand over her protectively.

"Titan, platz." Addison whispered and Titan laid back down, placing his head back on her. He grumbled but stopped his growling. "Just peachy." She said louder to her brother.

"Can...Can I come sit by you?" He asked with uncertainty.

"You might need to keep your distance for a few more minutes. Titan needs to finish doing his thing before he will allow anyone near me." Addison said.

"Addie, you are quite pale. Are you sure you are, okay?" She had never heard so much concern in his voice. He was usually always so happy and even if he was worried, he covered it up with humor.

"The doctor said it is a normal response. Titan helps counter it. Just give us a minute." Silence fell around her, and she began to relax again.

Titan began to nuzzle her neck and she patted his head. He shifted off her and she slowly sat up. Addison ignored the eyes on her and leaned back against the tree, letting out a heavy sigh. Titan laid his head back in her lap. She finally looked across to where Danny's voice had come from and saw both Danny and Ashton watching her with anxious expressions.

"Can I help you gentlemen?" She asked as calmly as she could after seeing Daniel's friend. She had not realized he was there.

"The doctor said what is a normal response?" Danny asked as he slowly moved closer.

"Do not worry about it, Danny. I am fine and I have Titan." Addison gave him a forced smile. Danny settled down next to her as Ashton took a seat facing them. Titan inched farther onto her lap and watched Ashton closely.

"What is it that Titan does?" Ashton asked curiously.

"That sir, should be obvious." Her voice rose in pitch with her anxiety. She cleared her throat and tried again. "He is doing it right now." Addison closed her eyes and breathed in the scent of wildflowers that surrounded the lake. Titan settled more heavily on her legs, and she began to relax.

There was a long pause before Danny spoke again. "Addie, do you always ride like that?"

Addison laughed. "That depends on what you mean." She looked over at her brother. "Yes, I ride Spartan that fast if not faster most days. When bareback, Spartan tends to run slower. Yes, we take jumps frequently but usually with a saddle. And yes, I ride in my custom-made riding attire because seriously, have you tried to ride sidesaddle in a dress? It makes for a much slower and more uncomfortable ride." Addison watched as Danny's eyes widened. "Do not worry, big brother. I have only fallen twice, and Spartan led Joshua and James back to me while Titan stayed nearby. A few stitches and a quick reset of the bones and I was back to riding within a few weeks."

"You what?" Danny sounded horrified.

"I am only kidding." Addison padded Danny's leg. "It was two ribs, and I was back in the saddle in two weeks." She mumbled. Ashton chuckled and Titan cocked his head at him. "Now, seriously, what brings you and Jack back?"

"Jack is hosting a two-week long house party in a few weeks. He invited me and told me to invite some of my friends along." Danny shrugged as if it were no big deal.

"Steh auf." Addison said, and Titan got up. She stood and began to pace. A house party? For two weeks? Why was she not notified of this sooner? How was she going to get everything ready in time and how many guests were expected? Titan began to whine again. He jumped in front of her, but she walked around him. He began to bite at her pants, and she tried to push his head away. "Nein, Titan." She snapped.

Addison changed her course and walked toward the lake to get Titan to leave her alone while she thought. She got to the end of the dock and turned around to start her return pace back.

Titan did not like that she wasn't paying attention to him and jumped up on her. He had done that before when he could feel her anxiety rise and she wasn't paying attention. However, this time it sent both of them into the lake. Her head broke the surface as she gasped for air. The water was freezing.

"Titan!" She yelled at the dog as he swam circles around her.

Danny and Ashton were running towards her as she was pulling herself back onto the deck. "Are you okay?" Danny asked, dragging her away from the edge.

"Just get that goofball out of the water." Shivering, Addison pointed to Titan as he was continuing to whine and swim in circles. Once Titan was back on dry land, Titan shook the water from his black and tan coat. "Hier." Addison's stern tone had Titan slinking towards her. A few feet from her he dropped onto his belly and crawled the rest of the way to her side. She hugged him tightly. "Time to go home." She whispered. Danny reached down and helped her to her feet. "We need to hurry home. I am sure Jack is going to be ecstatic when he discovers a few things."

"Would you like help mounting?" Danny asked.

"I don't require any assistance to get on my horse." Addison called over her shoulder as she ran towards Spartan. He was facing away from her, and she used her momentum to vault herself up over Spartan's rear and land on his back. She looked back to see Danny and Ashton gawking at her with open mouths. "Come on, gentlemen. I said we need to hurry. Titan, fuss." She tapped Spartan's sides, and he galloped forward, Titan right beside them.

It did not take long before she heard hoofbeats coming up fast behind her. "Addie, that was dangerous." Danny said pulling even with her.

"That wasn't dangerous." She glanced over at him. "Spartan and I have been together for a few years now and we share a special bond. Would you like to know what is dangerous?" Addison swung her leg over Spartan's back and continued to ride with both legs over one side. The nervous look on Danny's face was priceless and she laughed. Addison straddled Spartan again before continuing. "Trying to figure out how to clean out, load and shoot a gun by yourself. I nearly shot Titan by accident."

"You did what?" Danny's face had paled. "You tried to teach yourself how to shoot a gun? Addie, please tell me you are joking."

"I sure did. You can even ask Joshua. And I did not just try, I succeeded. Every Thursday for the past nine months, I practice." Addison smiled sweetly at her brother who looked sick. "I'll race you home." Addison called as Spartan took off across the field.

Addison was freezing cold and just wanted to change into something dry. She could hear the other two horses following close behind her. Spartan slowed his pace as he entered the stable yard. Joshua came running out and grabbed hold of Spartan's reins.

"Miss Addie! What happened? You weren't trying to stand on Spartan again, were you?" The boy sounded worried as he took in her drenched appearance.

"I promised you and your father after the broken ribs that I would give up on that endeavor and I would never break a promise." Addison gave Joshua a hug. "Titan pushed me in the lake again. If you can get him bathed in time for bed, I will make sure Mrs. Harvey cooks up some of your favorite sweets." She gave Joshua a wink and a huge smile spread across his face.

"Yes, Miss. And Mr. Danny, My Lord, I can take your mounts in as well." Joshua offered.

"Thank you, Joshua." Danny said quietly. "Does Addie really go shooting?"

"Every Thursday, sir." Joshua said with pride in his voice. "Titan, hier." Joshua said in a firm tone and Titan ran back to the boy.

Addison heard mumbling and she smiled as she walked out of the stables heading for the servant's entrance. Heavy boots on the ground behind her let her know that her brother was right behind her. As they entered the kitchen, it was in complete chaos.

"Mrs. Harvey, what is going on?" Addison asked in concern.

"There you are." The older woman said, relief evident in her voice. "Lord Blackwell is asking for the housekeeper, and I wasn't planning on the additional three mouths to feed and..."

"Take a deep breath." Addison grabbed the frantic woman's shoulders. "I will speak with Lord Blackwell about the housekeeper. Make beef and vegetable soup with rolls for dinner. It will not take much time to cook and will feed several people. For dessert, we can have the pie we were saving for tomorrow night." Addison took control and began assigning maids to do various tasks.

She finally turned to Mary. "Mary, I need a bath drawn up, please. Titan shoved me in the lake. And could you please assist me for this evening as well." Addison rarely needed Mary's help since she never went anywhere and most of the time she was in Daniel's old clothes. But tonight, she was going to have to be the lady she had been raised to be.

"Yes, Miss." Mary scurried off and everything was back to running smoothly.

Addison continued through the kitchen and toward the stairs. "That was impressive Addie." Danny complimented.

"I have been running this household for three years, Daniel Blackwell. Keeping it in order is my job." Addison said over her shoulder as she climbed the stairs. At the top she turned to her right and began walking down the hall.

"Where are you going?" Danny asked.

"My room." Addison stopped and turned around to face him.

"The family wing is that way." Danny pointed down the opposite hallway with his brows furrowed.

"Yes, but my room is at the end of this hall." Addison turned around and continued walking to her room. She turned the knob and stepped inside before closing and locking the door, letting out a heavy sigh.

She couldn't blame Danny for being confused with all the changes with her. He was gone with no way to reach him. He had no idea about the attacks or her lingering fear about sleeping in her old room or being around men. She was going to have to tell him eventually, but she hated reliving those memories. It was bad enough that they haunted her in her dreams most nights.

An hour later, Addison was clean and in a 'proper' dress. She loved this dress. The emerald green color contrasted nicely with her tanned skin and auburn hair. It had a high waist that allowed the fabric to flow around her. Mary had expertly pulled her hair up into a beautiful twist. There were a few curls left loose around her face to soften the look. Addison felt confident and ready to face her brothers.

She slowly walked down the stairs. Just before entering the drawing room a maid caught her attention and gave her a nod. Conversation ceased as she stepped into the room. Her two brothers and Ashton turned to face her. Jack still looked irritated with her but at least he was no longer glowering. Danny's smile stretched all the way to his ears. Ashton kept his stoic expression, but something flashed in his eyes that she could not read.

"Dinner is ready, gentlemen. If you would please follow me." Addison started to turn back to the door, but Jack's scoffing stopped her.

"The housekeeper or butler is supposed to announce dinner, Addison." Jack looked at her as if she were an idiot.

Addison clenched her jaw, and she met his glare with one of her own. "I am sorry. We can wait until you hire new ones then. I am not that hungry anyway." Addison moved to the couch and sat down. She picked up the book she had been reading the night before and opened it.

"What are you talking about, Addison?" Jack crossed his arms over his chest.

Addison turned the pages finding where she had left off. "I mean, shortly after father passed away our dear butler, Mr. Brown, fell ill and died as well. Mrs. Brown left to live with her daughter. I wrote to you telling you about the vacant butler and housekeeper positions, but since they have not been filled yet, I am guessing you did not read that letter either." Silence. Addison continued to read her book.

"So, who has been doing the job of butler and housekeeper?" Jack asked.

"I have." Addison didn't look up as she turned another page.

She was able to read four more pages before Jack finally spoke again. "I will look for replacements in the morning. Let us just head into dinner." Addison looked up and caught Ashton's eyes on her. He gave her a small nod and she lowered her gaze again.

"My dearest sister, can I please escort the queen of this palace into dinner?" Danny bowed to her as he offered her his hand. She placed her hand in his and allowed him to help her to her feet. They followed Jack out of the drawing room with Ashton bringing up the rear. "What has been going on this last year, Addie?" Danny whispered to her so that no one else could hear.

Addison glanced over at him with a tight smile and shook her head. "It will take more than this small walk to the table to tell you everything." They remained silent for the rest of the walk to the dining room. Danny gave her a small smile before he pulled her chair out for her.

An uncomfortable silence filled the room as dinner got underway. Addison just wanted this to be over with so that she could escape to her room. She couldn't take this kind of quiet anymore.

"Jack, I heard you are planning on having a house party?" Addison tried to sound like it was an exciting prospect.

"Yes, my guests will start arriving in two weeks. Until I get a new housekeeper, I will need you to continue to manage things." Jack did not even look at her.

"How many guests are you expecting? Do you have any specific activities you wish to have?" Addison's anxiety started to climb a little.

"I have six guests coming on top of any that Daniel has invited. We plan to have the mornings to do what we want before joining you for whatever activities you choose." Jack glanced at her briefly before taking a bite of his roll.

"I only invited Ashton so that is only seven guests total." Danny supplied.

Okay so only seven additional people. She could do this. Being in charge of activities would be daunting, especially since she didn't know anyone's preferences or what was acceptable for gatherings such as this.

"How many females and how many males? That way I can plan activities accordingly." Addison put her spoon down and took a sip of water.

"All gentlemen." Jack said. Addison choked on her water. Tears leaked from her eyes as she continued to cough. She couldn't seem to stop. Danny got up from his chair and moved to her side, patting her back.

"Excuse me?" She wheezed out in disbelief as she took another sip of water to clear her throat.

"I said that we will have seven male guests here for a house party. We will do our own thing in the mornings and then spend the afternoons and evenings with you." Jack gave her a hard look. "I expect you to act the part of a lady while my guests are here, Addison. I know for a fact, that father employed tutors for you."

Addison was struggling to breathe. Hopefully, the gentlemen at the table would assume it was from nearly choking to death. Seven gentlemen? Here at the house? There was no way she was going to survive this.

"Excuse me." Addison stood from the table and practically ran from the room.

Chapter 3

Ashton Fenwick watched as Miss Blackwell entered her room. Daniel stood in confusion as he watched his sister disappear down the guest wing. The maid that Miss Blackwell had called Mary came up the stairs and stopped when she saw them.

"This way Mr. Blackwell, Lord Fenwick." She began walking down the family wing. She showed them to their rooms before hurrying off.

Ashton gave Daniel a nod before stepping into his room. He couldn't help the smile that spread across his face as he pulled off his wet coat. Pulling the dog out of the lake had left his shirt and coat soaked.

Miss Blackwell was not what he had expected from all the stories he had heard about her over the years. Daniel had painted her as a mischievous child. Not a beautiful grown woman.

His mind wandered back to earlier that day, while he changed into dry clothes. He had not expected to be accosted within ten minutes of arriving at his friend's home.

Daniel had been his friend from the first year of school. As they grew older, they often spent breaks together. Especially, over the last few years.

Daniel's father became very sick. It had been hard on Daniel and Ashton did his best to be there for his friend. Then the death of Daniel's father had caused Daniel to spiral down into a dark place, becoming consumed by his grief.

Ashton suggested going on a trip where they would travel to new places and see the world; hoping to provide Daniel with a distraction. Daniel had jumped at that idea and the day after his father's funeral, the two of them had left. They originally planned to be gone for only a few months, but they postponed their return a few times. They ended up being gone for a year.

Once they returned, Daniel's older brother, Jack, invited them to their country estate for a house party. Ashton did not see a reason to go home yet, so he accepted the invitation and travelled with the brothers.

Their arrival had been unexpected to say the least. A footman had stepped out of the front door with a confused expression. Jack had asked for Mrs. Brown and the young man had become flustered. He had run back inside.

A boy around twelve came running around the side of the house not long after that. Seeing it was Jack and Daniel, the boy had paled before running back the way he had come. Jack was fuming that not even his sister was there to greet them.

Several minutes passed before a woman had yelled Daniel's name. Turning around to see who it was, Ashton found himself nearly knocked to the ground. Whoever it was, was so excited to see Daniel that they literally wrapped themselves around Ashton. Her body had tensed before she slowly lowered herself back to the ground. When she had stepped back, Ashton found himself looking into gorgeous green eyes.

She was younger than Daniel and himself, but not by much. She had long auburn hair that hung in a braid down her back. She was stunningly beautiful. Ashton couldn't help his growing smile as he thought of her surprised expression when she realized he was not her brother.

His smile slipped from his face as he remembered the look of complete terror that filled her eyes a moment later. She stumbled back and he reached out to grab her and pulled her back to him before she could fall. He could feel her shaking, her fear was palpable. Something bad had happened to the young woman, and he did not like it.

Ashton was confused with the tension that rose among the small group and why Jack had berated the woman. Before he could make sense of everything going on, Miss Blackwell was sitting astride a large brown stallion and she was gone, followed closely by a giant black and tan dog.

Ashton buttoned up his clean shirt as he thought about the dog and its behavior at the lake. It seemed to pick up on Miss Blackwell's distress. Something about the house party seemed to upset her. The look of confusion and worry on Daniel's face as they watched Miss Blackwell pace told him that this was not normal behavior for his sister. Then she and the dog had fallen into the lake.

Ashton nearly fell in trying to pull the large dog up out of the water. He was shaking the water from his sleeves when Miss Blackwell took off for her horse. She was not slowing down, if anything she was speeding up.

He watched in amazement as she vaulted over the horse's rear and landed on his back. Ashton's smile returned as the image of Miss Blackwell's dazzling smile came to him.

Daniel had been frustrated when Miss Blackwell rode off again. Ashton had to hold back a laugh as they raced after the crazy woman as she galloped across the field heading back to the house. She was a puzzle. She still hadn't really acknowledged his presence. Usually, his title garnered him more attention than he wanted.

After they got back to the house, he watched in amazement as, once again, Miss Blackwell seemed to transform. When they first arrived at the house, she was the overly excited younger sister, then a terrified young woman, then hot tempered. At the lake she had seemed anxious and fearful, then a daredevil, then intriguing. Now she was confident and took charge. In less than five minutes, she had calmed an overwhelmed cook and brought order back to the household.

To say Ashton was fascinated by Miss Addison Blackwell would be an understatement. He found himself wanting to know everything about her and discover what other sides she had to her.

Ashton pulled on his dinner coat and tugged at the cuffs. A smile spread across his face as he remembered how beautiful Miss Blackwell was in her men's clothes. She had pulled the look off amazingly.

Ashton shook his head to clear the image of Miss Blackwell from his mind as he stepped into the hallway. He was not there to get to know Miss Blackwell. He was there to help his best friend through his grief and to avoid his own mother's constant match-making attempts.

Ashton walked swiftly down the stairs and into the drawing room. Both Jack and Daniel were already there. "So, tell me Daniel, how was your travels?" Jack asked as Ashton sat in a chair near the brothers.

"It was good. We spent the last several weeks near the coast." Daniel responded stiffly. Ashton could see that there was something bothering him. He did not have to wait long before Daniel got right to the issue. "What did Addison mean when she said you burned her letter?"

Jack let out a tense breath as he ran his hand through his black hair. Jack had always been more serious than Daniel, but at that moment, Ashton could see a tension and tiredness in him that seemed to add years to his appearance.

"Father's illness and death was hard on all of us. Unlike you, I had to stay and take over the household. I stayed in London. It was easier to not have the reminders of what I had lost." Jack shook his head slightly. "I was not in a good place after the funeral. When I received a letter from Addison, it was too hard to read it. I did not want any reminders of father, and Addison was another reminder. I knew Mr. and Mrs. Brown would take good care of her and if she needed anything, they would send me word. Mr. Drake was also great at his job, so I did not need to make any visits back here. Father doted on Addison, and she was always with him. I could not deal with the pain of seeing or hearing from her when thoughts of Addison always brought thoughts of father."

Daniel glared at his brother who returned his glare with a scowl. Daniel wasn't the only one of the family that was struggling with the previous Lord Blackwell's death. A noise at the door drew everyone's attention. Miss Blackwell stood in the doorway in a beautiful dark green colored gown that matched her eyes. Her hair was expertly twisted up on her head with a few curls framing her face. She took his breath away.

"Dinner is ready, gentlemen. If you would please follow me." Miss Blackwell said. As she started to turn back to the door, Jack scoffed. She slowly turned back to them.

Ashton sat and watched in irritation at the way Jack talked to Miss Blackwell. He was impressed with the way Miss Blackwell handled Jack's hostility towards her. When Jack finally said they could have dinner, Ashton was beyond frustrated with the man and confused about what had happened to the siblings.

From all the stories Daniel told him over the years, all three of the Blackwell siblings were close. They played games, wrote to each other, and spent as much time as possible together. Daniel had slowly stopped talking about his family after his father became ill. Now, Miss Blackwell was a chameleon, Daniel had bouts of depression, and Jack was distant.

Ashton felt a small stab of jealousy as he watched Daniel escort Miss Blackwell to the dining room. He would have loved to escort her himself. Shoving the unwanted feelings down, Ashton followed behind them as they moved out into the hallway.

Daniel whispered something into his sister's ear, and she gave a small shake of her head. Daniel looked even more upset than before as they all took their seats.

The tension was so thick that Ashton was finding it hard to sit still. All he wanted to do was head outside so he could breathe. Daniel frequently glanced at his sister who looked more and more tense. Jack seemed not to notice anyone.

Dinner continued in silence until Miss Blackwell spoke. She paled as the conversation progressed. Even though Jack was speaking to her, he never looked at Miss Blackwell. Daniel's jaw muscle kept flexing as he watched her.

Miss Blackwell went ghostly white as she choked on her water. Daniel ran to her side, but Jack remained in his seat, eyes glued to his plate. Ashton fought the urge to run to her side and the desire to punch Jack in the face for his callous behavior.

"Excuse me." She stood from the table and practically ran from the room.

Daniel watched his sister leave and a muscle ticked in his jaw. When Ashton and Daniel's eyes met, Ashton could tell that Daniel was furious with Jack. Ashton made the decision to stay with Daniel as long as he needed him to in order to sort through whatever had happened during their year of travel.

"What are you doing, Jack?" Daniel growled out. "Why are you acting like this with Addison?"

"She is running around like she is still a child. Her actions today have shown her to still be impulsive, reckless, and hot-tempered. As the hostess, she will be required to show some dignity and restraint." Jack slammed his hand on the table.

"Have you noticed anything different about Addison since we have been back?" Daniel snapped. Jack didn't say anything as he glared at Daniel. "Addie looks haunted. After father's funeral, even with her tears and grief she still had that spark in her eyes, but it is no longer there, Jack. She is guarded and at times fearful. Addison was never afraid of anything. Something has happened during the last year that we do not know about, and I intend to find out what." Daniel stormed from the room.

Ashton quickly excused himself and followed Daniel as he went upstairs. He finally caught up to Daniel as he banged on Miss Blackwell's bedroom door. There was no answer.

Daniel ran his hand through his hair. "Something is wrong, Ashton. I have never seen Addie get so upset by the prospect of visitors. Or be so anxious. She was always carefree and fearless."

Ashton did not know what to say. He had only glimpsed Miss Blackwell once at the funeral. He didn't even think they had been introduced. "Maybe she went to the kitchen." He finally suggested and they made their way back downstairs.

The kitchen had several maids running around and the cook was finishing up with something on the stove. He and Daniel paused just inside the room as Daniel scanned the occupants. Someone caught his attention and Ashton's gaze followed his friend's. The maid that showed them to their rooms was wiping off a dish.

"Mary." Daniel called and the maid looked up, surprised.

"Mr. Blackwell. My Lord." She turned to them and curtsied. Daniel motioned for her to come closer. She kept her eyes directed to the ground as she moved to stand in front of them.

"Have you seen Addie?" Daniel asked anxiously.

Mary's eyes snapped up to Daniel's and she became flustered. "Miss Addie? Has something happened to her?"

"During dinner she seemed to become anxious and then left quickly." Daniel again ran his hand through his hair.

"If she was anxious, sir, she would go to find Titan, if he wasn't with her already." Mary responded. Ashton could see the worry in the maid's eyes. Something was definitely not right with Miss Blackwell and Ashton's own anxiety began to climb.

"The dog?" Daniel asked and the maid nodded. "No, he wasn't there with her." Mary's eyes widened as if that news was a shock. "If Titan wasn't with her, where would he be?"

"He would most likely be in the stables, sir." Mary glanced towards the door on the opposite wall. It was slightly ajar. Ashton began heading for it as Daniel thanked Mary and followed him outside.

They walked quickly across the yard and entered the stables. The young stable hand was cleaning a saddle as they walked in. He glanced up and jumped to his feet before giving them a quick bow. Daniel waved the boy off and he resumed his work.

Daniel moved over to the brown stallion's stall and peeked over but shook his head. Miss Blackwell was not hiding with her horse then. Daniel and Ashton began silently checking all the stalls. Ashton became more tense as the time ticked by and they still had not found Miss Blackwell.

"Can I help you with something, Mr. Blackwell?" The boy finally asked.

"You're James' son, Joshua, correct?" Daniel asked, taking a step in the boy's direction.

"Yes, sir." The boy put his supplies down and stood. "Are you looking for something? Maybe I can help."

"Yes, Joshua. We are looking for Miss Blackwell, have you seen her?" Ashton asked as he moved to stand next to Daniel.

The boy's brow furrowed. "No, sir. I have been waiting for her to come and get Titan."

"So, Titan is still here?" Daniel asked as he looked around for the large black dog. "She was upset after dinner and left rather quickly. Mary said she would go to Titan."

"If Miss Addie were upset, Mr. Blackwell, she would be with Titan. Usually, he sleeps with her in the house, but I didn't see her come get him." Joshua said as he moved towards a door off to the side.

He gestured for them to follow him as he led the way outside and around to the back of the stables. There was an enclosure that was attached to the wall of the barn. It had straw strewn on the floor.

As they approached, they saw a large dark figure lying in the hay. It wasn't until they reached the fence that they recognized the dark form of Miss Blackwell lying in the straw with the dog. She seemed to be sleeping.

"Oh, no. Miss Addie, not again." Joshua said sadly.

A breeze blew and Ashton saw Miss Blackwell shiver. It wasn't freezing out, but it wasn't warm either. In her light evening gown, Miss Blackwell had to be feeling the night's chill much more than he was.

Ashton took his jacket off and slipped inside the open gate. The dog lifted his massive head off Miss Blackwell and growled. Ashton froze for just a second before moving even slower as he tried not to upset the dog, but still be able to put his coat over Miss Blackwell.

Chapter 4

Addison ran out of the kitchen making a beeline for the back of the stables where Titan had an enclosure. She flung the gate open, and the large dog was right there. She knelt in the fresh straw and wrapped her arms around Titan's neck and allowed the tears to fall. She did not know how long she had sat there when her tears finally dried but she was exhausted.

Panic attacks always made her feel drained of energy. She laid down and Titan cuddled up to her. She put her arm around his neck and closed her eyes. It was a cold night, but Addison didn't have the strength to get up and go inside. She scooted closer to Titan, absorbing his warmth. This would not be the first time she had slept outside with him. Addison closed her eyes and tried to relax.

"If Miss Addie was upset Mr. Blackwell, she would be with Titan. Usually, he sleeps with her in the house, but I didn't see her come get him." Joshua's voice came from the other side of the wall, pulling her from sleep. A few moments later, footsteps approached. "Oh, no. Miss Addie, not again." Joshua sounded pained.

Titan lifted his head a little off her as he growled. "Easy boy, I'm just going to put this on your girl, so she isn't so cold." Mr. Ashton's voice was soft as something was draped over her arms. Titan relaxed again as he put his head back down on her shoulder.

"What is going on with her Joshua? Addie never used to get upset when it came to social gatherings." Danny asked quietly.

"It's not really social gatherings she has an issue with sir. It's men she doesn't know, that she struggles with." Joshua sounded so sad. Addie squeezed her eyes closed. Danny needed to know. But she didn't know if she could be the one to tell him, so she let Joshua continue.

"I think it started when the steward, Mr. Drake, attacked her when he found her going over the books right after the funeral. I'm not sure why he was so upset, but he beat her up pretty good by the time Mr. Brown found them in the study."

"What? Why wasn't Jack or I notified of this?" Danny asked angrily.

"From what I know, Miss Addie did send a letter to Lord Blackwell when she was able to write again. But like I said, that was only the start of her anxiety. The nightmares and panic attacks came after the break-in." Joshua explained.

"Break-in?" Danny and Mr. Ashton said in unison. Mr. Ashton sounded like he was still in the encloser with her and Titan.

"Something had spooked the horses. My father and I got up and were trying to settle 'em down when we heard screaming. Father grabbed his rifle and ran for the house. When we were able to get the front door open, we saw them." Joshua's voice became soft. "There were two men there. One was holding Miss Addie's legs down while the other sat on top of her. They saw us and took off. Father took several shots at 'em, but we never did find them.

"Miss Addie's face was covered in blood and there was blood on the grand staircase. We think she fell down the stairs. She was dazed and tried to fight whoever touched her. The doctor had to sedate her in order to clean her up and stitch the cut on her head. Mary stayed with her for several nights before they moved her stuff to the opposite side of the house. Mary said the memories were too much for her and the nightmares were bad." Joshua sniffed. "Father brought home Titan for her to be her protector since she lives up at the big house by herself. But Titan doesn't just protect her, he is able to sense a rising panic attack in her and is able to calm her."

"That's why she ran out here." Mr. Ashton's voice said softly. "She had a panic attack thinking about seven unknown men being in her home."

"Seven! Why would Lord Blackwell do that? I was with her when she wrote the letter to him explaining the break-in. She even said she asked him to either come back or allow her to move to London with him. He should know about her fear of men." Joshua sounded shocked and angry.

"What happened before you and your father showed up? Did they hurt her?" Danny sounded like he was in shock.

"She won't tell us. She has only said that they didn't hurt her in...that way." Joshua cleared his throat.

"It is only going to get colder. She cannot stay out here all night. Will the dog bite us if we try to move her up to her room?" Danny asked.

"If you take her and he isn't able to follow, Titan probably will bite you. The dog is smart, though, if he knows you are taking her to safety and allow him to follow, you shouldn't have an issue. He only responds to German." Joshua said.

"Ashton, you are going to have to carry her. My shoulder is not fully recovered from that fall last week. I will get the dog." Danny said as he moved closer. "Hier Titan. Let us get Addie up to her bed. You can lay with her up there."

Addison felt Titan move away from her just before arms slipped under her and lifted her up. She shivered and the arms tightened around her. She laid her head on Mr. Ashton's shoulder. She was too tired to fight and for some reason she knew that Mr. Ashton wouldn't hurt her.

Before she knew it, she was being put down on her bed. Her eyes flitted open and connected with ocean blue ones that were filled with concern. Titan plopped down on the bed beside her, and she gave a small smile to Ashton before she closed her eyes again. Someone pulled the blanket over her, and she snuggled more under it.

"Thank you, Ashton." Danny let out a heavy sigh. "I cannot believe what Addie has been through since father passed away. I should have stayed. I should have been here."

"Hey Dan, do not beat yourself up over the past. If you had stayed, maybe things would have turned out differently, but you didn't and you can't change that. Miss Blackwell reached out to your brother multiple times, but he seems oblivious to everything." Mr. Ashton kept his voice low.

"I'm going to stay here tonight to make sure she is okay." Danny said.

"Do you want some company?" Mr. Ashton asked.

"Thanks Ashton." The room went quiet except for Titan's snoring. Addison's exhaustion finally pulled her into a deep sleep.

* * *

Addison was back in her old room. There was the sound of heavy boots stomping down the hallway and men's laughter. The sounds stopped, and Addison sat up. Who was in the house? Did Jack come home for a visit? The door crashed open, and she froze in fear as two men walked in. When they spotted her sitting there, the evil smiles on their faces made her blood run cold.

The first man marched over to the bed and reached for her. Addison tried to get off the other side of the bed, but he grabbed her arm and yanked her towards him. He wrapped his arms around her and tried to kiss her. Addison screamed and turned her head so that his lips ended up touching her cheek instead of her lips. He continued to kiss her along her neck as she struggled against him.

"Addie! Wake up!" Danny's voice cut through the man's evil laugh as he shoved her towards his friend. She tripped over her feet, falling against the fireplace. "Addison, open your eyes." Danny's anxious voice yelled again.

Addison sat up gasping for air as she looked around frantically, fully expecting to see the two large men in her room. It was still dark outside, and Danny sat on the edge of her bed while a tall shadow stood just over his shoulder. Danny reached a hand towards her, and she flinched as she tried to back away from him.

Tears started to fall as she slowly got off the bed and sat on the floor. Titan pressed his head against her face and neck as he whined. Addison tried to take slow deep breaths, but they just ended in sobs. A hand softly touched her shoulder and she jumped. Danny was crouched next to her with tears in his eyes. Addison reached for him, and he gathered her into his arms. She clung to her brother as the tears continued to come.

"I'm so sorry Addie. I should have been here." Danny whispered into her hair. "I'm so sorry."

Danny held her tight until her tears slowed. Her crying finally stopped and her shaking set in. A blanket was draped over her, and Addison looked up. Blue eyes met hers and she squeezed her eyes closed. Why did he have to see her right now? Danny ran his hand over her hair. She winced as one of her hairpins stabbed into her head.

"Here. Let me help." Mr. Ashton said softly. His hands started pulling pins out of her hair, releasing them from their hold. When he was done, he moved back a few feet, giving her distance.

"Thank you." She whispered as she leaned more comfortably against Danny. "I'm sorry I woke you."

"Really? You just had a major nightmare. And I mean major. It took me several minutes to wake you up and you are apologizing for waking me. Addie, please do not ever feel sorry for waking me. Ever." Danny pulled her tighter against his side. Titan laid down close to her legs and whined.

Addison reached down and ran her hand over Titan's head. "How did Titan take it this time?" she asked quietly.

"The dog? He was the one that originally woke us. He started pacing on the bed and pawing at you. When you did not wake up from all that, we got worried and then you screamed." Danny kissed the top of her head. "What did they do to you?"

Addison's heart rate started to accelerate. Flashes from that night started to come back. The hands. The lips on her. The things they said they were going to do to her. Titan stood up and began pacing again.

"Dan, the dog." Mr. Ashton said pointing to Titan.

Titan began to nudge her, and she stood up. Both Danny and Ashton did as well. "Hier, Titan." Addison said as she climbed back onto the bed. She laid down on her back and allowed Titan's large head to settle on her chest. "He can sense it." Addison let out a slow breath.

Danny sat down next to her and ran his fingers through her hair like he used to do when they were kids. Addison closed her eyes and took a few deep breaths. "Do you remember when we were kids and I refused to let you climb up into my favorite tree?" Daniel asked and Addison couldn't stop the laugh that surfaced at the childhood memories. "I will take that as a yes then. You were so angry with me."

"Was this the time I smeared honey all over the tree branches or the time I threw rocks at you till you fell and dislocated your elbow?" Addison smiled up at him.

"I was thinking about the honey incident, dear sister." Danny chuckled. "I threw you in the lake for making me all sticky. You ended up getting sick from being in the freezing water."

"You personally helped Mrs. Harvey make me soup and you stayed with me until I got better." Addison yawned.

"I also promised you that I would always protect you." He swallowed hard. "I failed you, Addie and I'm sorry."

Addison sat up and caught sight of Mr. Ashton sitting in a chair in the corner watching them. She ignored him and looked at Danny. His eyes were cast down and his jaw was clenched. "Listen to me, Daniel Blackwell. The men from the break-in did nothing to harm me physically. Well, nothing that was major. I got away from them when they came into my room, and I tripped on my way down the stairs. I was injured from my fall. James and Joshua came in and scared the men away. I am perfectly fine." Addison tried to reassure her brother, but he gave her a hard look.

"They may not have harmed you physically but judging by your panic attack at the mention of Jack's friends spending a fortnight here and your nightmare, I would bet anything that those men mentally hurt you. As your brother, it is my job to watch out for you." Danny grabbed her hand and squeezed it.

"Danny, you are probably exhausted from travelling and staying up with me. You should go to bed. We can talk more about this tomorrow." The look on his face let her know that he was about to argue. "I am fine. Really, I am. It was just a stressful day." Addison climbed off the bed and held open her door. Danny slowly walked to the door but paused just before leaving. "I promise I am fine. The doctor said this is perfectly normal after experiencing something so…shocking. I have Titan now and everything is fine." Danny nodded and stepped into the hall. Addison was about to shut the door but remembered the other man that was in there with her. "You too, sir. Out."

Mr. Ashton stood from his chair and moved slowly across the room to the door. He stepped out into the hall next to Danny. "If you need me, just come to my room, okay?" Danny said. "And in the morning, I will move into the room next to yours. Then we are going to talk."

"I will instruct a maid to switch the rooms in the morning. All the other guests will be placed in the family wing with Jack." Addison yawned. "Good night, gentlemen." She said as she closed and locked the door. She climbed back into the bed and pulled the covers up. "Good night, Titan." The dog laid across her as sleep over came her again.

Chapter 5

Addison woke up feeling refreshed. She stretched and let out a soft sigh. Addison looked at the clock near her fireplace; 5:30am. It had been a very long time since she had slept so well. Titan was pacing by the door needing to go out, so she dressed quickly in a light green morning dress. She put her boots on and slipped out the door with Titan on her heels.

The sun was just starting to rise when Addison let Titan outside. He took off across the yard letting out several barks. Addison turned back to the kitchen with her hands on her hips. Mrs. Harvey wasn't up yet but Addison had too much energy to just sit around. Plus, she did her best thinking when she was working, and she had a lot of thinking she needed to do. With the house party starting in two weeks, she needed to get rooms prepared, meals planned, activities scheduled, and so many other things.

Addison pulled out a large bowl and set it on the prep table as she began to cook breakfast. She had made the dough for biscuits and was starting on the bacon by the time Mrs. Harvey walked into the kitchen. They talked about meals for the next two weeks and what needed to be purchased to feed all the extra mouths.

Several maids took breakfast out to the breakfast room while Addison helped clean up. When she was done, Addison and Mrs. Harvey made their way to the breakfast room with the last two dishes full of fruit. As they entered the room, Addison noticed that all three gentlemen were already sitting at the table. Addison put the bowl of fruit on the side table before turning back to the room.

She skipped over to Jack and dipped into a deep curtsey. "Good morning, Lord Blackwell." She straightened up and pressed a quick kiss to Jack's cheek before turning to Danny. "Beautiful morning isn't it, Mr. Blackwell?" She curtsied to Danny who was holding back a laugh and kissed his cheek as well. Addison twirled as she went back to the side table and dished up some eggs and a piece of toast. She turned around and saw everyone watching her with various degrees of surprise. She set her plate down and did a small curtsey in Ashton's direction. "And good morning to you too, sir." She said with less enthusiasm.

"Addison, you should address his lordship by the proper title." Jack said with a confused look still on his face.

"Lord, huh?" Addison mumbled. Lord Ashton's eyes sparked with humor as he watched her. Addison dipped into a deeper curtsey. "Good morning, My Lord." She gave him a small smile and she noticed a hint of dimples on his cheeks as she took her seat. Mr. Ashton gave her a wink before turning back to his food.

She felt a blush rise to her cheeks as she raised her fork to her mouth. She was chewing her second bite when Danny spoke. "You seem to be in a much better mood this morning Addie."

"It's amazing what sleep can do for a person's outlook on life." Addison smiled over at Danny before taking another bite.

"How much sleep were you able to get?" Jack asked in surprise.

"Umm. I was up by five thirty, so three hours? Maybe four?" Addison furrowed her brows as she tried to think how many hours she had actually slept.

"You are this chipper after three hours of sleep? How much sleep do you usually get?" Jack's brows drew together.

"Miss Addie." Mary stood in the doorway with an anxious expression on her face.

Addison stood from her place as she shoved another forkful into her mouth. "I'm sorry gentlemen I must be going." As Addison passed Jack, she paused as he studied her. "Jack, I don't usually sleep." She shrugged her shoulders as if it were no big deal before continuing towards the door.

"Wait, Addie. You have only had a few bites to eat. Surely whatever it is can wait until you eat." Danny took a step towards her.

"Sorry Danny, I wish I could. I have so much I need to do if I want to get a ride in this afternoon." Addison left the room quickly, meeting Mary just outside the door. Titan sat there waiting. "Fuss." Addison said and Titan moved to her side.

Out in the hallway, Addison and Mary moved down the hall towards the entry way. "Miss Addie, where would you like all the guests to be staying?"

"We need to move Daniel's things to the room next to mine. The other guests will be staying in the family wing with Jack. The farther away from my room the better." Addison slowed her steps as they approached the study.

"Miss, even if we move Mr. Blackwell next to you there are still two guests that can't fit in the family wing." Mary rung her hands nervously. She had taken Addison's attack as a failure on her part. Addison had tried multiple times to convince Mary that none of it had been her fault, but Mary still carried the guilt.

Addison hadn't thought about the number of guests to rooms. There were six bedrooms in each of the wings. With Jack in the family wing only five rooms would be available. "Let us move Danny's friend across the hall from him and Jack's extra friend at the far end of the guest wing. That way Daniel and his lordship can be some sort of buffer and I will make sure to have Titan close by." Addison took a deep breath. "Everything will be fine." Mary nodded her head before heading up the stairs quickly.

Addison slipped into her study and pulled out several books as she started to go over the menu that she and Mrs. Harvey had planned. She was going to have to let Mrs. Harvey know to go ahead and send someone to pick up the supplies as soon as she knew she didn't need to get anything else for the activities portion. What kind of activities do you usually do for a house party full of gentlemen? Addison had never been to a dinner party or anything like it.

She let out a puff of air and looked over at the clock. She had already been in there for an hour. She sighed heavily and rubbed her hand down her face. This was harder than she thought. Deciding to take a break from the party planning, Addison pulled out her ledgers and notes about the tenants. She needed to visit several of them today on her ride.

Addison glanced down at Titan who was sleeping under the desk at her feet. She opened the estate ledger and added up the weekly expenses and reviewed the last month. She had been at it for a few hours when a knock sounded at the door. "Enter." She called while continuing to look over her notes. Titan squeezed out from under the desk and stood at her side.

Mrs. Susan Gracie had a baby a few weeks ago and needed a few things. The Gracie home was also having its roof repaired before the rainy season started. She needed to check on its progress. Old Mr. Harold needed help with his fence before his sheep started to escape again. Maybe Joshua would be willing to help her with the fence. She made a note to order the supplies they would need. And finally, there was the Martin's. She needed to make sure that Mrs. Martin had been following the doctor's orders so she could recover. The Martin's had four young children that depended on their mother while their father worked here at the main house. She had contracted a cough that she couldn't seem to get rid of.

A throat cleared and Addison glanced up. "Oh, gentlemen, what can I do for you?" Addison got to her feet as she looked at Jack, Danny, and Lord Ashton as they stared at her.

"What are you doing in here, Addison?" Jack asked with a slight accusatory tone to his voice. Titan let out a growl.

"Titan, platz." He laid down so that he could see the men around the side of the desk. "I am looking over the estate accounts and my notes, Jack." Addison sat back down. "I have ordered several repairs for some of the tenant's lodgings. I need to go check on them this afternoon on my ride along with collecting the rent. I was also going over the meal plan for your house party. Is there anything else you would like to add to the list before I send someone to the village for the purchases?" Addison looked back down at her books and made a few more notes.

"Ordering repairs. Visiting tenants to collect rent. All those are the steward's responsibilities." Jack said, crossing his arms over his chest.

Addison sat back in her chair and raised her eyebrow. "I am well aware of that fact, Jack. Now, what can I help you with? I am terribly busy at the moment."

"I came in here to go over the books to see how Mr. Drake has been handling things. I have not had a report from him in a long time, but since my solicitor hasn't said anything about any issues with the property, I didn't concern myself with it." Jack moved closer to the desk.

"Mr. Drake has not been to the property in almost a year. If you want his address, I am sure I can figure out what jail he was taken to. As for the estate's records, they are all here." Addison pointed to the shelves behind her and on the desk. "This is the book that has all the rent records in it. Each tenant has their own book that catalogs any and all complaints, accomplishments, needs, and my observations on what they could use. This book has all the records for employee pay. Each servant has their own book as well. If you have any other questions, I will be back in an hour or two." Addison put her books back in their places while taking the rent book with her. "Fuss." She walked around the edge of the desk and headed for the door.

"You are doing the job of the steward as well?" Jack asked in a soft voice.

"I did send you a letter after I found out Mr. Drake was stealing from father." Jack looked so upset that Addison moved to his side. She placed a hand on his arm and when he looked at her, guilt showed in his eyes. "Jack, it is okay. It gave me a purpose. I really have not minded organizing all the records and caring for the people here. But I really do need to go." Addison squeezed his arm. She turned back around and met Danny's wide-eyed stare. She patted his arm as well before heading to her room to change.

Addison was descending the grand staircase in her preferred riding attire when Danny and Lord Ashton stepped from the study. They stopped their conversation as they caught sight of her. She continued her descent even though she felt self-conscious as she caught Lord Ashton looking her up and down. She was wearing her pants with her knee-high hessian boots and her new riding coat. She stopped beside Danny and shyly looked over at Lord Ashton. There was an intensity in his eyes that caused her stomach to do a little flip.

"Mind if we join you, Addie? I could use a ride." Danny asked.

"Of course. But I leave in ten minutes. If I am not in the stables by the time you two are ready to go, my first stop is the Gracie's home." Addison smiled at her brother.

"Miss Addie! I have the things you requested." Mary came hurrying down the hall carrying a large saddle bag.

"Thank you, Mary. I should be back in time to help prepare the rooms for our guests." Addison accepted the bag. "Have the two rooms been switched yet?"

"Yes, Miss." Mary curtsied before heading back down the hall.

Danny and Lord Ashton were halfway up the stairs by the time she was done talking with Mary. "Oh, Danny." She called up after them. Both gentlemen stopped and turned to face her. "Your things have been moved to the room next to mine." Danny smiled and gave a nod. They turned to continue heading upstairs to get changed. "My Lord?" Addison called up after them again. This time her voice shook slightly. Lord Ashton turned around with a raised brow. Addison did her best to not fidget nervously, but her hands still started to shake. Titan lifted her hand with his head, and she rubbed his ear. "Due to the number of guests and the number of rooms, your things have been moved to the room across from Danny's. If you would prefer a different room just let Mary know and she can relocate you, again." Addison turned around and walked out the front door without waiting for a response.

Her cheeks flushed as she closed the door behind her. Why was she blushing? Sure, Lord Ashton was handsome with his amazing blue eyes and light brown hair. From what she knew from almost tackling him the other day and him carrying her up to her room, he was strong.

Addison shook her head. She had decided months ago that men were not going to be a part of her life anymore. The man she loved and admired most died slowly in front of her over the course of two years, her brothers abandoned her when she needed them most, a man she worked with and trusted nearly killed her, and she was attacked in her own home by two random men. No, men only brought heartache or trouble.

Titan stuck to her side as she walked to the stables and unlocked Spartan's stall. She was nearly done saddling him when Titan let out a warning growl. "Easy, boy. I mean no harm." Addison's heart picked up speed at the sound of Lord Ashton's voice. "You saddle your own horse too?" He sounded impressed.

"A week after father gave Spartan to me, I got tired of waiting for the stable hands to have an extra moment to do the job. I had Joshua teach me and it has worked out better for everyone." Addison finished with the last strap and turned around. Her breath caught as her eyes met Lord Ashton's. There was that intensity again. Titan nudged her hand, and she blinked several times before looking down. She ran her hand over his large black head slowly.

"Do I still make you anxious?" Ashton asked in a soft voice.

"A little, I guess." Addison shrugged her shoulder as she grabbed Spartan's reins. "I do not mean to offend you, My Lord. Logically, I know you will not hurt me. It is just…my brain triggers…memories."

"I understand, Miss Blackwell. I am glad that you know I would never hurt you." He took a small step closer while looking at the ground before he raised his eyes back up to meet hers. He looked like he was going to say something else, but Danny's sudden arrival stopped him.

"I'm here. I'm here." Danny came running into the stables out of breath. "Is she still here?"

"I'm still here, Danny." Addison rolled her eyes but smiled. "But I was just heading out. Saddle up boys." Addison led Spartan outside.

"Oh, come on, Addie. You can wait a few minutes while we get our horses saddled." Danny followed her out still trying to catch his breath.

"I told you; I am on a very tight schedule. I have to get back as soon as possible so that I can finish up everything I need to. You should be able to catch up easily enough. Now hurry up, you are wasting time." Addison put her foot in the stirrup and swung into the saddle. "Fuss, Titan." Addison kicked Spartan into a trot and aimed him towards the Gracie's home.

It wasn't long until quick hoofbeats were heard coming up behind her. She smiled over at Danny when he pulled even with her. They rode in silence for several minutes before he spoke. "I'm glad you moved my room next to yours, but I thought you would be more comfortable having that wing to ourselves?" Addison knew what he was getting at. He was wondering why she had moved Lord Ashton into the guest wing as well.

"In an ideal situation, you are correct. But Jack has so many guests coming that two of them will have to be in the guest wing. After considering my options I chose the lesser of two evils. At least with you in the room next to me, his lordship across the hall, and Titan in my room, I can have three security measures in place." Addison explained her logic in placing them where she had.

"I am a security guard now?" Lord Ashton laughed. "I can live with that." Addison's cheeks burned.

"I also called you the lesser of two evils, My Lord." Addison looked over at him. He was smiling as his eyes sparked with humor. "Now, I should update you two on the Gracie family. Their roof has started to leak, so I ordered repairs to be done. We are going there to check on the status of the repairs. They should have been done yesterday." The Gracie's home came into view and Spartan picked up his pace. Once next to the hitching post Spartan stopped. "Wait here. They do not want a lot of people in the house right now." Addison dismounted and turned to Titan. "Bleib." She issued the command before pulling the saddle bags off Spartan's back. Addison moved to the front door of the small home and knocked.

It took a moment before the door was pulled open a crack. A tired looking woman peered out but when she saw that it was Addison, she opened the door fully. "Oh, Miss Addie! I am so glad to see you. Come in, come in." The woman pulled Addie in before closing the door.

Susan's long blonde hair was a mess and her eyes drooped with fatigue. Addison was close with Susan Gracie even before Susan got married. She used to work as Addison's lady's maid, but once she married Ted Gracie, Susan had resigned. Addison set the saddlebag down before giving the tired mother a hug.

"How is your little girl doing?" Addison kept her voice low just in case the baby was sleeping. "I brought you some things for you and the baby."

"You really didn't need to do that, Miss Addie. You do so much for us already." Susan tried to protest but Addison started to unpack the things she brought anyway. She pulled out several different food items and three baby blankets that she had made. "These blankets are beautiful." Susan breathed out.

"How are you and the baby doing Susan?" Addison asked again.

Susan's shoulders slumped. "Evelynn doesn't sleep well at night. She only seems to sleep when someone is holding her. Ted has been trying to help, but he needs his rest so he can work in the fields."

Addison's heart went out to the woman. She was only a few years older than Addison, but her husband worked early in the morning and all day. "Would you like me to stay for an hour to watch Evelynn so that you can get a little rest?"

"I couldn't ask you to do that, Miss Addie." Susan started to tear up.

"You did not ask, I offered. Now, bring me the baby and go rest. You need it." Addison smiled as she settled into the rocking chair next to the fireplace. Susan went into the other room and brought out a little bundle of blankets before passing the bundle over to Addison. She wiped the tears off her face as she mouthed a thank you to Addison. "Oh, Susan? I know you do not like a lot of people in your home right now, but my brother and his friend accompanied me this morning. Would it be okay if they came in as well?" Addison asked and held her breath.

The baby was only two weeks old and Mrs. Thompson, the midwife, told the new parents to limit the baby's exposure to people for the first several weeks to avoid the child getting sick.

"Oh course, Miss Addie. It's the least I could do for all the help you have given us. The roof was finished last night, and we couldn't be more grateful to you." Addison smiled, happy that the repairs were done on time. "I will let them know they are welcome to wait inside." Susan headed outside and Addison turned her attention to the infant in her arms. She had thick black hair on her tiny head and her face was relaxed as she slept peacefully. Susan returned, followed by Danny and Lord Ashton. "Thank you again, Miss Addie. If she wakes up just come and get me."

"Not a chance, Susan. I told you I would take care of Evelynn so you could get some sleep and I meant it. Now, go to bed." Addison smiled at the woman who gave her a tearful nod before disappearing into the back room.

"Is this why you planned on a few hours for collecting rent?" Danny whispered as he moved closer to her.

"Baby Evelynn has never been one for sleeping much. I had the feeling that Susan would need a little help this morning. I try to come and help when I can." Addison kept her voice low so that it didn't carry to the back room as she glanced at her brother. "And the repairs to their roof were finished yesterday."

"That's great news." Danny said. The small home became quiet except for the soft creak of the rocking chair as Addison closed her eyes and rocked the baby.

Thirty minutes ticked by before Evelynn began to whimper. Addison stood up and put Evelynn to her shoulder, patting the tiny little girl's back. Evelynn settled back to sleep, but Addison continued to pat her back. "You seem to be a natural with babies, Addie." Danny whispered.

"By natural you mean spending every other day here for hours since the day Evelynn was born, then yes, I am quite the natural." Daniel laughed and Evelynn jumped at the sudden noise. "Now, shush Danny. I am trying to keep this little angel asleep."

Addison heard a quiet chuckle from across the room. She had almost forgotten that Lord Ashton was there. Addison rotated so that her back was towards the confusing young lord. She moved slowly to the window and saw Titan lying in the grass in front of the house, watching the front door with his head on his paws.

A small smile touched her lips. She had developed such a strong bond with Titan in such a short amount of time. She could not imagine life without him by her side.

"Penny for your thoughts." Lord Ashton whispered. He had moved closer to her but still left enough space between them that she did not feel anxious.

"Even as a Lord, I don't think you can afford the number of thoughts coursing through my head." Addison glanced over at him to see him studying her.

He gave her a lopsided grin and a dimple appeared on his left cheek. "Looks like I need to do some investing so I can afford to hear what is going on in that head of yours." Addison's stomach did another flipflop and she felt a blush creep up her neck.

Addison glanced over at Danny who was watching them with a thoughtful expression. She cleared her throat and looked at the clock. It had been nearly an hour. Thank goodness. Lord Ashton was causing her to feel uncomfortable with all the butterflies in her stomach and his disarming smile.

She stepped away from the window and made her way to the back room. As quietly as possible she entered the room Susan was sleeping in. Addison gently laid Evelynn into the cradle next to the bed and moved to Susan's side. She softly touched the woman's shoulder. Susan's eyes fluttered open.

"I need to get going. I put Evelynn in her cradle, and I will make sure the front door is locked. I just wanted to let you know that I was leaving. Now, go back to sleep." Addison whispered and Susan's eyes closed again. Addison snuck back out to the front room. Danny and Lord Ashton were standing close together talking in hushed tones. She walked up to them and put her hand on Danny's arm. "Time to go. You gentlemen head out first. I need to lock up." They gave her a nod and walked out.

Addison locked the door behind them and moved silently up to the attic. She moved to the small window that faced the back of the house. She eased it open slowly. A smile spread across her face. She had always wanted to try this. Addison whistled two short whistles and waited until she saw Spartan trot around the edge of the house, Titan not far behind him. He stopped directly under her.

Good boy. She climbed out the window and dangled her feet down the wall holding onto the windowsill. She grunted as she used one of her hands to quickly close the window and grab the windowsill again. Glancing down, Spartan was still right below her. She only needed to drop about two feet onto his back.

Her heart began to beat fast. She took a deep breath and let go. One of her feet landed on Spartan's back, the other on the saddle. She swung her arms wildly trying to keep her balance. Deciding it was a lost cause, Addison turned and dropped her weight into the saddle. *I cannot believe that worked!* She yelled in her head.

Addison nudged Spartan forward as she laughed. She could not believe she did not end up on the ground, dazed. Titan danced around Spartan, clearly just as excited as she was that she was uninjured. They made it to the front of the house before a voice behind her caused her to jump.

"What was that, Addie? You could have really hurt yourself." Danny snapped at her.

Addison turned in her saddle to face him. "But I wasn't, so stop worrying."

"Addie, hanging out a two-story window over a horse is dangerous." Danny continued.

Addison rolled her eyes. "When you have two near death experiences in a short amount of time, one learns to embrace life and take chances. Susan needed her rest. She does not feel safe when the front door is unlocked. I found an alternative route out of the house that allowed her to sleep comfortably." Addison shrugged her shoulders. "Plus, dear brother, I remember you teaching me how to climb down the vines near my window on the third floor so I could escape whenever I got in trouble."

"You have to admit Dan, it was quite impressive." Lord Ashton said from her other side.

"Really, Ashton? If that had been your sister dangling out a window, would you think it was impressive?" Danny was clearly not happy with Addison's little adventure.

"I would most likely be upset that she put herself in harm's way but secretly impressed with what she did." Ashton commented.

Daniel grumbled while Addison kept quiet. She kicked Spartan to a gallop and the gentlemen kept pace. The rest of her stops passed by quickly. Danny and Lord Ashton remained quiet as she conducted her business. She was able to get the rent and check in on a few other tenants as they went.

Finally done and ready to head home, Addison gave Spartan his head. She needed to shake Danny's reprimand off. He had never scolded her before, and it made her feel horrible. She urged Spartan on, and he flew through the meadow that separated the tenant cottages and the stables. Gravel flew as Spartan came to a stop in front of the stables. Joshua came running out to meet her.

"Everything all right, Miss?" Joshua asked anxiously.

Addison looked back the way she had come and saw her two escorts racing across the meadow. "Just fine, Joshua. Please give Spartan a good cool down. We rode hard today."

"Yes, Miss. Do you want me to keep Titan out here?"

Addison shook her head as she turned toward the house and began walking, not bothering to wait for Daniel and Ashton. Titan stayed glued to her side as she entered the house.

She quickly found Mary in one of the bedrooms being cleaned for the guests and started helping her prepare it. She heard Danny calling for her, but she ignored him. Mary remained silent, but she kept giving Addison questioning looks as they continued.

Addison was not ready to hear another lecture. She had lived completely without people judging her for so long. She worked hard every day to keep this place running and the people happy. She did not need someone judging her for having a little fun. Especially, her brother who had been king of mischief all their growing up years.

Chapter 6

Once she could no longer hear Danny calling for her, Addison quickly ran to her room to get changed. She discovered several abrasions along her forearms from her adventure climbing out the window. She put her pale green dress back on and sat on her bed next to Titan. Addison took a deep breath. She couldn't avoid Danny forever.

"Fuss." She said as she headed for her door with Titan at her side.

She quietly walked to the kitchen and let Titan out the back door. She made herself a quick sandwich and heading back to the study. She opened the door to find Jack sitting at her desk going over a few of her books. She hesitated at the doorway until he looked up. She moved across the room and put the rent logs back into its spot.

"I am impressed Addison. Your records are quite thorough." Jack said as he watched her.

"Thank you." she said quietly as she wrapped her arms around her middle. She kept her gaze on the ground, too afraid to look at him. The silence between them grew and Addison stepped towards the door. "I will see you at dinner." she said quickly and left the room, heading for the library.

She hoped that no one was up there at the moment, and she could at least have a few minutes of peace before she needed to meet with Mary for their lesson. Her hopes were quickly dashed when she stepped into the room. She let out a sigh as Danny and Lord Ashton stood at her entrance.

She gave them a nod of acknowledgement before taking a bite of her sandwich and moving to the shelves. Addison finished her sandwich as she slowly looked through the books. A book on Astronomy caught her eye. Addison pulled the book off the shelf and moved to the window seat.

It was her favorite place to sit and read. She unfolded the blanket she always had waiting there. Addison spread the blanket over her legs and settled back comfortably. She cracked open the book she had read to her father years ago and began to read.

She jumped a little when soft male voices reached her ears. She glanced over to see Lord Ashton and Daniel talking quietly. She turned back to her book as a blush touched her cheeks. She had forgotten they were there. Would she ever get used to having others around?

After thirty minutes, a hand touched her shoulder and she looked up startled. Danny stood there with an unreadable expression. "Can we talk?" he asked softly. Addison turned back to her book as she shrugged. She was still not in the mood to be lectured about climbing out the window. Daniel lifted her legs off the bench and sat down holding her legs in his lap so she couldn't go anywhere. "You have been avoiding me." He stated.

Addison let out a frustrated breath and slammed her book closed. She gave her full attention to Daniel. "You do realize, Daniel, that since father got sick three years ago, I have been my own keeper? Even before he became ill, I was treated as someone with a mind and father allowed me to do many things that most fathers would never allow their daughters to do." He blinked a few times in surprise but didn't say anything.

Addison pulled her legs off Daniel's lap and stood, facing him. "I am not trying to hurt you, Danny. Really, I am not. But the reality is that I have been on my own for a long time and I do not take kindly to being treated like a child. I have kept the estate from ruin. In fact, I have made it more profitable. I have survived more than anyone knows. I have made my own decisions for a long time. Just remember that we are all adults and you and Jack do not get to dictate my actions." Addison turned to leave but smacked into someone.

Looking up she met Lord Ashton's eyes. "Your brothers are only concerned for your safety, Miss Blackwell. No one is trying to dictate your choices." Lord Ashton said softly.

"And you, My Lord." Addison sneered as she pointed a finger into Lord Ashton's chest. She kept stepping closer to him and he kept stepping backwards. His hands were raised in a show of no harm, but Addison's anger had been lit. "Have no right to make excuses for them. They left me alone to watch my father die and then they completely abandoned me after father passed. Not once did they think about me or what I needed for three years."

Lord Ashton's eyes widened in surprise. Addison closed her eyes and took a deep breath. She stepped away from Lord Ashton and left the library. She needed to find a place to be alone, to get herself under control.

*   *   *

Ashton watched as Miss Blackwell turned away from him and stormed out of the library with her head held high. He had never seen someone so mad that he felt as if their glare would stab daggers into him.

He took a deep breath and looked over at Daniel. Daniel stared at the empty door with a look of torture on his face. Stepping away from the wall he was now up against, Ashton walked over to Daniel. His friend finally looked up at him before dropping his head in his hands.

"She is right. I never thought about what she needed. Father's death probably hit her the hardest, yet I was so selfish. I did not give her a second thought. We used to write to each other all the time, but as father became more and more sick, I stopped responding to her letters. Eventually, she stopped writing." Ashton took a seat next to his friend. Daniel groaned. "How could I be such an idiot?"

"Grief affects people in different ways. I have seen people who withdraw into themselves while others isolate themselves from all reminders. I have seen people become more involved in different causes in order to deal with their grief. You and Jack seemed to withdraw. Unfortunately, your sister was left completely alone as a consequence. I am not saying what you and Jack did was okay, but you cannot change it. All you can do is try to make up for it." Ashton placed a hand on Daniel's back and gave him a small smile when he finally looked up at him. "And she is definitely right about the fact that she is not a child anymore."

"Are you saying you find my sister attractive?" Daniel asked as he wiped his face.

Ashton cleared his throat and felt heat rise to his cheeks. "I am just saying she…" Ashton got to his feet. "So, how do you plan on making up your absence to Miss Blackwell?"

"I do not know." Daniel took a deep breath as his shoulders slumped. "Any ideas?"

"Sorry, my friend. I have no idea. I have never had to deal with anything like this. Maybe just be honest with her about how you were feeling and apologize?" Ashton shrugged. "While you think on it, I am going to go for another ride." Daniel nodded and Ashton left the library as he set out for the stables.

Ashton walked into the stables and found young Joshua brushing a horse. "Good afternoon, My Lord." Joshua smiled at him as he bowed. His eyes flicked over to the brown stallion's stall before quickly going back to Ashton.

If he were a betting man, he would bet his entire inheritance on Miss Blackwell being inside the stall with her horse. "Good afternoon, Joshua. I am going to go out for a ride."

Joshua nodded his understanding. "Would you like me to saddle your horse for you?"

"That will not be necessary. I will be going bareback today." He heard a small gasp come from the stall but kept his face neutral, even though he wanted to laugh.

Not many people had the skill or desire to ride bareback. He had taught himself how to when he was twelve and stuck at home with nothing else to do.

Ashton moved over to his horse's stall, which was right next to Miss Blackwell's horse's. Leonidas was a large grey stallion that stood 16.5 hands high. "Hey Leonidas, you ready for a good ride boy?"

Ashton ran his hand along Leo's sleek neck as he heard rustling in the stall next to his. "Leonidas?" Miss Blackwell asked curiously.

"When I got Leo five years ago, I debated between calling him Spartan or Leonidas. Leonidas seemed to fit him the best." Ashton kept his back towards her as he continued to pet Leo. There was a long stretch of silence, but he could tell Miss Blackwell was watching him. "I'm planning on going for a ride, would you care to join me, Miss Blackwell?"

"Um." she said hesitantly. Ashton turned to look at her as he draped his arm over Leo's withers. Miss Blackwell was biting her lip with a look of indecision on her lovely face.

"You can say 'no' if you do not wish to go." Ashton gave her a smile.

Miss Blackwell rolled her eyes, but a smile tugged at her lips as she fought it. "I love riding, but unfortunately, I am not dressed for a ride." She glanced down at her light green dress with a frown.

"If you wish to go, I will wait for you." Ashton said quietly. Miss Blackwell's eyes danced with excitement as she looked over at Spartan and then back to him. Without saying a word, she left the stables.

Ashton watched her go, not knowing if she intended on riding with him or not. He decided to wait a few minutes before heading out just in case Miss Blackwell did want to ride. He busied himself with checking Leonidas's hooves and getting his bridle on.

Not fifteen minutes later, Miss Blackwell came back through the stable doors with a radiant smile on her face. She opened her horse's stall door and the horse laid down. Ashton watched as she climbed onto the horse's back and the horse stood back up. She held on to the horse's mane, but he did not see a bridle or reins.

"Ready?" she asked as her horse walked out of the stall.

Ashton led Leonidas out to a stump before using it to get on him. "Where are your reins?" He asked. Miss Blackwell was sitting on her horse with no reins and no saddle, and he was not sure if he should be concerned or not.

"I do not need them. I have trained Spartan to respond to different pressures on his sides." Miss Blackwell smiled at him. "Titan, hier." She said and the dog immediately came to stand next to her horse. "Fuss."

Ashton nodded to her, and she began to trot out of the yard. It had been a long time since he had enjoyed riding bareback. He closed his eyes and allowed the sun to warm his face as he let Leonidas move freely.

He felt Miss Blackwell watching him, but he refused to look over at her. He was intent on waiting for her to speak first. Ashton did not want to make her feel uncomfortable or anxious. He was honestly surprised she had even come with him.

"Leonidas is an interesting name." She said after they rode in silence for a long while.

Ashton smiled over at her. "I loved the idea of naming him after a powerful leader. Leonidas just seemed to fit." He shrugged. "And you Miss Blackwell, how did you come up with the name Spartan?"

"When Spartan first arrived, he fought everyone. Father was ready to return him, but I convinced him to allow me to work with him. It took a while, but father finally relented. It took a month to gain Spartan's trust. Spartan was a fighter, so I named him after the military I was reading about in a book." Miss Blackwell leaned forward and patted Spartan's neck.

Silence once again fell between them, but it wasn't uncomfortable. Miss Blackwell seemed content just to ride. After a few more minutes, Ashton looked back over at her. Her eyes were closed, and she had her face turned up toward the sun. She was so beautiful.

"Miss Blackwell." She turned and looked at him. "I am truly sorry for overstepping in the library. I should not have intervened." He swallowed as he watched her for any reaction.

Her face softened a little as she watched him. "I am sorry as well. I should not have directed my frustrations with my brothers at you. You were only trying to help your friend and I was very rude to you." Her cheeks pinked prettily as she looked down at her hands.

"You have every right to be upset with them. I do not know how I would have handled it if I were in your position." Ashton commented.

Miss Blackwell laughed lightly, but there was no humor in it. "One learns to adapt even though there can still be some strong feelings buried."

"You are a very strong woman, Miss Blackwell."

Ashton's eyes met Miss Blackwell's. His stomach did a flip as he got lost in her mesmerizing green eyes. They held each other's gazes until Titan barked as he ran after something in the grass. Miss Blackwell blinked a few times before turning her attention forward.

"Tell me, My Lord, do you have any siblings?" she asked as she refused to look back at him.

"No, it is just me. Once at school though, I met a scrawny boy named Daniel that became the closest thing to a brother I could get." Ashton answered. "He would even read me the letters he received from his younger sister."

"He didn't." Miss Blackwell's wide eyes were back on him.

Ashton laughed. "Oh, he sure did. Well, most of them. He also talked about her nonstop, even when we travelled together. There was one letter I remember that threatened him. It said if he forgot to bring home a birthday gift for her again, she would make sure he slept in the haunted attic with the ghosts and spiders. Daniel explained to me that he hated spiders and even though he knew the plan, she would still somehow lock him up there. The next time we went to town we hunted for the perfect gift. He was paranoid that it would not be good enough and land him in the attic." Ashton watched as Miss Blackwell's face turned red with embarrassment.

"Well, if he had not forgotten the previous two years, I would not have had to take such drastic measures. And I still have the horse figure." Miss Blackwell laughed. "Out of everything that I have received throughout the years, it is one of my favorites."

"I'm glad you enjoy it." Ashton felt proud of himself. He had been the one that found the horse figure and showed it to Daniel. They had to go in on it together because Daniel did not have enough coins with him to purchase it.

*   *   *

Addison loved that horse. It was one of her most precious treasures. She leaned back so that she was laying on Spartan's back as they continued walking towards the lake.

Lord Ashton wasn't as scary as she had originally thought. She was glad she had agreed to come on this excursion. She almost declined, but riding had always helped calm her thoughts and she could not pass it up. She glanced over at Lord Ashton; he was watching her.

He gave her his dimpled grin before asking her another question. They asked questions back and forth as they slowly made their way around the lake. Addison had not realized how lonely she had been over the years. This ride and conversation had been the longest time she had spent with anyone capable of conversation in years.

On the far side of the lake, tears began to sting her eyes as all the loneliness over the past years hit her. She rolled off Spartan and took several deep breaths. Lord Ashton was suddenly beside her, grabbing her arms with a worried expression on his face. Titan's large head pressed into her face.

Addison tried to smile at Lord Ashton so that he wouldn't think anything was wrong, but a traitorous tear slipped from her eye. Lord Ashton cupped her cheek and gently wiped the tear away with his thumb only for more to replace it.

"I'm sorry if I said anything to upset you, Miss Blackwell." Addison shook her head. "Then what has upset you?" His voice was soft as he studied her face.

"I am sorry. I did not mean to cry." Addison closed her eyes tight, willing her tears to stop. She felt him pull her gently to him as he hugged her close. Addison wrapped her arms around his waist as she continued to fight for control. "I am sorry." She whispered again.

"Shh." Lord Ashton said as he continued to hold her. "No need to apologize."

It took several minutes but she finally felt in control enough to move away from Lord Ashton and stand. He allowed her to put space between them and Addison was grateful that he did not try to keep her there.

"What is the matter, Miss Blackwell?" His brows were furrowed as if he was trying to figure out a great puzzle. Addison shook her head and looked down at Titan, embarrassed about her breakdown. "Please?" Lord Ashton asked.

Addison took a deep breath. He had been so kind to her, the least she could do was be honest with him. "I just…" This was harder than she thought. "I just did not notice how lonely my life has been until I realized that this was the longest conversation I have had in over three years. My normal conversations have consisted of speaking to the maids about duties, lessons, or Joshua for a few minutes about Spartan or Titan." She gave Lord Ashton a small smile. "Thank you."

Lord Ashton was quiet for a long moment before speaking. "I'm glad to help in any way I can." He bowed as he gave her one of his lopsided smiles that showed off his dimple. Addison smiled back at him. "Now that you seem back in better spirits, shall we finish our ride, My Lady?" Addison nodded and they both remounted.

Addison was surprised that Lord Ashton had not asked to assist her onto Spartan, but then she remembered he had been there when she had told Daniel she did not need any help.

The rest of the ride was filled with laughter and more questions. She learned quite a bit about Lord Ashton. She felt a little bad that she did not talk much about herself.

Lord Ashton did not seem to mind as he told her all about his childhood and some of the pranks he and Daniel had done while in school. She told him a little about growing up and spending a lot of time at her father's side and learning how the estate was run.

He was attentive and asked follow-up questions periodically, but sensed her reluctance to talk about certain things, so he avoided asking more details about them.

By the time they returned to the stables, dinner was ready. Addison thanked Lord Ashton again before rushing upstairs to change before Jack saw her.

At dinner, Addison noticed that Danny was much quieter than he normally was, and he kept his eyes on his plate. She felt bad for having yelled at him earlier.

She found him after dinner and apologized, but he told her that she had been right to feel like she was abandoned. He promised to make it up to her as best he could.

Chapter 7

The next week and a half flew by in a blur. Addison had busied herself with getting the house ready for guests and planning the dreaded house party along with keeping up her lessons with the servants. The only time she had to relax, was on her rides.

She either rode with Lord Ashton, Daniel, or both. Daniel was trying really hard to make up for not being around the last several years and she appreciated it.

On one of their rides, Daniel had broken down and told her about his difficulties with father's illness and death. She understood his struggle to cope with the loss of their father. They were able to comfort each other through some of the grief.

Having someone to talk to was like a light in the darkness, pulling her out of the dark abyss that had swallowed her over the last year. Her life had changed a lot in the last two weeks, and she had never felt so happy.

She also found that she felt more comfortable around Lord Ashton. Her anxiety over him being at her house was gone. However, that feeling was going to be short lived because the guests for the house party were to arrive the next day.

Addison tried not to let tomorrow's events ruin her peace for tonight. She dressed in a cream colored evening gown and headed down to dinner. This last week she hadn't needed Titan so much. He was often nearby but wasn't glued to her side anymore. She had asked Joshua to keep Titan for the evening since he had decided to roll in some manure earlier.

Addison was running late and knew that her brothers would be waiting for her in the dining hall instead of the drawing room. She made her way to the dining room and paused before entering. She took a deep breath, squared her shoulders, and stepped into the room. Four gentlemen stood at her entrance and Addison froze. Jack motioned for her to take her seat. She hesitated for a moment before moving quickly to her chair.

"Addison, this is my friend Mr. Oliver Hansen. Oliver, this is my sister Miss Addison Blackwell." Jack made the introductions quickly. Addison gave a quick curtsey before taking her seat.

Her hands were beginning to shake, and she was concentrating on trying to keep her breathing normal. She glanced at the occupants at the table to find everyone looking at her. Had she missed something? Mr. Hansen looked at her with an expectant look, Jack with a look of confusion while Danny and Lord Ashton looked at her with concern.

Danny tapped his fork and Addison realized they were all waiting for her to start eating so that they could. She quickly grabbed her fork and took a bite of what she thought was green beans but was not sure of what she actually put in her mouth.

She felt so overwhelmed that she could not taste anything, and her stomach clenched uncomfortably. Jack and Mr. Hansen began to speak about business, which Addison was grateful for. She was not at all up to having a conversation.

By the time the meal was nearly done, her nerves were in tatters. Mary came into the room and made her way quickly to Addison's side.

"Miss, Joshua needs to speak with you right away." Mary whispered anxiously.

Addison nodded once before getting to her feet. All four gentlemen stood as well, which caused her to flinch. She recovered quickly and began walking with Mary. "Excuse me gentlemen, I must see to this immediately." She said in a small voice as she headed for the door.

"Is everything all right, Addison?" Jack asked.

Addison stopped beside him and glanced back at the table. Lord Ashton met her eyes, and she could almost hear him asking her the same thing. She quickly looked back at Jack. "I just need to have a quick word with one of the servants. I should not be gone long." Jack gave her a nod and she walked from the room.

At the door, Addison glanced back at Lord Ashton one more time. He gave her the tiniest of nods as he retook his seat. Addison's heart skipped a beat and warmth spread through her. That small gesture had a calming effect on her.

She gave herself a mental shake. Lord Ashton was not really concerned for her. He was just her brother's friend, nothing more. And here she was, allowing herself to think that the tiniest of nods meant something more.

As they approached the kitchen, Mary pointed outside. Addison noticed for the first time that Mary was pale. Addison ran outside to find Titan pacing anxiously next to Joshua who sat on the ground holding his arm as blood continued to seep out from under his hand.

"What happened?" Addison asked as she ran to the boy's side.

"Something got into Titan. Father had to help me get him into the kennel. He just continued to whine and pace. We were cleaning the saddles when Titan became frantic. Father and I went to see what got him all riled up and when we got there, Titan had chewed through some of the fencing and got himself caught. As I was freeing him, my arm caught on the wire. Father ran for the doctor, but I can't get the bleeding to stop." Joshua's face was devoid of color.

"Can you walk, Joshua?" Addison asked quickly. He nodded. Addison helped him to his feet and she guided him inside. "Titan, fuss. Mary, hot water and fresh rags. I am taking him to the guest room across from mine." Addison used the servant's staircase to avoid walking past the dining hall. Titan stayed next to her as she helped Joshua upstairs to the room.

Joshua sat on the floor panting from the effort of climbing the stairs. Mary entered the room a few moments later with Addison's requested supplies. "I'm going to clean it while we wait for the doctor, okay?" Addison told Joshua. He was looking worse by the minute. "Here lay down. You will be more comfortable." Addison laid Joshua's head on the pillow she pulled from the bed.

Addison spent the next twenty minutes scrubbing the blood off of Joshua's arm. The gash was deep and would most definitely need stitches. She sent Mary to get the strongest alcohol in the house while she applied pressure to the wound.

Mary returned with a thick glass bottle. Addison didn't even look at the label before she poured it over the wound. Joshua screamed in pain and Addison put another clean rag over the wound as she continued to apply pressure.

Tears rolled down her cheeks as she watched Joshua fighting back tears. The door behind her burst open. James and the doctor came running in.

"What is going on in here?" The doctor demanded angrily.

"I cleaned the wound with hot water. It was caused by a metal fence so I also poured this on it to fight any infection that might set in." Addison glanced up at the two men before looking back at Joshua. "It is really deep and won't stop bleeding. I have been applying pressure for several minutes now."

The doctor knelt down on the other side of Joshua and motioned for her to lift the rag. His lips pulled into a grim line when he saw the wound.

"You have done well Miss Blackwell. We can take it from here, though. You should get cleaned up." The doctor's voice had softened, and he gave her a small smile. "I will come down and talk with you once I am finished with the boy."

Addison gave him a nod before getting to her feet. Mary walked across the hall with her with a fresh pot of hot water. Addison brushed the back of her blood covered hand over her cheek to wipe the last of her tears away as Mary filled the water basin on the table and left Addison to clean herself up.

Addison washed her hands thoroughly to make sure all the traces of blood were cleaned up. Ten minutes later, Addison felt like she could rejoin her brothers. She walked from the room with Titan at her side.

She went first to the dining room but found it empty. Addison tried to think of where they would go. Deciding to check the drawing room, Addison and Titan made their way down the hall. She rested her hand on Titan's back as she entered the room. Jack and Mr. Hansen stood near the far window in quiet conversation while Danny and Lord Ashton sat on the couches.

Before any of them noticed her, Addison crossed quickly to Danny and Lord Ashton. They looked up at her as she quickly took a seat on the couch next to Danny, so her back was facing Jack and his friend. Titan laid on the floor across her feet.

"Is everything okay, Addie?" Danny asked quietly.

Addison nodded then shook her head. She let out a heavy sigh and then nodded again. She glanced over at Lord Ashton who was studying her with his brows furrowed. He made a motion to her cheek, but she did not know what he was trying to tell her. Danny grabbed her chin and turned her to face him.

"Is that blood on your cheek?" Danny whispered and quickly pulled his handkerchief from his pocket before wiping at her cheek. He finally stuffed the blood-stained cloth into his pocket. "What happened?"

"Titan was going crazy and chewed through his kennel fence. Joshua was cut and bleeding. His father rushed to get the doctor, but Joshua could not stop the bleeding. I took him upstairs to clean him up." Addison whispered in Danny's ear.

Lord Ashton cleared his throat just as Jack and his friend walked over. Titan let out a warning growl as he stood protectively in front of her.

"Addison, why is the dog in the house." Jack asked. She could see the irritation in his eyes. He hadn't been as hostile towards her lately and she thought they were starting to understand each other better, but apparently not.

"Titan stays with Addie, Jack." Danny said sternly.

"That is a very large dog." Mr. Hansen said with a tight smile and forced laugh.

Addison forced a smile on her face even though she felt like crying in the corner. She did not want to be near this stranger. Titan turned and laid his head in her lap while keeping an eye on Mr. Hansen. Addison looked down at Titan's large black and brown face and dark brown eyes. She slowly ran her hands over his ears and reminded herself to just breathe.

"He seems rather attached to you, Miss Blackwell. How long have you had him?" Mr. Hansen asked her.

"N-nine months. I-I have h-had him for n-nine m-months." Addison stuttered out and she closed her eyes against the sting of tears. If this is how she reacted with one strange man, how was she going to handle six?

A knock at the door drew everyone's attention. The doctor stepped inside. Addison got to her feet and walked around the far side of the couch to avoid having to walk anywhere near Mr. Hansen. She stepped out into the hall with the doctor and closed the door to the drawing room.

"How is he?" She asked.

"He is doing better. His father took young Joshua home. He did receive several stitches, but everything should heal nicely. I told James that Joshua needed a few days of rest." The doctor, Mr. Thompson, gave her a smile. "How are you doing, Miss Addison? You seem to be having a bit of a struggle in there."

Addison shook her head. Her hands were still shaking, and she was pretty sure she was pale. "You know how I am around meeting new...people. Titan is with me so I should be fine." Addison tried to smile but could not seem to muster one.

"Miss Addie, I mean this in the kindest way possible, you are as white as a sheet, you are shaking like a leaf, and you were stuttering. You are near an attack, again. Would you like me to leave you something to help you sleep?" He watched her with kind but worried eyes. He and his wife had been the ones to help with her injuries after both attacks. They had all developed a good relationship over the months of her recovery.

"No. No thank you. I do not like being so deep asleep that Titan cannot wake me." Addison looked down at the dog at her side.

"I think you should retire for the evening then. Putting yourself into situations that induce your panic attacks will only make them worse, Miss Addison."

"I will. Thank you for taking care of Joshua. Please send his bill here, I will take care of it." Addison shook Mr. Thompson's hand as they walked towards the front door.

"I will be back in two days to check on Joshua's arm and on you." The doctor patted Titan on the head. "And you keep this girl safe."

Once the doctor left, Addison returned to the drawing room. This time when she entered, all four men watched her enter with questions in their eyes. She allowed her gaze to meet Danny's. He looked like he wanted to say something, but he kept silent. Her gaze slid over to Lord Ashton, who watched her closely. She blinked before turning her full attention to Jack.

Jack crossed to her and grabbed her arm, pulling her farther from the group of men standing together. "Addison, what is going on?"

"Joshua was hurt, and the doctor came to give him stitches." Addison answered him quietly.

"What is going on with you? I have never heard you stutter before or go from normal to ghost white in the matter of seconds." Jack sounded worried. Was he actually concerned about her? She doubted he even knew about the break-in, since he had not canceled the house party yet.

"I just have a headache. Dr. Thompson gave me something for it before he left." Addison felt slightly guilty for lying to Jack but if she stayed, she was afraid that she would end up unconscious on the floor.

"Perhaps you should retire for the evening. We have a big day tomorrow with preparing for the house party." Jack offered as he guided her to the door. "Go ahead and get some rest tonight. I will let everyone know that you are feeling under the weather."

Tears pricked at her eyes again. "Thank you, Jack." Addison whispered before raising up on her toes and pressing a kiss to his cheek. "You are the best."

Addison glanced once more back at the gentlemen standing near the couches. Danny and Lord Ashton both had looks on their faces that told her they would find her later. She did not even look over at Mr. Hansen before she turned towards the door and left.

Titan followed her all the way up to her room. She changed out of her gown and into her dark brown dress she used when working outside in the garden. Remembering Joshua had mentioned that Titan had eaten through the fencing, Addison sat on the floor and looked Titan over for any cuts. She let out a sigh of relief when she found none.

She patted his side as she stood back up and double checked to make sure her door was locked. Addison climbed into bed and Titan jumped up beside her. She lay there with his head on her shoulder for a long time. Her eyelids began to grow heavy, and she finally fell asleep.

Chapter 8

It was late and Addison couldn't sleep. She wandered the empty halls of her home for hours. The absence of her father's racking cough made the house seem even more depressing than when they constantly filled the air.

Addison finally found her way to her father's study. She sat down at the oak desk and ran her fingers over the smooth wood. Tears fell as she recalled memories of sitting next to this desk as her father worked and she played or studied. Sometimes she would even sit in his lap as he told her all about what he was doing and what all the numbers in the books represented. Addison folded her arms on the desk and laid her head on them as she sobbed.

When her tears finally dried, she sat up and stared at the book at the corner of the desk. She sniffled as she dragged the book to her and opened it slowly. She absentmindedly flipped through the pages as she traced over her father's familiar handwriting. About halfway through the book the handwriting changed.

Mr. Drake took over the records when her father became too ill to see to them. As she turned page after page, Addison started to notice discrepancies in the records. She wiped her cheeks as she paid more attention to the ledger. She pulled out extra paper and a quill as she began making notes of what she found. She was startled as the door opened. Mr. Drake stood frozen as he stared at her sitting at the desk.

"What are you doing in here, Miss Blackwell?" Mr. Drake's voice was uncharacteristically stiff, but he gave her a smile. When he noticed the book and paper in front of her, he slowly closed the door behind him. He clicked his tongue as he walked towards her. "You shouldn't have done that." Addison was frozen in fear. Mr. Drake's voice was cold, and his eyes flashed with anger.

Before Addison could register what was happening, Mr. Drake grabbed her by her hair and yanked her from the chair. His other hand clamped around her throat and squeezed.

Addison scratched at his hand as she tried to loosen his grip. Panic set in as her vision began to fade from the lack of oxygen. Just before she lost consciousness, he slammed her head on the desk.

A hand grabbed her shoulder and shook her while another one covered her mouth. She began to fight back with what little strength she had left.

"Addison, wake up!" Danny's voice cut through the office as she struggled against Mr. Drake as he inflicted blow after blow. Another hard shake and Danny calling her name.

Addison opened her eyes to find a hand over her mouth. She was about to scream when she noticed Danny leaning over her. His hand was covering her mouth. She slapped his hand away as she gasped for air.

She sat up and glared at him. "What are you doing in here? I locked the door." She panted out.

"Did you forget I can pick locks? Titan was barking up a storm, and you wouldn't open the door. We had no choice but to break in." Danny said worry evident in his voice.

"We?" Addison pressed a shaky hand to her forehead as she tried to get rid of the lingering effects of her dream.

"Ashton and I." Danny brushed the hair back from her face and she flinched.

Of course, Danny brought Ashton with him. Addison closed her eyes and took several slow breaths. Titan nuzzled her face and she leaned into him. The dreams were getting worse and coming more frequently. Maybe Dr. Thompson was right and putting herself into these high stress situations made her reactions stronger.

"You guys can go back to bed. I am fine now." she said tiredly.

"I am not leaving, Addie. You haven't had a nightmare in several days and then this one." Danny said stubbornly. Addison groaned and looked at her brother. They had lit a few candles so at least she could see him clearly. "I'm staying here with you tonight."

"I am fine, Daniel. Seriously, you can go back to bed, in your own room." Addison got off the bed on the opposite side from Danny. She looked up to see concerned blue eyes watching her. "Hier." Addison said and Titan jumped off the bed. "Fuss." She moved past Lord Ashton and headed for the door.

"Where are you going?" Danny's anxious voice asked.

"I'm getting up for the day." Addison pulled the door open. The hallway was completely dark.

"It is three in the morning, Addie. We will leave you and you can go back to sleep." Danny followed her out and grabbed her arm to stop her.

"I will not be able to sleep." Tears brimmed in her eyes, and she refused to look up at Danny's face. The fear from her nightmare was still pressing on her making her shake and struggle to breathe normally.

"I am sorry, Addie. We will let you sleep." Addison kept her gaze directed at the floor even when Daniel tried to meet her eyes by leaning down. "Please, Addie, look at me." Danny's voice broke at the end and Addison looked up at him.

Addison wiped at the stray tear that slipped from her eye as she shook her head. "I can't." She tried to pull her arm away, but he tightened his grip. "Danny please. I do not want to go back there. I am too tired to fight him again." She whispered.

"Fight who?" Danny looked confused now.

"Mr. Drake. I cannot go back to sleep. I will be fine. I will go over the ledgers or something until everyone wakes up." Addison tried to reason with her brother to let her go. She did not want to fall back into her nightmare.

"You had another nightmare." Lord Ashton's deep soothing voice said quietly from her doorway. He looked like he was puzzling over something.

Addison looked over at him as another tear slipped from her eye. "I always have nightmares."

"You seemed to sleep better after you and your brother talked about happier memories last time. Maybe it could work again." Lord Ashton suggested.

Before Addison could say anything, Danny was dragging her back to her room. "Ashton's right, you did. Let us try it." Addison sat on the bed and watched the hope in Danny's eyes grow as he waited for her.

Sighing in resignation, Addison climbed under the covers as Titan jumped on the bed next to her. "I hope you both know how terribly awkward this is." She heard Lord Ashton chuckle and Danny settled onto the bed next to her with his back against the headboard.

"Just be quiet and listen while I recount our childhood." Danny said with a wide smile.

"I can't wait." Addison said sarcastically.

Daniel started recounting the time when he pushed her into the lake when she was ten. She swam under the dock, and he began to panic when she did not surface. Daniel had dived into the lake after her. Every time he came up for air, she would duck under the surface. The lake was so murky that he could not see her when he was under the water.

After fifteen minutes of searching, Daniel had climbed out of the lake and sat on the dock with his legs hanging over the edge. He continued to look for her while giving his legs a break. She had grabbed his ankle causing him to scream and scramble backwards before falling off the edge of the dock. At that point, Addison climbed out of the water and ran away yelling how she was going to tell father what Danny had done.

Addison laughed softly as her eyes began to droop. Danny started in on another story, but she fell asleep before he really began.

* * *

Addison yawned and stretched her arms over her head. She blinked her eyes open slowly. It took her a moment to realize that her room was bright from the sun coming through her window. She bolted upright and reached for Titan. Titan wasn't lying beside her.

Addison climbed out of her bed in a panic. Where was he? She caught sight of a piece of paper on her nightstand. She picked it up and read it. Relief and frustration filled her. Danny had apparently taken Titan outside this morning so that she could have more sleep.

Addison glanced at the clock. It was nearly two in the afternoon. Jack was going to kill her. Addison threw the letter back on the side table and quickly dressed in a light blue dress. She braided her hair instead of taking the time to stack it all on top of her head and headed downstairs.

She needed to find Titan and then she was going to hunt down Danny. He should have woken her up. There was too much that needed to be done.

The house was quiet as she made her way downstairs. Addison headed for the kitchen. There was the normal hustle and bustle of Mrs. Harvey preparing a meal. Addison grabbed an apple on her way through the organized chaos.

Once outside, Addison let out a long whistle. She waited anxiously on the back step for Titan to appear. After several tense minutes, she was starting to worry until she heard faint barking.

She let out another whistle and waited. Another bark came, this time closer. She scanned the meadows until she saw two men walking and a large black figure running towards her.

Titan nearly knocked her to the ground in his excitement to see her. She wrapped her arms tightly around his neck and he instantly settled down. He probably sensed her anxiety.

"How did you sleep, Addie?" Danny's cheerful voice made her blood boil.

She should have been up hours ago. He had let her sleep in and now Jack was most likely mad at her. Not to mention, he took her dog. Addison stood slowly and faced Danny. He held up his hands as if trying to ward off an animal attack.

"Addie, hold on." He said desperately.

"Hold on, Danny? You want me to hold on?" She took a step towards him, and he took a step back. She drew her hand back and threw her apple at him, hitting him in the chest.

"Ow." Danny's eyes widened as he rubbed where the apple had struck him. "Really, Addie?"

"You let me sleep in and you stole my dog. I have responsibilities today, Danny. I do not have the luxury of sleeping in." She fumed.

"Do you hear yourself, Addison? You have not had a decent night's sleep in who knows how long, and you are mad at me for allowing you to sleep peacefully? And I did not steal your dog. I have been taking him out every couple of hours for a quick run before bringing him back to your room." Danny shot back at her.

Hours? Did he just say every couple of hours? "How long have I been asleep?" Addison's anger was quickly changing to dread.

"Roughly thirty hours. You fell back into a deep sleep after the nightmare. I heard Titan scratching at your door later that morning when I was heading down to breakfast. I took him out and returned him before eating. Jack said to let you rest. He did not want you to get sick with the house party starting." Danny took a tentative step towards her.

"That means, everyone has already arrived?" Addison asked as she crouched next to Titan. Danny nodded. Addison closed her eyes briefly before opening them and looking into Titan's brown intelligent eyes. "I can do this, right?" she asked the dog in a quiet voice. Titan's knub of a tail wagged. "You are right, buddy. We can do this." Addison straightened up and squared her shoulders.

She turned back to her brother and gave a weak smile. "Thank you for taking Titan out and allowing me to sleep. But if you ever let me oversleep again, Daniel Blackwell, I would start checking my bed before I go to sleep if I were you."

"Addie, that's not funny. Last time the snake actually bit me." Danny narrowed his eyes at her.

"Wait, what?" Lord Ashton laughed.

"Addison got mad at me. She put a snake in my bed, and it bit me." Danny explained.

"It was nonvenomous, and the bite was not even that bad. It bit me too as I was catching it." Addison smiled sweetly. "My threat still stands big brother. Fuss." And with that, Addison turned around and walked inside. Titan walked at her side as she headed for the study. She needed to put in a few notes about a few of the tenants that she wasn't able to mark down earlier.

An hour later and Addison was finished. She headed back outside, wanting to at least see Spartan and give him a treat or two. She was halfway to the stables when seven horses rode up. Several of the riders had seen her walking so it was too late to turn around.

A small whimper escaped her lips and Titan was immediately on alert. Jack dismounted and Addison stopped walking. Jack led the group up to her with a smile on his face. At least he wasn't mad at her for sleeping a full day and a half away.

"Addison, I'm so glad to see you up." Jack pulled her in for a hug. Addison was too terrified to hug him back. "These are my friends. Lord Percy, Lord Trenton, Mr. Hansen, Mr. Royce, Lord Blake, and Lord Channing. Gents this is my sister, Miss Addison Blackwell." The gentlemen all bowed, and Addison did her best to curtsey, but it was more of a quick bob.

One of the gentlemen stepped forward as if he were going to offer his arm to her but Titan stepped in between them and growled. The man stopped in his tracks as he eyed the large dog. He swallowed hard before stepping back and lifting his eyes to her. Addison still could not move, and she was having a hard time breathing.

"Miss Addie! There you are. You asked to see me about Spartan?" Joshua's voice called across the yard and it snapped her out of her fear-induced trance.

"Yes." She called back. Turning to Jack and his friends, she dipped into another curtsey. "Pleased to meet you all but I must be going." She did not look back as she hurried to the stable.

Once inside, Joshua grabbed her arm and pulled her to a bale of hay. He had her sit down and handed her a cup of water. "Take nice slow breaths, Miss." he said softly as Titan licked her hand.

Addison did as Joshua instructed her. She concentrated on her breathing and after several long moments she felt calm enough that walking back to the house didn't seem so daunting of a task. Joshua had disappeared but Titan stayed by her side. She was shaking uncontrollably, and Titan whined as he licked her hands.

Twenty minutes passed and Addison was nearly back to normal. Danny and Lord Ashton came running into the barn with Joshua on their heels. Addison rolled her eyes at them before turning back to Titan. Danny moved to her side and placed an arm around her but didn't say anything.

Breathe, Addie. Come on girl, nice and slow. Addison coached herself. She could do this. She just needed to figure out how. Danny squeezed her shoulders, and she looked up at him.

"What happened? You were your normal fiery self earlier." He kept his voice soft.

Addison stood and walked over to Spartan's stall. She ran a hand down his neck as he laid his head over her shoulder. "I came out to see Spartan since I overslept," Addison shot Danny a glare. "I did not get my normal ride in. I was almost here when Jack and his friends came back from whatever they were doing." Addison swallowed hard and took a deep breath.

"I am going to talk to Jack. Maybe we can at least limit the number of 'friends' you encounter at one time for a few days, until you feel more comfortable around them." Danny quickly walked to the door but stopped. "Ashton and Joshua will stay with you until I get back." Addison whirled around to protest, but Danny was already gone.

Lord Ashton stood not too far off, with his hands behind his back. "I can step outside and wait there if you wish."

Addison rolled her eyes at him. "You can do whatever you want, My Lord." Lord Ashton moved to her side and leaned his shoulder against the side of the wall. Addison glanced over at him as she continued to pet Spartan.

"You have most of your color back." He was studying her with so much intensity that it brought a slight blush to her cheeks. "Well, maybe a little more than your normal color."

Without thinking Addison smacked his chest like she did when Danny teased her. Her eyes went wide as she realized she had just hit a titled gentleman. "I am so sorry. I did not mean too." She stopped trying to apologize when Lord Ashton started to laugh. She felt her cheeks heat even more and she turned back to Spartan.

"Please forgive me, Miss Blackwell." Lord Ashton started to say.

"It's Miss Addison." Addison interrupted him. "Miss Blackwell makes me feel so old."

A smile tugged at Lord Ashton's lips. "Very well. Forgive me, Miss Addison. I did not mean to make you feel uncomfortable in any way." Addison turned to face him fully as she studied him.

Why was she not falling apart with him standing so close? She couldn't even function the other night with Mr. Hansen standing nearly ten feet away.

Male voices snapped her out of her thoughts and Lord Ashton quickly looked at the door. With no warning, he pulled her to him causing her to hit his chest. He pulled Spartan's stall door open and pushed her inside before closing it.

"Get down." He whispered as he took a relaxed stance and ran his hand down Spartan's head. Addison ducked down and seconds later, several men came into the stables.

"Lord Fenwick, we did not expect to see you here." Mr. Hansen said in surprise. "We were hoping to find Miss Blackwell. Have you seen her?"

"Mr. Hansen, always a pleasure." It sounded to Addison as if Lord Ashton meant the opposite of what his words said. "As you can see, Miss Blackwell is not in here."

"You have been here for several weeks, have you not?" There was a pause before Mr. Hansen continued. "What have you learned about our elusive Miss Blackwell?"

Addison shivered. She had a very uncomfortable feeling about Mr. Hansen. "I didn't realize Miss Blackwell belonged to any of us." Lord Ashton said coolly.

"Oh, come now, Lord Fenwick. We are all here for the same reason. By the end of these two weeks, she will belong to one of us." Mr. Hansen and the other men with him laughed and Addison covered her mouth.

"You must have more knowledge about this house party than I do because I was under the impression that I was spending the fortnight with a friend and his family." Addison looked up from her crouched position to see Lord Ashton's clenched fist sitting on top of the stall door.

"Lord Channing and I were at the club when Lord Blackwell mentioned that his sister had come of age, as well as her coming out of mourning, and that he needed to bring her to town for the season. Channing suggested a little get-together with eligible gentlemen before the season so maybe Lord Blackwell could avoid all the hassle. It only took a few hours to convince him and here we all are, vying for the young Miss Blackwell's affection." Mr. Hansen said as he moved closer. "Since you are obviously not here to win the prize, be a good chap and share with us what you have learned about her."

Lord Ashton's hand slowly lowered on her side of the gate. Addison slipped her hand into his and held tightly as she rested her forehead against the back of his hand. He gave her hand a quick squeeze.

Her anxiety started to rise, and she held onto Lord Ashton's hand as if it were her lifeline. Addison couldn't believe what she had just heard from Mr. Hansen. Was that really the only reason Jack was back? He was trying to get rid of her.

If he did not want to deal with her, then he should have just left her alone. She was happy in her life here. She had learned to take care of those around her and she put everything she had into making sure everyone was happy and thriving. She was even teaching the servants how to read and write.

"Miss Addie is not a prize to be won. She is smart and kind. You should be working to prove yourself worthy of her, not deceiving her into liking you through lies." Joshua said angrily. Addison could kiss the boy for defending her.

"Leave the boy alone." Lord Ashton's voice held a threatening edge to it. "He is protecting the lady of the house. I would take his actions as a glimpse into Miss Blackwell's character to inspire such loyalty in her staff."

"I will be speaking to Lord Blackwell about your disrespect, boy." Mr. Hansen sneered.

"Ashton, I just finished talking with Jack. And…Oh, Mr. Hansen, Lord Channing, Lord Percy. I did not expect to see you all out here." Danny's voice went from relieved and excited to cold and emotionless. Lord Ashton squeezed her hand again. "Jack was just about to start a game of cards. I am sure he is looking for you gentlemen."

There was a tense silence before Addison heard footsteps leaving the stables. Addison closed her eyes and held tighter to Lord Ashton's hand. She was struggling to breathe again at the thought of having to marry one of the men that Jack invited.

She was vaguely aware of the stall door opening beside her. Lord Ashton's hand shifted slightly in her hold just as a heavy weight landed on her legs. Her eyes flew open. "Ow, Titan. Vorsichtig." The dog looked up at her while whining. Addison let go of Lord Ashton's hand and pushed Titan off her legs.

"Are you all right, Miss Addison?" Lord Ashton asked softly. He was crouched next to her with Danny standing directly behind him.

Addison nodded as she tried to get to her feet. Lord Ashton grabbed her arm as he helped her stand. Titan leaned his weight against the back of her legs causing her to stumble forward. She fell against Lord Ashton's chest and his arms came around her. She looked up into his blue eyes. They were searching hers for something and Addison could not pull her gaze from his.

"Titan, stop pushing Miss Addie around. You are going to hurt her one of these days." Joshua scolded the dog as he rushed over. He grabbed the dog's thick leather collar and pulled him away from her.

Addison cleared her throat and took a step away from Lord Ashton. Her heart was racing again, but not from an impending panic attack. She felt her cheeks warm as she moved past Lord Ashton on her way out of the stall.

Lord Ashton confused her. She was normally so anxious around men but when she was around him, she felt calmer. She could see a glimpse of the confident fun girl she was before the attack and break-in.

"What did they want?" Danny asked with obvious disgust in his voice.

"I take it you don't care for my suitors then?" Addison asked as she watched him. Did he know about Jack's plan?

"Your what?" Danny yelled. Several of the horses were startled at his outburst.

"Lord Blackwell is trying to marry Miss Addie off." Joshua growled out still angry at the thought of it.

Addison smiled at the boy as she moved over to him. She pulled him into a hug which he returned. "My hero. I cannot believe you stood up to him." Addison gave him a squeeze. "But we need to talk about proper etiquette when speaking to those that out rank you. I do not want you getting into trouble."

"Yes, Miss. But Lord Blackwell can't do this to you." Joshua pulled back to look at her.

"Do not worry Addie. Even if Jack set this whole thing up to find you a husband, you will not have to marry anyone unless you want to." Danny said firmly. "Jack is your guardian, but your marriage requires both Jack's and my signatures to be approved."

Addison looked from Danny to Joshua to Lord Ashton. All of them had matching scowls on their faces. She bit the inside of her cheek to keep from laughing. It had been so long since she had anyone looking out for her and it felt strange. The three of them looked ready to go to battle in order to protect her.

If only Jack felt the same way as Danny. No, Jack wanted to show her to all his friends in order to marry her off. Addison paused. Would it be so bad to marry?

Addison thought about Jack's friends. They were all at least ten years her senior; if not older. She did not like the idea of being married to someone who is that much older than she was. She didn't think she was even ready to marry in the first place, not with her recent experiences still affecting her.

Jack wouldn't allow her to stay away from their guests, so she was going to have to figure out a way to cope with them being around her. What were things she did to reduce her stress? If Jack wanted her to show off to these men, then she would do so.

They could all go riding, but she would have to go sidesaddle. She could at least still take many of the jumps she usually did. She loved reading and mind puzzles. A plan started to formulate in her mind. She was not like most young women her age who spent their days doing needlepoint or practicing the piano forte. She had developed other skills.

"You have that look on your face again, Miss Addie." Joshua crossed his arms over his chest as he narrowed his eyes at her.

"What look?" She fought the smile that tugged at her lips.

"The look that usually comes before you do something that you probably shouldn't." Joshua gave her a pointed look.

Addison laughed as she headed for the door, Titan right beside her with his tail wagging. "If Jack wants me to show off for our guests, so be it." She called over her shoulder.

"This isn't going to be good." Joshua mumbled.

Chapter 9

Addison's whole body was filled with tension as she sat at the full table during dinner. Titan sat next to her with his head almost level with the table. His attention was on the nine men that sat around the table eating their meal.

Her earlier determination to show off her true self was quickly overshadowed by her fear as soon as two of the men approached her in the hallway. Titan's growls kept them at a distance, but they still put her nerves on edge.

"Miss Blackwell, you have been quiet this evening." Lord Channing turned to her.

Addison fought her rising panic and took a sip of her water before answering. She was proud of herself for not spilling her glass with how bad her hands were shaking. "You are assuming this is not normal for me, My Lord." Several of the gentlemen laughed.

"She has you there, Lord Channing. We do not know anything about you, Miss Blackwell. Tell us something about yourself that not many people know." Lord Percy smiled at her.

"Something many people do not know?" she asked in a shaky voice and Titan laid his head in her lap. Lord Percy nodded.

She drew strength from Titan's comforting presence. All nine men were watching her expectantly as she thought of how to answer. *Be strong, Addison and show your true colors.* She reminded herself. "When I was fourteen, I discovered a snake in the garden and thought it was fascinating. I tried to share my discovery with my brother, but he was not as enthusiastic as I was."

Silence fell around the table and Addison glanced briefly at Danny, who was glaring at her. Lord Ashton was sitting right next to him, and Addison caught the hint of a smile cross his face as he took a bite of his food. Addison took another bite of her own food as the silence continued.

"Miss Blackwell, tell us about your rather large and intimidating companion." Lord Blake requested.

Could she not just eat in peace? "I would hardly describe Daniel or Jack as large or intimidating." Addison took another bite without looking up.

A choking cough sounded to her right and she looked over to see Danny patting his chest as he tried to clear his throat.

"I think Lord Blake was referring to your dog, Addison." Jack sent her a warning look.

"My apologies." Addison forced a smile. "Titan is a dog with four legs, black fur with brown markings, brown eyes, and a strong protective instinct. He is loyal to a fault."

Addison affectionately stroked the dog's head. Her comments were once again met with silence. She was sure Lord Blake wanted to know where and why she got him, but she would never tell this lot about her need for Titan.

Before anyone could ask her another question, Addison looked at Jack. "Jack, what are your plans for tomorrow?"

Jack began to go over the gentlemen's plan to ride into the nearby village in the morning. He asked her to accompany them, but she declined. She explained she had some things to go over with the new housekeeper, Mrs. Jankins. Jack did not push the matter considering today was Mrs. Jankins's first day on the job.

The night continued with Jack's friends attempting to pull her into conversation while she gave them bland or obvious answers. Mr. Hansen was beginning to get frustrated with her. A vein pulsed in his neck when she deflected his attempts to bring her into a conversation with him.

Jack allowed her to retire early, and she hurried up to her room. She closed the door and locked it. Titan immediately jumped up on the bed and settled in while she changed into her brown work dress. The fabric was coarse and uncomfortable but there was no way she was going to be in her night gown if her brother and his handsome friend came in.

Tapping her lip, Addison looked around the room as she thought. Her lock was proving inefficient to keep people out of her room. Her eyes caught site of her wardrobe and a smile slowly spread across her face.

She spent the next twenty minutes pushing and pulling the wardrobe in front of her door. Addison finally sat on her bed, exhausted. It had been much heavier than she had expected, and she was breathing hard from the effort of moving it.

Now she just needed to make sure Danny and Lord Ashton couldn't get past her new barricade. They were probably still downstairs with everyone else. What was she going to do while she waited for them to come up to bed?

Lord Ashton's suggestion about reliving good memories had helped keep the nightmares at bay so Addison went to her small bookcase near the window and pulled out her old journal. She lay on her stomach across the end of the bed next to Titan as she began to read.

A couple of hours passed as Addison read. She smiled at how mischievous she used to be. She had been so full of life and adventure. A knock at the door had her head snapping up. She waited quietly for a moment before another knock came. She remained still. She heard quiet voices and then the sound of doors closing.

Danny was in his room. How was she going to get him to attempt to break into her room? She could scream, but that might bring more than just him into the room. Titan shifted and Addison looked at him. An idea popped into her head and a big smile spread across her face.

Sitting up, Addison faced the door and Titan. "All right Titan. You ready to get Daniel's attention?" She asked the dog quietly and his tail wagged. "Gib Laut." She commanded in a firm voice while keeping her voice low.

Titan let out a loud bark. Addison repeated the command several more times and Titan barked after each one. She added the 'spin' command to the mix. Titan was getting increasingly excited with the game, and he started to continuously bark as he jumped around the room.

A hard knock sounded at the door, which just caused Titan to bark even more. Addison grabbed for Titan's collar to start settling him down. The knocking became more insistent, but Addison remained silent.

She heard metal scratching the lock on her door and she held her breath. The handle turned but the door did not swing open. She heard a thump against the door and the wardrobe shook a little, but it held firm.

Addison jumped off the bed and pushed the wardrobe until the door could open a crack. Her fingers were nearly smashed as the door hit against the back of the wardrobe. Danny's face appeared in the crack.

"Can I help you?" she asked innocently.

"Open the door, Addie." Danny demanded. He did not look happy.

"Sorry, but no." Addison fought a smile as she watched his frustrated face as he tried to shove the door open more. "You can go back to bed now, Danny. And I assume Lord Fenwick, is it?"

Daniel stopped trying to push the door open as he furrowed his brow. "Of course, Ashton is here. He heard Titan barking too."

Addison rolled her eyes. "You do realize, brother, that you have not actually introduced me to his lordship? I have heard you call him by his given name and Jack mentioned his title. I think I heard Mr. Hansen call him Lord Fenwick earlier today, but I haven't had an introduction."

"You're right." Danny laughed. "Addie this is Lord Ashton Fenwick. Ashton, this is my sister Miss Addison Blackwell. Now, that we have that out of the way, can we come in?"

"Pleasure to finally meet you, My Lord. And no, you cannot come in." Addison smirked at her brother. "I am completely fine."

"Titan was barking, Addie. Please let us in." Danny strained against the door again.

"Having you two in my room is inappropriate, Daniel." Addison smiled at her brother. She reached through the crack of the door and flicked his forehead. He gave her a glare but stopped pushing on the door. "I was playing with Titan. He got excited and started barking. Plus, I needed to make sure you could not get in if I did have another nightmare."

"You got him to bark so that I would try to get in here to test whatever you have in front of your door?" Danny sounded mildly irritated. A laugh behind Danny had Addison fighting her own grin. Danny turned to the hallway. "Don't encourage her, Ashton." He turned back to look at her. "I thought you grew out of torturing me, dear sister?"

"I am not trying to torture you, Danny. I need to know that no one can enter my room. Who's to say that someone else can't just pick the lock like you do? Thank you for testing my new lock. Now go to bed."

"At least she didn't scream to get us here to try to break in." Lord Ashton said as Danny backed away from the door.

"I thought about it." Addison admitted. She laughed as she heard Danny groan. She closed and relocked the door before pushing the wardrobe back into its new place. Addison blew out her candles and climbed under the covers. "Hier, boy. Time for sleep." Titan laid down on the bed and Addison smiled as she fell asleep.

Addison woke to a knock on her door. "Who is it?" She called as she rubbed the sleep from her eyes.

"Mary, Miss. Mrs. Jankins is asking for you." Mary called through the door and Addison jumped out of bed. Glancing at the clock it read 7:30.

"Tell her I will meet her in the study in thirty minutes." Addison called back.

She dressed in her dark blue riding habit before she worked on moving the wardrobe. She managed to move it enough for her and Titan to slip out. She let out a sigh and moved quickly down the stairs.

Instead of going all the way to the kitchen to let Titan out, Addison opened the front door. Titan took off towards the back and she laughed. She was in a really good mood with not having any nightmares that kept her up all night.

Addison went into the study to wait for Mrs. Jankins. Not five minutes later she arrived. Addison studied the woman her brother had hired to take care of the house and staff. Mrs. Jankins looked to be in her early sixties with her greying hair pulled back in a severe bun at the back of her head. She was thin and not very tall. She had a serious expression on her face, but her brown eyes held kindness.

"Mrs. Jankins, I am Addison Blackwell. I have been running this household for nearly a year on my own. I am glad Lord Blackwell has finally found someone who can take up the mantle, but I also have certain expectations when it comes to how things are to be run." Addison smiled at the surprised look on Mrs. Jenkins's face. She gestured for the older woman to take a seat and they got to work.

They spent several hours going over Addison's records and routines for the household. Mrs. Jenkins was pleasantly surprised with Addison's organizational skills and the level at which she had taken care of everything since the last housekeeper left. She was also surprised but very happy when Addison mentioned that each servant was being taught how to read and write.

Addison felt like she and Mrs. Jenkins could work well together. It was just after two in the afternoon when Addison called it a day, and Mrs. Jenkins hurried off to check on preparations for dinner.

Addison walked out the front door and took a deep breath of the fresh air. A storm appeared to be building in the distance. *Great*. She quickly made her way to the stables. If she were to get her ride in before the storm hit, she needed to get going.

As she stepped inside the stables, the scent of fresh straw and leather hit her, and she began to relax. She smiled at Joshua as she saddled Spartan and led him outside. Titan trotted out beside her, ready for a run.

"Are you sure, Miss Addie? A storm is coming." James followed her out with a look of uncertainty.

"I will not be gone long, James. I skipped yesterday's ride and I need this." He gave her a reluctant nod as she tapped Spartan's front leg. He laid down and she climbed into the saddle. Spartan got back up and Addison shifted trying to get comfortable. Sidesaddle was so uncomfortable. "You can call in the calvary if I am not back by dinner." She sent him another smile.

Spartan galloped out of the stable yard and towards the meadows and hills. Addison closed her eyes and breathed in the heavy scent of the impending storm.

It wasn't long until the old church came into view and behind it sat rows of headstones. At the metal gate, Addison dismounted, signaled for Titan to stay, and walked through the grounds until she came across her father's grave.

She knelt on the ground as tears began to fall. She missed her father dearly. He had not only been her parent, but he had also been her closest friend.

She had been so young when he had taken ill. At fifteen, Addison's whole world had shifted to taking care of him. Her few friends ended up moving away and marrying while she had taken care of her father. She did not regret her sacrifice. She couldn't. She loved her father.

"I have started to re-read my journal." She said aloud as if her father was sitting there with her. "I hadn't realized how much I have changed since everything happened." Warm tears continued to flow down her cheeks. She attempted to wipe them away, but they were immediately replaced. "I am not sure if all the changes have been good. Father, I do not even know who I am any more. I am so scared that I cannot even attend church or go into the village. I have only left our estate lands to come visit you." Addison wrapped her arms around her middle in a vain attempt to comfort herself. "Please, help me find true happiness, to be the woman you raised me to be."

A raindrop fell on her head as she wiped the last of her tears away. Looking up, she noticed that the dark clouds were now directly overhead. Letting out a sigh, Addison said good-bye to her father and returned to Spartan and Titan.

Mounting quickly, she aimed Spartan in the direction of home and let him run. She was halfway back when the skies opened up and the rain began to fall in great sheets. Even though the rain was cold, Addison couldn't help the smile that spread across her face.

She slowed Spartan to a walk so he would not slip on the wet ground as the rain fell harder. She could barely see in front of her. She let Spartan direct them as she turned her face to the sky.

Titan let out a single bark and Addison looked around. She caught sight of lights in the distance and knew it was the house. Addison was not quite ready to be home yet, so she pulled Spartan to a stop. She slid off his back and tied up his reins so that he would not trip on them.

Addison wiped the rain from her face. "Go home Spartan and get something to eat." She patted his shoulder, and he trotted off. She turned her back to the lights and began to walk.

This storm reminded her of the storm that raged inside of her; dark and cold and empty. She thought back to the night of the break-in. Those men had taken nothing. From the time she heard the crash to the time they burst into her room, had been short. They must have come directly to her room. Had they come looking for her? Nothing was broken except for the window they had used to enter the house. Who were they? What had they wanted?

Titan barked again and she looked down at him. He wagged his tail and did a play bow. Addison smiled as she remembered the girl she had been before; so carefree and ready to take on the world. She wished she could be that girl again.

Addison stopped in her tracks. Why couldn't she? She had read in her journal from four years ago that she spent hours dancing in the rain until her father had forced her inside.

She turned her face back up to the heavens and smiled. If Jack wanted to marry her off, this might be one of the last times she would be able to enjoy this simple pleasure. She had always loved the rain. Maybe, just maybe, it could wash away all of her fears and leave her feeling at peace.

Addison spread her arms out wide and began to spin. She laughed as Titan jumped around her. She ran through the puddles and mud as she played tag with Titan. His happy barking and her laughter mixed with the downpour.

She was shivering and out of breath as she pushed Titan before taking off in the opposite direction. She let out a scream as he jumped on her back knocking her to the ground. She rolled over and he began licking her face. Titan got off her and ran off as she continued to lay there, breathing hard and laughing.

She jumped when a figure suddenly appeared above her. Strong arms scooped her up and hugged her close. "Miss Addison, are you all right?" Lord Ashton's voice reached her ears. She wiped the rain from her face as she looked at the man sitting in the rain with her.

"Lord Ashton?" She started laughing. "Isn't this storm amazing?"

"Addison, you have had us all worried sick. Spartan returned nearly two hours ago." Relief and confusion shone on his face. He ran his knuckles over her cheek before cupping it. "Are you all right?" he asked again as he studied her face.

Addison shivered as she stood up. She looked down at him as he remained kneeling on the wet ground, watching her. "I am more than all right, Lord Ashton." She saw a movement and knew Titan was running towards her. Before he could tackle her again, she took off giggling as the dog loped after her.

"She's over here!" She heard Lord Ashton yell, and a voice answered him.

She ignored him and whoever he was with as she continued to play with Titan. The mud caused Titan to slip frequently which allowed her more chances to get away from him. Someone grabbed her arm and spun her around. Danny stood there completely drenched.

"What are you doing, Addison?" He said loudly in order to be heard over the rain.

"I am embracing life, Danny. I am having fun." Addison gave him a push and he slipped on the mud. He pulled her down with him and she laughed. "Tag. You're it." She said as she got to her feet and ran.

"Addie, that's not fair!" She heard Danny yell after her.

Titan barked as he followed her. She thought she heard footsteps behind her, so she glanced over her shoulder. Danny was right on her heels. She squealed as she ran faster. The ground suddenly dipped, and she lost her footing. She tumbled down a steep embankment.

"Addie!" Danny's panicked voice followed her as she rolled and slid down the hill.

Addison finally rolled to a stop. She lay there blinking up at the dark storm clouds and the falling rain. There was a moment of stillness before she started laughing so hard tears started to roll down her cheeks, mixing with the rain and mud. She was gasping for air from her laughing fit when Danny and Lord Ashton made it to her side. They knelt beside her as they tried to assess her for any injuries.

"Addison, where are you hurt?" Danny's worried voice asked her. "Addie, please answer me." Addison looked between Danny and Lord Ashton. Their worried faces made her laugh even harder.

"I can't tell if she is crying or laughing." Lord Ashton commented as he brushed her wet hair from her face.

"Both." She wheezed out. She finally was able to stop laughing. She wiped the rain and tears off her face. "I lost track, whose it?" she asked, trying to get up.

Danny and Lord Ashton each grabbed one of her arms as they helped her to her feet. "I think we are done for the day, Addie. You are shivering."

Addison laughed as she turned to climb the hill. They were about halfway up when Addison looked at Danny. "Fine. But do not be surprised if there is a new friend in your bed tonight."

Lord Ashton stopped climbing and laughed. The mud under his feet was so slick that he started to slide. He fell to his knees as he slipped all the way down the hill.

Addison started laughing again and her own feet slipped out from under her. She let out a squeak as she slid down the hill. She was still laughing when she hit something hard. She looked over to see Lord Ashton still on his back, chest heaving.

"Are you all right?" he asked as he continued to laugh, and his blue eyes sparked with amusement. Addison grinned at him.

"You two are hopeless." Danny called down from halfway up the hill right before he let out a curse and began sliding towards them.

Lord Ashton grabbed her around her waist and rolled, putting his body between her and Danny's. She felt the moment Danny collided with Lord Ashton's back. She looked up into Lord Ashton's face and knew he was just about to ask her if she was all right.

"Don't you dare ask." Addison warned. Lord Ashton smiled at her. "You have a little mud right here." Addison laughed as she wiped his cheek, only making it worse. She bit her lip to keep from laughing harder.

Once they were all back on their feet, they stood looking up the steep hill. "How are we going to make it up the hill? It's too slippery." Danny asked, his earlier amusement fading.

She looked up the hill. Titan paced at the top. "I have an idea." Addison patted Danny's arm as she shivered again. "Titan, hier!" She called up to him.

Titan picked his way carefully down, only sliding a few times. Addison began to climb the hill towards Titan. When she met him, she gripped his collar. "Weiter." She commanded and he turned around, heading back up. After several minutes and several near falls, she made it to the top. She lay on her back to catch her breath.

"Addison?" Danny called up. "That's great that you got up, but what about Ashton and me?"

Addison sat up and peered back down at the two men standing at the bottom. The rain had lightened up quite a bit, but it was still enough to keep the hill slick.

She grabbed Titan's collar and looked him in the eyes. "Titan, bring seil." She said as she began shivering again. The dog took off through the meadow. She looked back down the hill. "Give me a minute. I have an idea on how to get you two up here." She pulled her knees to her chest and closed her eyes. She rubbed her hands up and down her arms trying to warm herself. Now that she wasn't running around, she was really feeling the cold.

Something pressed into Addison's face, and she slowly opened her eyes. Titan's nose was sniffing her. She uncurled herself with a groan. A rope lay in the grass next to her. Addison looked at it for a long moment before it registered what the rope was for. Grabbing it, Addison moved back to the edge. "Danny?" She called down.

"Addie? Where have you been?" Danny stood and looked up at her.

"I am throwing d-down a rope. I will let you k-know when I g-get the other e-end secured." Her teeth were chattering as she tossed down one end of the rope. After Danny grabbed his end, Addison looked around to see if there was anything she could tie her end to but found nothing.

She tripped over a rock that was mostly buried in the ground. Seeing no other option, Addison sat on the wet ground and wrapped the rope around her back, gripping the rope tightly. She pushed her feet against the rock as she sent up a prayer that she would have the strength to get at least one of them up the hill.

"Okay!" She yelled.

The rope pulled tight, and she tightened her grip on it. It bit into her back and palms as the other end was being pulled. Tears stung her eyes. She was so cold, and her hands felt almost numb.

She questioned her choice to play in the storm but could not bring herself to fully regret it. She hadn't laughed like that in years, but at the same time, she was so very cold.

A warm hand covered hers on the rope and she looked up surprised. Blue eyes full of worry studied her. Lord Ashton sat down next to her as he took the rope from her. Addison didn't say anything, and she didn't move. Lord Ashton called down to Danny and she saw his muscles tighten as he held the rope as Danny climbed up.

She stared down at Titan who lay across her lap. A hand cupped her face and turned her to look at them. Danny looked anxiously at her. She gave him a smile even though her teeth were chattering. "Y-you ready to h-head home?" She asked as she tried to push Titan off her lap. He didn't budge.

"Titan, steh auf." Lord Ashton said firmly. Titan whined before slowly getting off Addison's legs. "We need to get her back home and warmed up."

Addison looked over at Lord Ashton. Was that real concern in his voice? She was fine. She could get home on her own.

Addison got to her feet and stumbled forward. She wrapped her arms around herself. Something was draped over her shoulders and she tugged it tight around herself relishing its warmth. She took a deep breath and smiled at the smells that accosted her nose. It was an unusual combination of scents, but she liked it. It smelled like a combination of leather and...mint?

She continued walking without saying anything. She could see the lights of the house. Addison's shivering was getting worse.

"Addie?" Danny asked tentatively. "How are you doing?"

Addison laughed. "B-better than ever." She pulled the large coat tighter around her. "Just a little c-cold."

They got to the door that led to the kitchen and with a shaking hand Addison opened the door. When she stepped into the warm kitchen, a startled Mary dropped the bowl she was holding.

"Miss Addie!" She cried out as she ran to her, completely ignoring the broken bowl on the floor. "What happened?"

"I-I played with T-Titan in the rain. D-Danny shoved me down a hill and we got s-stuck at the bottom b-because of the r-rain. Titan h-helped me up and then I-I had to rescue the g-gents." Addison smiled as Mary's eyes widened in shock.

"I did not shove her down the hill. She ran over the edge." Danny corrected her.

"You are back to your normal shenanigans, I see. But my word, Miss Addie. You are covered in mud and shivering." Mary smiled at her.

"A w-warm bath and something w-warm to eat and d-drink is all I need." Addison laughed. Mary nodded before calling for several maids to start preparing baths for the three of them. "Oh, M-Mary, I need y-your help moving m-my wardrobe." Addison called over her shoulder as she headed up the servants' stairs. Mary followed her with a confused look on her face. Addison explained what she had done, and Mary laughed.

Together they were able to push the wardrobe enough for the tub to be moved into her room. While the bath was being filled, Mary lit a fire to warm Addison up.

Once the bath was ready, Mary helped Addison get out of her wet clothes and into the steaming water. Addison bit her lip as she slowly lowered herself into the water. It felt hot on her cold skin, and she let out a hiss.

"It's really good to see the old you coming back to us, Miss Addie." Mary commented as she helped scrub the mud out of Addison's hair. "We all have been worried that this house party might make everything worse."

"This house party is ridiculous. I nearly have a panic attack whenever I am with Jack's friends. Mr. Hansen and Lord Channing specifically make my skin crawl." Addison shivered for effect causing Mary to laugh.

"What of Mr. Blackwell's friend? He seems nice enough and he is handsome too." Mary gave Addison a large smile.

"Lord Fenwick is nice, and Titan does not seem bothered by him. I do not know why but I don't feel panicked when I am near him. He seems to respect the fact that I cannot be around men very easily and he gives me the space I need." Addison took a deep breath and let it out slowly.

"The way he looks at you is rather adorable." Mary finished rinsing Addison's hair.

"What do you mean?" Addison asked confused. How did Lord Ashton look at her?

"Every time you are in the same room as him, he can't keep his eyes off you, Miss Addie. The look of concern in his eyes when they stepped into the kitchen behind you rivaled that of Mr. Blackwell's. He was watching your every move. When you started joking about being shoved down the hill and having to rescue them, the cutest dimple appeared on his face." Mary sighed. "I haven't noticed him smile unless you are in the room."

"He is just my brother's friend. His concern was because I was shivering with cold. Anyone would be concerned." Addison tried to reason away what Mary had said, even though her stomach did a summersault and her heart picked up its rhythm. "I can't imagine any man admiring me after seeing my childlike behavior today."

"I wish you would have invited me to join you. I would have loved to see the old Miss Addie." Mary held out a towel for Addison as she climbed out of the now murky water. "Please tell me she is here to stay."

"That is my hope, Mary." Addison smiled as Mary helped her into a clean, long-sleeved wool dress. She had worn this particular dress during the winter. It was dark grey in color with very little embellishments on it, but it was warm. "Do you know where Titan ran off to?"

"I believe Lord Fenwick volunteered to take Titan to the stables to get cleaned up." Mary answered as she left Addison's room.

Dinner would be announced soon, and Addison was beginning to feel anxious. If she were to face all of Jack's guests, she wanted Titan by her side.

Chapter 10

Addison left her room determined to go to the stables to find Titan. As she was passing Lord Ashton's door, she heard scratching and whining. She paused and listened. The whining increased and the scratching became more insistent.

Why would Titan be in Lord Ashton's room? Addison knocked on the door and waited anxiously. After a moment, the door cracked open. A black nose stuck itself through the crack just before the door flew open and crashed into the wall. Titan jumped up on her, nearly knocking her down.

"Titan, platz." Addison laughed at the dog's excitement. Addison glanced back at the open door and saw Lord Ashton watching her with a lopsided grin on his face. Titan settled into his place at her side with his rearend wagging with his stubby tail. She ran her hand across his wet back.

"I took him to the stables, but Joshua was unable to get him cleaned up. Titan just kept trying to get back to the house. I brought him up here and did my best to get him clean so he would be ready for dinner." Lord Ashton scratched the back of his neck as a light blush touched his cheeks.

"You gave Titan a bath?" Addison's eyes went wide. Titan was difficult at best to give a bath too. She noticed that Lord Ashton was still in his wet and muddy clothes from earlier.

"Well, I..." Lord Ashton cleared his throat before meeting her eyes. "He was a mess and I figured Lord Blackwell would draw the line at a muddy dog at dinner."

Addison could not control her smile anymore. "Titan is a nightmare to give a bath too."

"I figured that out." Lord Ashton chuckled. "He seems excited to be done though."

Addison looked down at Titan's still wagging tail and tongue that was hanging out of his mouth. "Thank you, My Lord. I do not know what I would do without him with me tonight." She looked back at Lord Ashton and their eyes met. Addison's breath caught at the intensity of his gaze. "I will see you at dinner, Lord Ashton. Fuss." Addison curtsied before turning and continuing down the hall. She could feel his eyes on her until she made it to the stairs. Once she was down on the ground floor, Addison was able to take a full breath.

Hearing voices coming from the dining room, Addison made her way in that direction. Jack had made it clear that the gathering was going to be less formal and more relaxed. They were to meet in the dining hall instead of the drawing room for meals.

As she entered, she noticed that everyone but Lord Ashton was there. She made her way to her seat quickly. Titan's wagging tail and happy demeanor changed to one of alert protectiveness as she sat.

"Miss Blackwell, we were wondering where you had disappeared to." Lord Percy smiled at her. Addison gave him a weak smile as she picked up her fork.

"Is everything okay, Addison?" Jack asked with a hint of concern in his voice. "Danny told me about this afternoon."

Addison could not stop the smile that spread across her face as she looked down the table at Jack. Running and playing in the rain had been amazing. She had felt like the downpour had washed a lot of her stress and grief away. "I am more than okay, Jack."

Conversation among the gentlemen picked back up and Addison focused on her food. She still felt a bit chilled from the rain and anxious with all the guests present, but she felt lighter than she had in years.

Her father's two-year long illness had taken its toll on her in a way she hadn't realized. Reading her journal had shown her just how much she had withdrawn from life.

A noise at the door had Addison peaking up through her lashes. Lord Ashton made his way over to where Daniel was sitting and took his seat. He glanced over at her and gave her a wink. Addison's cheeks flushed and Lord Ashton's eyes twinkled with laughter, even though his face remained stoic. Addison quickly looked back at her plate and tuned back into the conversations around her.

"What is that smell?" Mr. Hansen said in disgust. "It almost smells like wet..." His voice trailed off and Addison caught his subtle glance in her direction. Addison's grip on her fork tightened. He was most definitely talking about Titan. "I'm surprised, Lord Blackwell, that you allow your sister such liberties." Mr. Hansen had lowered his voice, but Addison still heard him.

Jack's response was quieter, and she was unable to make it out. Addison tried not to react. She would let the comment slide to keep the peace. She really did not want to draw attention to herself if she could avoid it.

There were more comments made by several of the gentlemen about Titan being in the house and Jack's lack of control over her. Addison counted to ten as she bit her tongue. Her earlier anxiety about being in the same room as all the gentlemen was fading as anger began taking over.

"Miss Blackwell, do you always dress to match the weather?" Lord Percy asked.

"Excuse me?" Addison set her fork down as she looked over at the gentleman.

"Your grey dress? I can only assume you are matching the storm clouds outside, either that or someone died." Lord Percy smiled at her, oblivious to her raised hackles.

Silence filled the room as she continued to stare at the man as he took another bite of his food. She clenched her jaw so tightly that her teeth began to hurt.

Titan began to whine as he turned his attention to her. He had never seen her this angry before and didn't know how to react. She slowly placed her hand on his head before letting it run down his back.

"Are you saying I look like I am in mourning, Lord Percy?" she finally asked with a raised brow.

"Addie, he most likely does not know." Danny whispered to her, but she ignored him.

"That dress does have that air about it." Lord Percy started to realize how tense the atmosphere in the room had become.

Lord Channing cleared his throat. "You seem different than your normal self, my dear Miss Blackwell. You appear to have a glow about you."

That did it. How could any of these men know what her 'normal' was? "You are assuming you know me well enough to know my 'normal,' sir."

"Addison, calm down." Jack said quickly.

"Calm down? How do you know if I am calm or not? No one here knows me, Jack. Not even you." Addison stood from her chair causing everyone to stand as well. "You and Daniel have been absent from my life for over three years, and I have known these gentlemen for less than a week, yet you all assume to know my 'normal' dressing habits and my 'normal' behavior and moods."

Addison took a deep breath. "Fuss." She snapped out as she began to head for the door. Just before stepping into the hall, she turned around to face the room again. She could feel her blood boiling. "That is going to change starting tomorrow. Breakfast will be served at 6:30 in the morning. By 7:00, I expect to see every one of you up in the nursery dressed in your riding clothes." She turned back around and headed for the stairs.

"Now we've done it." Danny said with trepidation.

Once in the entry way, Addison changed her mind. Instead of going up to her room, she walked out the front door and slammed it behind her. Titan seemed uncertain about leaving her side.

"Voraus." She said and he ran off into the grass quickly.

As soon as he finished his business, she was going to go to her room and figure out what she was going to do to have everyone learn more about her. She did not even know why she had said that. She had been so mad that her mouth just ran away from her.

Several minutes passed and Titan was still just sniffing around. The front door opened behind her, but she refused to look. Titan's head snapped in her direction but after a second, he went back to whatever he was doing. So, whoever followed her outside was not a threat. Addison felt eyes on her, but she continued to glare out over the front lawn.

"Even when my mother is mad, I don't think she could shut down a room full of men like you did." Lord Ashton's voice was soft.

Addison let out a sigh and leaned her back against the pillar she was standing by. She looked at Lord Ashton as he leaned back against the opposite pillar. She studied him as he crossed his arms over his chest.

"Lord Blackwell seems nervous, and Daniel is absolutely terrified. According to Daniel, you had a look in your eyes that spells suffering." Lord Ashton sounded curious.

"Hardly." Addison scoffed. The wind picked up and she shivered. Lord Ashton pushed off the pillar as he unbuttoned his coat. He walked over to her slowly. He grabbed her hand gently and pulled her towards him. He wrapped his coat around her shoulders before meeting her questioning gaze.

"Better?" he asked quietly looking down at her.

"Yes. Thank you." Addison's voice was barely above a whisper. As if to belie her words, she shivered again.

Lord Ashton began to rub his hands up and down her arms.

Addison stood still, not knowing what to do. She was not afraid of Lord Ashton and Titan did not seem threatened by him either. Addison closed her eyes. Maybe if she couldn't see his mesmerizing blue eyes and his crooked grin, she could think more clearly.

A couple of minutes passed, and Addison found herself leaning forward slightly. She rested her head against Lord Ashton's shoulder and felt his hands move from her arms to her back. He stood still, not saying anything.

After another minute, Addison let out another sigh. "I cannot believe I did that." She muttered to herself. "I cannot believe I challenged a room full of men. What was I thinking?"

Lord Ashton's arms tightened around her. "You had every right to get angry. I was getting angry, and they were not even aiming their barbs at me." He chuckled softly. "You are definitely a force to be reckoned with, Miss Addison." Addison leaned back as she looked up into his face. "And I am looking forward to seeing what other amazing sides of Miss Addison Blackwell are revealed tomorrow."

Addison rolled her eyes as she took a step back. Lord Ashton's arms fell to his sides as he watched her with a smile. Titan came back onto the porch and nudged Addison's hand.

"I don't know if there is anything amazing about me, My Lord." Addison pulled the coat from around her shoulders and handed it back to him. "Thank you for the jacket and the conversation." She dipped into a curtsey before heading back inside. She was about to close the door but turned around to face him. He was watching her with an unreadable expression on his face. "Good night, Lord Ashton." Addison said quietly before closing the door and quickly making her way upstairs.

She made it to her room without running into anyone else. She changed for bed and lay under the covers. Mary had made sure the fire in her room was going, which kept the chill away. Addison stared up at the ceiling long after she blew out her candles.

Her stomach fluttered as she thought about her time out on the porch with Lord Ashton. He had come looking for her. Had she really leaned on him?

Addison let out a groan. He probably thought her a complete freak. A raving mad woman one minute and then leaning up against him for warmth the next. Embarrassment filled her. He offered her his coat and she had taken advantage of his kindness by putting them in a potentially compromising situation.

What if someone had found them like that? Her reputation and his would have been ruined. How could she feel so at ease around him, enough so that she used him as a source of comfort? Whatever was going on needed to stop.

She could not trust him anymore than any other man. Every man in her life has left her and she didn't think she could handle it if Lord Ashton did as well. She let out another groan and Titan climbed on top of her legs. Closing her eyes, Addison willed herself to fall asleep.

Addison woke before the sun rose in the sky. She let out a soft moan as she stretched and got out of bed. She changed into her dark green riding habit and headed for the door.

With the storm yesterday, she needed to check on the Gracie's roof. Hopefully, the repairs held. Addison really needed to repair Mr. Harold's fence as well. It would have been a miracle if the storm hadn't knocked it completely down.

Addison stepped out into the hall and paused. The house party. She had nearly forgotten about it and that she was supposed to teach all the gentlemen a little about herself.

An idea began to form in her head about what she was going to have the gentlemen do in order to understand her better. She smiled at the prospect of finding out their characters as well. As she passed Daniel's door, she knocked loudly. After a few minutes, his door finally opened. He looked like the walking dead as he stared at her in confusion.

"Good morning, Danny." She smiled at him brightly.

"The sun isn't even up yet. What do you need, Addie?" He grumbled as he rubbed a hand over his face.

"It is time to get up Danny. The day is starting, and you are wasting precious time." Addison was fairly bouncing with excitement. Daniel groaned as he looked at her. "Do not give me that, big brother. You should be grateful that I let you sleep in." Addison laughed at the look of horror on his face before starting to head for the kitchen.

"You and Ashton would get along famously." Daniel muttered under his breath just before closing his door. "He never slept past the sunrise."

Addison walked into the kitchen and like normal, Mrs. Harvey wasn't there yet. She let Titan out and started making toast for everyone. If they wanted to know more about her, they were going to eat what she usually did. She was almost done when Mrs. Harvey entered the kitchen.

"Oh, Miss Addie. Good morning, dear." Mrs. Harvey moved over to help Addison pull the fruit preserves from the pantry. "What would you like for breakfast today?"

"Morning, Mrs. Harvey. We will be eating my usual today." Addison smiled at the older woman. Mrs. Harvey raised her brow in question. "The gentlemen have been making comments about my 'usuals' and my 'normal'."

Addison rolled her eyes. "Today they all will be experiencing a day in my shoes. Starting with their meals."

Mrs. Harvey chuckled. "In that case, I will start making their sandwiches for lunch. What would you like for dinner?"

"Soup and rolls, Mrs. Harvey. Just soup and rolls." Addison grabbed the tray of toast before turning around to see Mrs. Harvey watching her. "They all presume to know me, including Jack and Daniel. They have not really been around since they went off to school. All they know is the young girl I used to be. They have no idea the woman I have become. Jack set this whole house party up to find a man for me to marry. He doesn't know what I want; he doesn't know my hopes or my dreams." Addison ranted. Her earlier frustrations coming back.

"Then you show them just how strong and amazing you are Miss Addie. And don't forget that it is Thursday." She gave Addison a meaningful look. "Outshoot the lot of 'em and I will have a special something for you when you get back." Mrs. Harvey gave her a wink before pulling items out for picnic lunches.

"Thank you, Mrs. Harvey." Addison smiled. "Can you have Mary bring the strawberry preserves to the dining room when she wakes up?" Mrs. Harvey nodded, and Addison continued walking with the toast to the dining room.

Addison just put the toast on the sideboard with the grape preserves when she heard noises behind her. She grabbed a slice of toast and smeared a generous amount of preserves on it. Taking a bite, she turned around to see Daniel, Jack, Lord Ashton and Lord Percy watching her. All of them looked like they were asleep on their feet.

"Morning gentlemen." Addison said with a bright smile. "You all look rather chipper this morning." She took another bite of her toast.

"What's for breakfast, Addison?" Jack yawned as he moved to the sideboard, but when he saw what was there, he froze and looked at her.

"My usual breakfast." Addison bit her lip to keep from laughing. "Toast and water." Mary came into the room with wide eyes and quickly put the strawberry preserves next to the toast. "Right on time, Mary. Eat quickly gentlemen, we have a lot on our schedule today. Remember to meet in the nursery when you are finished."

Addison grabbed another slice of toast and began eating it on her way out of the room with Mary. She caught Lord Ashton's eye as she passed, and he bowed his head to her with a smile on his lips.

Once in the hall, Addison led the way upstairs towards the nursery. "What is going on, Miss?" Mary asked, confused.

"They all think they know me, but they do not. Today they are going to spend a day doing what I usually do. But I cannot have nine men going through my estate books. So instead, they are going to do a few puzzles that my father gave to me before he became too ill to continue our game. After that, they will be meeting me in the study. I need your help to set some things up." Addison explained to Mary.

They spent the next twenty minutes setting up the puzzle. The puzzle she had chosen was one of the last ones her father had given to her. Her father gave her a piece of paper with lines at the top with difficult math problems along the bottom half of the paper. The answers to the problems were then written under the lines at the top of the page. She had to use those numbers to decode a message with the numbers representing a letter's place in the alphabet.

Addison laughed to herself as she watched all nine gentlemen warily step into the nursery. They stood near the door as if they were afraid to come any farther into the room.

"How was breakfast?" Addison's question was met with silence. She smiled at them as she tried not to laugh at their unimpressed expressions. "Are you ready for the next order of business?" Still nothing from them. "Since I can't have the nine of you going through my estate logs and financial books, I have devised a little game to fill the time while I finish what I need to do." A few of the men scoffed, but she ignored them. "Now, are you going to be doing this challenge as a single group, two separate groups or individually?"

The gentlemen looked between each other before Jack looked back at her. "As one group."

"Perfect. This should go quickly then." Addison moved to a stack of papers. She picked them up and set them out on a long table that Mary had helped her pull out. "There are five math problems that I have created. You must solve the problems before using them to figure out your next clue. The problems are numbered, so keep them in order."

Addison grabbed Mary's arm and pulled her with her as she walked towards the door. Her heart rate picked up speed as she neared the gentlemen. Swallowing hard she managed to make it out of the room without panicking. Addison turned back around. "Good luck, gentlemen." Addison smiled before walking quickly away.

* * *

Addison sent Mary off to the stables to have her inform James and Joshua that they needed to have everyone's horses saddled and ready by eleven.

She stepped into the study and closed the door. She let out a sigh before making her way behind the desk. She got lost in her books and was startled when a knock came at the door. She called for whoever it was to enter as she continued to read over her notes about Mr. Harold's fence. It really needed to get done today. It was a good thing she had a plan to make quick work of it. If it was just her and Joshua, she would plan on it taking a few days to be completed.

A throat cleared and she looked up. Nine men stood frustrated in front of the desk. She glanced over at the clock. It was just after eleven. She was going to be late.

Addison closed her books and put them away quickly before turning back to the gentlemen watching her. "I'm glad you were able to complete that challenge. Follow me. We are running late."

She was anxious to get out of such a small room. She felt trapped with all of them in there with her. She only had to look at the right corner of the desk to see evidence from the last time she had been trapped in the study. The blood stain had been impossible to get out, but she refused to replace her father's desk. She glanced down and caught sight of the stain and memories flashed through her mind. She pushed past the gentlemen, desperate to be out of there.

"I'm sorry, Miss Blackwell, but what does any of this have to do with getting to know you?" Mr. Blake asked, irritation in his voice.

Addison didn't slow her steps as she headed out the front door. "Well sir, my day starts before the sun most days. That puzzle you did was one of the last puzzles my father gave me before he died." Addison smiled as Titan came running up to her. She paused long enough to press a kiss to his great big head.

"Fuss." As she approached the stable yard, she noticed nine horses saddled and ready to go, but Spartan was not among them. "Mount up gents, I will be right back." Addison called over her shoulder as she entered the stables.

She spotted Joshua and James mucking out the stalls. "Morning, Miss Addie." Joshua smiled at her.

"Good morning James, Joshua." she greeted, as she moved to Spartan's stall. She busied herself with tacking up Spartan for the ride. "James, can I steal Joshua this afternoon?" James nodded and Joshua ran to saddle up a horse so he could be ready to go when she was. She scrunched her nose as she placed the sidesaddle on Spartan's back.

"Addison?" Jack asked and Addison looked over at the door to see all of the gentlemen entering the stables. "James, why aren't you saddling Addison's horse for her?"

Addison turned to glare at her brother with her hands on her hips. "I prefer to saddle my own horse, Jack. James knows this about me." Jack's eyes widened and Addison turned around to finish.

Addison led Spartan out into the stable yard and to a more open area, away from the other horses. Titan was glued to her side as he eyed the gentlemen warily. "Can I assist you on your horse, Miss Blackwell?" Mr. Hansen stepped towards her with a smile that made her skin crawl.

Titan let out a growl as Addison turned to face the man fully. She didn't even try to smile at him. "There is no need for anyone to assist me, sir." she said firmly.

Addison tapped Spartan's front leg and he laid down. She settled herself into the saddle and patted Spartan's shoulder to let him know she was ready. He got to his feet and Addison looked at everyone. Several of the men's mouths were slightly open as they stared at her while Daniel and Lord Ashton were smiling.

Besides her, Joshua was the only other person on a horse at the moment. Addison gave Daniel a smirk as she nudged Spartan into a gallop, not waiting for the gentlemen to mount their horses. It did not take long for Addison to hear the thundering of horse hooves as her shadows for the day approached.

Time for lesson number two. She was a very capable horse woman. At least Daniel and Lord Ashton knew she could ride well. Spartan sensed her intentions and picked up his speed. She heard Jack yell at her to be careful, but she just smiled.

Joshua was just behind her as she took her first jump. The two of them had spent years jumping their horses as they visited the tenants. She heard his laugh of exhilaration as they landed and continued on their way.

It had been too long since she and Joshua had ridden like this. They took seven jumps before they spotted the Gracie's cottage. Spartan began to slow before coming to a stop at his usual spot next to the gate.

Addison slipped from the saddle while Joshua stayed mounted, grinning ear to ear with windswept hair. She turned towards the front door and took a step but was pulled back by strong arms.

Jack spun her around so fast she nearly fell before being crushed in a tight hug. "What were you thinking? Those jumps, Addison! You could have been hurt." Addison hugged her brother back. When he finally released her and stepped back to look at her, Addison could still see the fear in his eyes.

She reached up and placed a kiss on his cheek. "Jack, those were nothing. You should see the jumps I take when I ride astride. I have been doing this for years. Do not worry, I'm completely safe with Spartan." He let out a tense breath and shook his head. "You gentlemen stay here. Mrs. Gracie does not want strangers in her home. I need to check on the condition of the roof, since it was recently repaired."

Addison walked quickly towards the front door with Titan at her side. She stopped as she looked down at him. "Platz." She commanded and the dog laid down. "Bleib." Addison said before continuing to the door and knocking.

A minute later Mrs. Gracie opened the door with a smile. "Oh, Miss Addie. I had a feeling you would be by this morning. The roof held!" The young mother bounced the infant in her arms as she beamed at Addison.

"I am so glad to hear that. And how is Miss Evelynn today?" Addison smiled. She was so relieved to know that the roof no longer leaked.

"She slept through the storm! I don't know if it was the constant sound of the rain or what, but she actually slept." Tears gathered in Susan's eyes. She quickly blinked them away and then looked at something over Addison's shoulder, her smile slipping from her face. "Is that Lord Blackwell?" She whispered.

"Here let me hold Evelynn and you can go see him." Addison didn't give her much choice as she lifted the infant from her mother's arms. Susan had been all of their friends while growing up.

Addison watched as Susan marched up to Jack, pointed a finger at his chest and began scolding him for not being there for Addison. Addison's eyes widened in surprise; she had never seen Susan so angry before.

Addison blinked a few times before rushing towards Susan and putting herself in between the angry woman and Jack. "Mrs. Gracie, calm down. It is okay." She tried to soothe her friend.

"It is not okay, Miss Addie." Susan fumed. "It hasn't been okay. Not since that first night. You haven't been the same. Lord Blackwell should have been here for you instead of leaving you to pick up the pieces by yourself."

"Mrs. Gracie!" Addison said sternly, which got Susan's attention. "Why don't you take Evelynn inside. I will be there in a few minutes." Susan glared one more time at Jack before taking Evelynn from Addison and walking inside, slamming the door behind her.

Addison turned around to look at Jack. His brows were furrowed in confusion and there was pain in his eyes. "What was she talking about?" he asked softly.

"That is a conversation for a different time, Jack." Addison gave him a reassuring smile. She took a step back and looked over the shocked and confused faces of all the gentlemen.

"The roof repairs were a success, but I usually stay for a while to assist Mrs. Gracie with her baby. You gents will be following master Joshua to our next stop. Joshua will be in charge and will instruct you on the task you will be completing. My normal lunch has been packed into your saddlebags. I usually eat between jobs, so eat while you can."

Addison turned back to Jack, who was still studying her. She lowered her voice and whispered. "We will talk later, Jack." He nodded and remounted his horse. She waved as the group followed Joshua towards Mr. Harold's cottage.

Chapter 11

Addison was helping James set out five pistols on the table. There were five archery style targets already set out several paces away. This was the part of the day that Addison had been looking forward to the most. She had fallen in love with shooting. After a long day of dealing with her daily stresses, she found that shooting was a great way for her to unwind.

"Are you sure about this, Miss Addie? This isn't a typical activity that young ladies engage in?" James asked with a twinkle in his eye.

He was the one that discovered her trying to figure out how to work her father's old pistols. He had been impressed that she even wanted to learn the skill. After Mr. Drake attacked her, she wanted to be able to defend herself if needed.

"James, this is the highlight of my week. I am not going to pass on it just because some gentlemen might get their delicate feelings hurt." Addison gave him a wink and they both laughed.

Addison looked to the sky. It was late afternoon, and she was getting anxious to start. Addison had been using this particular clearing for target practice the past year and Joshua knew it well, so they weren't lost. James asked if she wanted her holsters, but she declined. She did not want them to know that she could use the guns.

Letting out an impatient sigh, Addison once again looked at the sky. It was going to get dark in the next couple of hours. She was debating taking a few shots when the sound of men's voices and horses reached her ears. Titan stood up from where he had been sunbathing and trotted over to her.

Joshua came through the trees with a huge grin on his face. "Miss Addie! The whole fence got finished."

"That is great news Joshua!" Addison smiled at the boy. "It is nice to know that we will not have to spend three or four days working on it next week. Did they give you any trouble?" Addison asked just as the rest of the party walked into the clearing. They all looked tired and were covered in dirt and sweat.

"A little, but Lord Fenwick and Lord Blackwell put them in their place." Joshua laughed.

Addison watched as the men approached. Mr. Hansen and Lord Channing glared at her while Jack, Danny and Lord Ashton gave her tired smiles. The other gentlemen either avoided her gaze or had stoney expressions.

Lord Channing stepped closer to her than the others, and Titan moved, putting his body between hers and the approaching man.

"Are we to assume, Miss Blackwell, that there was a reason for having us do the job of a laborer?" Lord Channing ground out through clenched teeth.

"Yes, there is Lord Channing. You see, you boys have saved me and Joshua four days of work." Addison glared at the man. "And before you ask, the answer is yes, I would have been in the dirt fixing the fence. I have done it before, and I will probably be doing it again."

Jack cleared his throat. "So, what is the next thing on your schedule, Addison?" He stepped up to the table that displayed the guns.

"I'm glad you asked." Addison pulled her glare from Lord Channing and smiled at the group. "Since you all have saved me a great deal of time mending the fence, I figured you could all use a little down time. We will be spending the next hour or two shooting." She watched the men's faces light up with excitement. "We have five pistols and five targets. We will have you in two separate groups. Each group will fire three shots and then we will tally up the scores. The lowest two shooters will be eliminated until we are down to three men. At which point it will be single elimination." Addison explained moving closer to the table.

"What is the prize for winning?" Mr. Hansen asked as his gaze traveled over her. Addison resisted the urge to shiver in disgust.

"Bragging rights?" Addison suggested.

"What about a kiss?" Lord Percy smiled and several of the gentlemen eagerly agreed with him.

"The winner gets a kiss from our lovely hostess." Mr. Hansen's smile spread even wider. Addison glanced at her brothers, but both looked too shocked to say anything.

Addison squared her shoulders. "I will accept your terms if I might add my own." When the gentlemen looked intrigued and several nodded for her to continue, she took a deep breath. "I will enter the competition when there is three men left." Laughter met her request.

"And what will you get if you win, Miss Blackwell?" Lord Channing was clearly mocking her.

Addison smiled as sweetly as she could. "I will give a kiss to two of you boys here." Addison saw the protest start on Mr. Hansen's lips. "Other than my brothers of course."

"Then its settle. A kiss for the winner or two kisses if Miss Blackwell wins." Mr. Hansen smirked at her.

Five men eagerly moved to the table and began loading their pistols. Addison slowly backed up as she observed those at the table. She was trying to gauge who would be her toughest opponents.

She bumped into someone and whirled around to find Lord Ashton's troubled gaze on her. Daniel and Jack moved to her side before she could say anything.

"What are you doing, Addison?" Daniel asked quietly as anger flashed in his eyes.

"You don't have to do this." Jack whispered.

"It will be fine. I have faith in the Blackwell Clan to save me from having to kiss any of those snakes." Addison gestured towards the group of men near the shooting line with her head. Jack pinched the bridge of his nose as if trying to calm himself. "Relax, Jack."

Gunshots filled the air and Addison turned back around to see how the shooters had faired. There was a chorus of cheers and laughter as guns were reloaded.

Addison felt a warm hand lightly touch her wrist and she knew that it was Lord Ashton. She resisted the urge to reach back and grab his hand. She wanted him to stay close.

Addison gave herself a mental shake. She was being ridiculous. She did not need a man in her life because all they ever did was leave.

Another round of gunshots pulled her attention back to the task at hand. She observed those that seemed more confident in their handling of the weapons. Mr. Hansen, Lord Channing and Lord Percy were all making great shots. Addison groaned.

Another light touch on her wrist and Addison took a half step back. She felt his warmth at her back and his proximity calmed her rising nervousness. "You're not getting nervous, are you?" Lord Ashton whispered just loud enough for her to hear. His breath caused her hair near her ear to tickle her neck.

Addison shook her head slightly just before the final shots were fired. She took a deep breath and stepped closer to her brothers. Now that the round was over and attention wasn't on the targets, Addison didn't want anyone to see how close she stood to Lord Ashton.

She glanced in his direction and saw him glaring at a couple of the gentlemen, but she could not tell which ones. The next line of shooters began stepping up to their mark and she found herself alone.

Titan positioned himself between her and everyone else and growled softly. She patted his side as she watched the shooters load their pistol, take aim, and fire.

She was surprised that her brothers were terrible shots while Lord Ashton had excellent aim. At the end of the round, Lord Trenton and Mr. Royce were eliminated.

Clean targets were put out and the next round started. This time Daniel and Lord Blake were eliminated, followed by Jack and Lord Percy. They were down to the final three.

Addison shook her hands out as she moved to the table. She was at the end with Lord Ashton to her left. At least she wouldn't have to stand next to Mr. Hansen or Lord Channing.

James was switching out the targets when Mr. Channing came around her right side. She immediately took a step to her left and bumped into Lord Ashton. She didn't move away from him as Lord Channing moved closer.

"Let me help show you how to properly load this." He reached for the gun in front of her.

"Thank you, sir, but I have been watching carefully to what everyone has been doing and I think I can manage." Addison tried not to grimace at his nearness.

Lord Channing made no move to leave, and Addison felt her anxiety creeping up. Titan picked up on it and immediately snapped at Lord Channing, who dropped the gun on the table and stumbled backward.

"Control your dog, Miss Blackwell." He snapped out.

"Considering you were invading the lady's space even after she told you she was fine, Lord Channing, I think the dog is entirely in the right for protecting Miss Blackwell." Lord Ashton said with a steel edge to his voice.

With Lord Channing back at his spot, Addison moved back to hers and busied herself with her weapon. She purposely fumbled with it a few times, which wasn't hard considering her hands were shaking from Mr. Channing's unwanted attention. The gentlemen ended up waiting on her for the round to begin.

When she was ready, they all took aim and Addison pulled the trigger just after the others. She had purposely aimed a little to the right and hit the second ring out from the center.

She took stock of the other targets and saw she was in third place. She didn't want to slaughter them just yet, so she aimed for the second ring again. This time hitting to the left. On the third shot, she hit the first ring from the center. Lord Channing was eliminated.

She busied herself with her weapon again, but she could tell Lord Ashton kept glancing over at her. She ignored him and focused on her target. If Lord Ashton and Mr. Hansen shot similarly to the previous round, she would need to get a few bullseyes to get into the final round.

They took aim again and this time Addison hit dead center. The field was silent for a moment before several of the gentlemen congratulated her on her good luck. She rolled her eyes inwardly. It was not luck. It was a year's worth of constant practice. Addison's second and third shots hit the first ring out from the center, effectively knocking Lord Ashton from the running.

Mr. Hansen smiled at her and gave her a wink. Addison shivered in disgust. "Stop playing with them Miss Addie!" Joshua yelled just before James clamped his hand over Joshua's mouth.

She reached around Lord Ashton and pulled the other two pistols over to her side. She loaded all three of them and turned to Mr. Hansen.

"Why don't you take your three shots and then I will take mine." Addison suggested. Mr. Hansen raised a brow at her but shrugged his shoulders.

He fired his three shots, two in the bullseye and one on the first ring from the center. He helped load the pistols for her. All five were now ready to shoot. He stepped back, giving her space with a smirk on his face.

Addison turned her back to him and took a calming breath. She could not lose this. She picked up the first pistol and aimed. She hit dead center again. There was silence all around as she picked up the second gun. She hit just to the right of her original shot but still in the center ring. Taking a deep breath, she grabbed the third gun and aimed. She pulled the trigger and hit to the left of the center hole but still in the bullseye.

Silence remained and she slowly turned around. All the men had their mouths slightly agape. Mr. Hansen was the first to recover from his shock and his face turned red. "Those were just lucky shots, Miss Blackwell." He accused.

"Oh really?" Addison said grabbing the other two pistols, one in each hand. She shot them, one right after the other, each shot hitting Mr. Hansen's bullseye.

Jack's smile was huge, and he walked over and pulled her into a hug. "I can't believe you hustled us in a shooting competition." He laughed. "Now you have your prize that needs to be handed out, dear sister."

Addison laughed. "Very well. As promised, a kiss to two of you boys, other than my brothers." Addison restated her wording.

She knew that Lord Channing and Mr. Hansen especially were not going to like who she bestowed her kisses on. Addison bent down and kissed Titan on his head causing his tail to wag. "One." She said to sputtering from several of the gentlemen.

Addison turned and walked towards Lord Ashton and Mr. Hansen who were standing side by side. As she approached, she made eye contact with both. She stopped in front of them but waited until Mr. Hansen began to shift uncomfortably.

"Excuse me." She said with a pointed look. Confused, Mr. Hansen and Lord Ashton stepped aside, and she walked up to Spartan. She gave his velvety muzzle a kiss. "Two." She turned around with a smirk.

Laughter shone in Lord Ashton's eyes while Mr. Hansen looked like he was going to burst a blood vessel. "That was not in the agreement."

"My sister said two boys. I do believe both Titan and Spartan are boys, therefore they fall into the terms she set, and you agreed to sir." Daniel crossed his arms over his chest and raised a brow, daring Mr. Hansen to push the matter.

Addison could see him grinding his teeth before he finally stormed off into the trees. The tension in the meadow was so thick she could cut it with a spoon.

She cleared her throat. "Thank you, gentlemen, for shooting a few rounds with me. Would any of you be up to a round of archery tomorrow? You can choose standing target practice or mounted."

Daniel laughed. "You taught yourself archery as well?

"Of course not." Addison rolled her eyes at her brother. "Father started teaching me when I was five. We moved to mounted target practice when I was seven."

"I have a feeling you would outshoot us at that as well." Jack commented as he draped his arm over her shoulders. "And father taught you to shoot?"

"No. He got sick before he was able to. He said for my twentieth birthday he would get me my own set of pistols if I could outshoot him before then."

"What other things did father teach you while we were away?" Daniel asked while laughing in disbelief.

"Just like you, he taught me to play cards." Addison tapped her lip as she fought a smile. "Do you recall my ninth birthday when you both forgot to bring me something, again." Their smiles grew as they nodded. "Father suggested we play a round of cards."

Jack suddenly straightened and turned to look at her. "That was when you lost the first six games and then won on the seventh, forcing us to be done for the night."

"I sure did." Addison said proudly.

"How did winning a hand at cards end the night?" Lord Percy asked, clearly amused by the story.

"She cleaned us out of all our spending money for the quarter. Father only laughed and called it a night." Daniel scowled playfully at Addison.

"How did you manage that?" Lord Ashton asked.

Addison tapped Spartan's leg and settled into the saddle while everyone watched her. Once Spartan had gotten back to his feet, she looked back at the crowd. "Father told me to lose as I learned their tells. Then I could clean them out."

"You cheated!" Danny accused.

"Oh no, big brother." Addison clicked her tongue. "You are just terrible at gambling." Laughter met her comment. Mr. Hansen reappeared still looking angry. "I must be getting back to the house. I have several more things that need to be seen to before dinner is served. You gentlemen are free to take the rest of the day off from my duties. And I will see you all at dinner." Addison said as she turned Spartan towards home. "Titan, fuss."

She trotted off with Titan at her side and made it to the stables before anyone else. She untacked Spartan and led him into his stall before heading back inside to make notes in the records, check on dinner preparations, and meet with a few of the servants for their reading lessons.

A few hours later, Addison was walking by the ballroom when someone reached out and grabbed her. They pulled her into the dark room. She was just about to scream when she saw laughing ocean blue eyes. Her heart was beating so hard she was sure he could hear it.

"You can't scare me like that." She smacked his arm as she whispered. They really should not be in a dark ballroom by themselves.

"I needed to speak with you." He whispered back as he took a step closer, which did not help her racing heart. Addison stood quietly waiting for him to say more as she studied him.

He smiled at her, and his dimple appeared. He reached up and tucked a few strands of her hair behind her ear. He cupped her cheek as he took another step closer to her. "You were amazing today, Miss Addison." Addison was having a hard time breathing with him looking at her like that.

Addison's breath hitched as his head dipped slowly towards hers. He was giving her plenty of time to back away. Did she want to back away? She couldn't help the feeling of longing that filled her.

She wanted him close to her. She needed to feel his strong reassuring presence next to her. A breath away from his lips touching hers, he paused, giving her one more chance to pull away. Even though her head was screaming at her to run, Addison rose up on her toes and closed the distance.

She felt him smile against her lips as he pulled her closer. At some point her arms had found their way around his neck. After several minutes, Lord Ashton pulled back allowing them to breathe. He rested his forehead against hers as he tried to catch his breath. Lord Ashton pressed a kiss to Addison's forehead as she leaned into him, and he wrapped his arms around her, holding her close.

"Have you seen Miss Addie?" Mary asked someone in the hallway and Addison tensed.

"No, last I saw her, she was up with Hazel in the nursery." Another maid answered followed by the sound of footsteps retreating back down the hallway.

Addison leaned back and looked up into Lord Ashton's face. His eyes were a stormy blue as he gazed down at her. "I should go." She whispered, regretting the fact that she couldn't stay.

"Addison, promise me you won't make any more wagers where you will be kissing other men." His breath tickled her neck as he whispered close to her ear.

"Is it really a wager when I already knew the outcome?" Addison asked as she took a step back out of his arms.

Ashton reached for her again and she allowed him to pull her back to him. "When I wanted to point the gun at every man there just to make sure he wouldn't win, it's too close to take a chance." Ashton whispered before pressing his lips back to hers.

Addison smiled as she pulled back again. "It is almost dinner time, My Lord. We should probably go before we are late. I think you will love what the cook has prepared."

"It is Ashton, if you don't mind, and I am worried that dinner will be another scant offering. You need to eat better if today's foods are examples of your usual meals." Ashton kept hold of her hand as he pulled her slightly more into the shadows.

"I have survived on those meals for over two years, Ashton. They serve me well and allow me to get everything done that I need to." Addison said defensively.

"Don't be surprised if I start requesting heartier meals, my dear Addison." He pressed a kiss to her hand. "I was a bit disappointed that you weren't wearing your breaches today." He muttered quietly.

Addison covered her mouth to try to keep her laugh quiet. "You are probably the only man on the planet who would ever say such a thing." Addison raised up on her toes and kissed his cheek. "Could you imagine the other gentlemen's faces if I had worn my riding clothes? Jack would have skinned me alive."

"You are right. The other gentlemen do not need to see how beautiful you are in that outfit." He gave her a crooked smile before pressing a kiss to her lips one more time. "You head out first and I will follow in a few minutes."

Addison smiled before turning for the door. She resisted the urge to look back as she stepped out into the hall. She made her way to her bedroom, needing a moment to compose herself.

Once safely behind her door, Addison closed her eyes and took several deep breaths. What had she just done? She had sworn off men since the day after the funeral when her brothers left without saying good-bye.

What was it about Lord Ashton that made her lower her guard around him? Sure, he was handsome with his brown hair, tanned skin, and ocean blue eyes. His dimpled smile caused her heart to skip a beat and he was observant and kind. Somehow, he knew what she always needed.

Addison pushed off the door and began pacing. She needed to get her head on straight. Men never brought any good to her life. They either abandoned her, or they attacked and hurt her.

Squaring her shoulders, Addison put her priorities back in order. There was no way she was falling for Lord Ashton Fenwick. That kiss was just that, a kiss. All be it her first, but still just a kiss. She would have that memory for the rest of her life, but she was going to keep her distance from Ashton from now on.

She could not let herself fall anymore for him than she already had because he would eventually leave too. Addison would have to learn to deal with it when he did. Chances were that she was just a diversion for him. Someone to pass the time with since she was the only female at this house party.

Addison moved to the door, determined to avoid Lord Ashton for the rest of the evening. Tomorrow she would come up with a plan to avoid him for the rest of the house party.

Addison walked into the dining room, late, with her head held high. As the gentlemen stood at her entrance, she reminded herself not to look over at Ashton.

She took her seat and waited for Jack to signal for the meal to begin. There was some grumbling about the soup and rolls for dinner, but Addison ignored the comments. She did not realize how hard it would be to keep her gaze from drifting to Ashton. She could feel his eyes on her throughout the meal.

When dinner was over, they all went to the drawing room. Addison did not feel like talking with anyone, so she moved to a single chair near the fireplace. She pulled out a book and pretended to read it. Luckily for her, the gentlemen all seemed to get the hint to leave her be and started forming small groups as they struck up conversations.

Addison turned a page in her book and glanced up briefly. Her eyes met those of Ashton's, and she quickly looked back at her book. She felt her cheeks warm as the memory of their kiss resurfaced.

Dash it all. Curse his amazing blue eyes. Addison scolded herself for looking up. Her heart skipped a beat as she continued to think about the feel of Ashton's arms around her and the feel of his lips. *Stop it, Addison. You do not need the heartbreak that would eventually come with getting attached to him.*

Addison got to her feet and took a step closer to the fireplace. Maybe she should just head to bed so she could put more distance between herself and Ashton. A soft knock on the door drew her attention.

Addison turned to see a footman leaning down to speak to Jack. When he straightened back up the blood in Addison's veins froze. His eyes met hers and she could not draw in a breath.

He gave her the same smile he had that night he had pulled her from her bed. He winked at her before turning and walking from the room.

Addison's ears started to ring, and she felt like she was drowning, unable to breathe. Someone called her name, but it sounded as if it were from a great distance. How was he here? Why was he here? Where was the other man?

A hand touched her arm and she jerked away. She looked around but everything was blurry. Where did he go? She needed to know where he was so she could get away. A hand cupped her face, and another grabbed her arm. She tried to back away, but they held firm. She looked at her attacker and was met with blue eyes that were full of concern.

* * *

Ashton noticed the sudden shift in Addison after she turned to face the room. He watched the blood drain from her face and her breathing came in short gasps. Lord Blake asked if she was feeling all right, but she didn't react or show any indication she had heard him.

Ashton stood up and moved to her side. Her eyes were filled with terror. Ashton was concerned she was going to faint. He reached out and touched her arm, hoping to pull her from whatever thoughts were consuming her. She flinched away from his touch with a small whimper. Her reaction and gasping breaths drew the attention of the whole room.

"Where is Titan?" Ashton asked while keeping an eye on Addison. "Someone, go get Titan and Joshua." He commanded and he heard several men run from the room.

"She's having a panic attack." Daniel said as he moved to stand near her. He too was a bit pale as he watched his sister's terror filled eyes and ghostly white face.

Ashton grabbed her arm and cupped her face trying to get her to look at him. Maybe he could help calm her down a little before Titan was found. "Addison, look at me." he said firmly. Addison turned to look at him and his heart clenched. He had never seen someone so scared in his life. "Daniel, I don't think she is aware of anything going on." Ashton commented softly to his friend who nodded in agreement.

Addison's eyes met his and held. Tears started to pool in her beautiful green eyes. Her face and lips were completely devoid of color. She continued taking shallow quick breaths. She reached up and grabbed hold of Ashton's forearm.

"Ash." Addison whimpered before her legs gave out from under her. Ashton caught her before she fell, and he swooped her up into his arms. Her eyes were now closed, and she was completely limp.

"Lord Fenwick, take her to her room. You, send someone for the doctor." Lord Blackwell started snapping out orders as he followed Ashton up the stairs.

Mary came running but stopped when she saw Addison in Ashton's arms. Her face, too, went pale. Ashton tightened his hold on Addison as he reached the top of the stairs. He could feel her incredibly fast heartbeat and it worried him.

What had caused her panic attack? She had seemed completely fine most of the evening. She did seem quieter and avoided everyone since…His steps faltered as he approached her door. He glanced down at her face, guilt filling him. Had he caused her panic attack by kissing her earlier?

Jack opened the door for him, and he walked inside. Ashton gently placed Addison on the bed. She whimpered again and Ashton brushed the hair off her face. Mary came running in and rushed to the other side of the bed.

"What happened?" She asked.

"We were in the drawing room. She was reading a book by the fire and then she just started breathing fast and lost all her color. Then she fainted." Daniel paced at the foot of the bed. Ashton looked back down at Addison. She was still incredibly pale.

"She hasn't had one this bad since right after the break-in." Mary said quietly to herself before looking over at Jack, Daniel, and Ashton. "Where is Titan? Wasn't he with her?" Just then the large dog, followed by Joshua came bursting through the door. Titan jumped on the bed, jostling Addison's limp form. He whined and started licking her hand, but she did not move. He eventually settled down across her legs.

"What happened to Miss Addie?" Joshua's worried voice filled the room.

"Something triggered her. Joshua, tell Mrs. Harvey to get the tea ready and have her send up some cool water and some rags." Mary took a deep breath and let it out slowly before looking over at the boy. "Don't worry, we will get Miss Addie up and moving in no time."

Joshua nodded once before racing out the door. Mary began to move around the room while Daniel continued his pacing. Jack had his arms crossed over his chest as he stared at his sister. Ashton ran a hand through his hair. He grabbed her hand and held it tightly. She had to be okay. He needed her to be okay.

"What caused her to have such a severe panic attack?" Jack asked as he ran a hand through his hair.

"I'm not sure, Lord Blackwell. She is able to hide her anxiety pretty well. Usually, Titan is able to sense a coming attack and alert her to it. Miss Addie described it as a pressure settling on her chest that makes her feel like she cannot breathe as memories consume her. Titan is able to pull her from her spiraling thoughts and keeps her grounded in the present. If Titan wasn't there, she could have just been too overwhelmed being in the room with so many men." Mary explained as she accepted the bowl of water and rag from a footman.

The footman stood in the room a moment longer looking at Addison lying on the bed with a hard expression. Ashton noticed a scar that ran down the side of his face. The man left quickly after he saw Ashton watching him and Ashton was left with an uneasy feeling.

Addison's grip tightened on his hand, and he returned his gaze to her. Her eyes were still closed, but her grip remained strong. A hand touched his shoulder, and he glanced over to see Daniel watching him closely.

"What memories?" Jack asked quietly.

"From the break-in, My Lord." Mary said with a furrowed brow. When Jack looked at her just as puzzled, Mary explained the events of the break-in to Jack. It was the exact same as what Joshua had told Daniel and Ashton.

Jack moved over to a chair and sat heavily in it as he covered his face. His shoulders slumped forward before they started shaking. Ashton could tell Jack was taking it really hard, harder than Daniel had. Several minutes passed in silence before Mary cleared her throat.

"She'll be okay. She always is." Mary gave them a reassuring smile even though her mouth was tight with worry. "I'm going to ask you all to leave though so I can get her settled."

Jack nodded and headed for the door. Ashton could not bring himself to step away from Addison. He wanted to be there when she awoke. Daniel grabbed Ashton's arm and gave him a gentle tug. Ashton pulled his arm from Daniel's grip roughly.

Daniel's eyes widened and Ashton took a deep breath. He knew he couldn't stay. He had no right to stay with her. He leaned down and pressed a kiss to Addison's forehead before turning and walking out of the room. Daniel caught up to him and yanked him into his room.

"What was that, Ashton?" Daniel asked angrily.

Ashton ran his hands through his hair before rubbing his face. How was he going to tell his best friend that he was falling fast for his little sister? He looked over at Daniel who stood with his arms crossed glaring at him.

"Dan, I..." Ashton groaned as he turned toward the window. He braced his hands on either side of the window and hung his head.

"She got to you, didn't she?" Daniel's voice was softer.

Ashton kept his head down as he mumbled. "From the moment she thought I was you." He took a deep breath before straightening and looking back at Daniel.

"Does she know how you feel?" Daniel asked as he moved closer. Ashton shrugged. He had tried to let her know that he loved her but after they kissed, she had become distant and then collapsed. "Is this some infatuation or are you serious about her?" Daniel was watching him closely.

"I don't think I could go a day without her." Ashton looked straight into Daniel's eyes. He needed Daniel to know that he was, in fact, very serious about Addison.

After a few minutes of tense silence, both men staring at each other, Daniel's serious expression turned to an amused smirk. "Who would have thought that the oh-so-eligible Lord Ashton Fenwick would fall hard for a hot tempered devious little sprite like Addison." He let out a laugh.

"Very funny, Daniel. Your sister did not really give me a choice. How did she even do it? One minute she was your intriguing little sister who mistook me for you and the next she has become the most important thing to me. Then she agreed to kiss the winner of that blasted competition she set up. I was ready to shoot the whole lot of them." Ashton began to pace. Now that he was putting words to his feelings, he sounded utterly mad.

"You are in deep, Ashton." Daniel clapped him on the shoulder. "But I won't lie, I don't know who else would be able to handle her. I swear some of the pranks you pulled at school are the exact same things I could see her doing." Daniel started heading for the door. "Come on Ashton, let's go talk with Jack. He should probably know you are in love with Addison." Ashton followed Daniel out of the room, and downstairs to find Jack.

Chapter 12

Addison groaned as she opened her eyes. She was back in her room with Titan lying next to her snoring loudly. The room was dark except for the faint light of the moon coming through the partially open window. She tried to remember how she had gotten up to bed and then all the evening's memories came back to her.

The new footmen that Jack had hired was one of the men that had attacked her the night of the break-in. She was just about to get out of bed to go talk to Jack about the man when a movement in the shadows drew her attention. It was slight but she could have sworn she saw something move. Her brows drew together as she focused her attention on that spot.

She was about to sit up when a shadowy figure lunged at her. A hand grabbed her throat and squeezed. She tried to scream, but her air was completely cut off and no sound came out.

Addison scratched at the man's hand trying to get him to release his hold on her. She was struggling to get away from him when Titan jumped to his feet. He stared at them for a moment before clamping his jaw down on the man's forearm. Her attacker let out a muffled cry of pain as Titan's growls grew more vicious.

The man backed up dragging Titan over the top of her and off the bed. He began slamming his fist down on Titan's head trying to get the dog to release his hold.

Addison rolled off the other side of the bed while gasping for air. She knew she needed to get away from here and fast. She held her aching throat as she stumbled in the near darkness. She was moving around the end of the bed when she tripped into the side of the fireplace as she tried to run to the door. A yelp sounded and she looked over and saw Titan drop to the floor.

She grasped the fire poker just as the man lunged for her again. Addison swung the poker with all her might, striking the man across the head.

He fell at her feet, and she jumped over his unmoving body before dropping to her knees next to Titan. Her hands were shaking as she reached for him but stopped. There was a knife sticking out of his side and he whined softly at her.

Tears burned Addison's eyes as she ran her shaking hands over Titan's side. His side was wet with blood. The man groaned and Addison jumped to her feet. She couldn't stay there any longer. She needed to get away. She ran for the door and yanked it open. She sprinted through the hall, down the stairs and out the kitchen door.

She paused for just a second before continuing to run out into the meadow. Addison didn't stop running as she raced through the field. She knew she could not go to the stables to get Spartan. It would take too long, and she was afraid he would catch her there. At least with it dark and her wearing her dark grey dress, it would make her harder to spot.

As she ran, she tripped over a rock and fell. She quickly got back to her feet, ignoring the dirt that now covered her dress and hands. Her lungs were burning but Addison continued to push herself. The sun was just beginning to show itself as she caught sight of the Gracie's cottage and changed her course, angling towards it.

Addison was out of breath as she approached the door. She could hear movement on the other side and let out a sigh of relief. She knocked quickly and waited anxiously as she bounced on her feet. Finally, after what felt like a lifetime, someone unlocked the door.

The door opened a crack and Addison pushed her way inside before slamming the door behind her. She locked it quickly before turning and pressing her back to the door.

"Miss Addie! What is the matter?" Susan asked in surprise.

Addison couldn't hold the tears back anymore and a sob broke from her lips. She slid down the closed door as she buried her face in her hands.

They had come back for her. The men from the break-in were in her home. One had tried to kill her, and he had killed Titan. Addison felt Susan wrap her arms around her shoulders as she cried.

Once Addison had stopped crying, she looked up at Susan. Susan had been the only person she had told everything to about that long ago night. What the men looked like. What they did and how they acted. Everything. Being Mary's older sister and a friend for many years, Addison had felt safe telling her about the terrifying event. She needed to tell at least one person.

She did not tell Mary because Mary would have freaked out more than she already had.

"They came back." Addison sniffed. "At least one of them. I think Jack hired him as a footman. He attacked me in my bed. Titan bit him but the man stabbed him." Addison's throat ached from being squeezed so hard, and she felt more tears begin to form again.

Susan's face paled. "You can't go back there." Addison nodded her agreement.

"But what do I do? I won't stay here. It is too close to home, and I won't put you and your family in danger." Susan helped Addison to the couch.

"I think I have an idea." Addison kept her gaze on her hands as Susan continued to speak slowly as if she was trying to figure out if her idea was going to work or not as she spoke. "I have a cousin that works on an estate a day's ride from here. She has said that if ever I need someplace to work, she could probably get me a position there. What if you pretend to be a maid and work there until I send word that it is safe to return?"

Addison thought about it for a few minutes before she nodded slowly. She needed to get going before anyone came looking for her. "Thank you."

"I will write her and send the letter today so hopefully in a day or two you can be safely away from here. But until then, you will stay here and if anyone comes looking for you, you can hide in the attic." Susan said nodding her head.

Addison was grateful for Susan. She was so emotionally exhausted, and her throat was killing her. Between the man squeezing it, running and her crying, it felt like it was on fire.

Addison spent the next several hours in a bit of a daze. Susan tried to get her to eat but Addison didn't really have an appetite and it was incredibly painful to swallow. She cuddled Evelynn while Susan cleaned the small cottage.

It was just after they finished their midday meal when a knock came at the door. Addison's barely acquired calm shattered, and she began to shake. Susan took Evelyn from Addison as she pointed her towards the ladder that led up to the attic. Addison moved quickly as she climbed up the ladder. She was sitting against the wall, out of sight, when she heard Susan open the door.

"Can I help you?" Susan sounded so calm and normal.

"Yes, ma'am." A man said. "Have you seen Miss Blackwell?"

"She was here earlier at her normal time, but as you can see, she isn't here now." Susan answered. "Has something happened?" Addison was impressed with Susan's acting skills. She sounded so sincere as she asked about Addison.

"Miss Blackwell has gone missing. Lord Blackwell is desperate to find her."

"What happened?" If Addison didn't know any better, she would have thought this was the first time Susan had heard Addison was not where she should be.

"We are unsure of the details, ma'am. All I know is Miss Blackwell is missing and Lord Blackwell is looking for her." The man said.

"I will keep an eye out for her. And please send word if she is found." There was a pause before Susan called out louder. "Could you by chance take a letter to the big house for me? I need to send it off to my friend, but I forgot to give it to Miss Blackwell this morning."

Addison heard a muffled response and then the door closed. Ten minutes later, Susan's head poked up through the attic entrance and told Addison that the coast was clear.

The rest of the day was uneventful. Addison spent her time helping Susan with the household chores and Evelynn to keep her mind occupied. But her thoughts kept returning to the events of the early morning.

She wanted to know what had happened to Titan. Was he really dead? And she wanted Ashton. Addison bit her lip to keep it from trembling. She really needed to remember that Ashton was not hers.

Towards the evening, Addison hid in the attic so that Susan's husband, Ted, wasn't aware that she was there. Apparently, he couldn't keep secrets. Being alone in the attic with nothing but her own thoughts was not helping Addison remain calm.

She was terrified to fall asleep in case she had another nightmare. As she lay on the wood floor, she thought about her brothers. Jack had sent some of the servants to look for her. That thought brought some peace to her. She felt guilty for not running to him or Danny, who was asleep right next door to her room. She had been so scared that her only thought was to get far away, and she still wasn't used to her brothers being home.

Addison closed her eyes and immediately amused blue eyes were staring back at her. She could picture all the details of Ashton's face. His thick dark brows, chiseled jaw, the dimple that made an appearance when he smiled. His soft lips as he had kissed her in the ballroom. She could almost feel his arms wrapped around her, holding her tight as she almost knocked them both to the ground the first day they had met.

Addison felt a tear drop off the end of her nose. She wished she could be back on the front porch with his comforting arms around her. She had felt so safe and protected. Addison knew she could never be with him, but for the moment, she allowed herself to dream of what could have been if she was capable of trusting again.

Addison awoke to Susan calling her name softly at the top of the ladder. Addison opened her eyes and sat up. Susan gasped and her eyes went wide.

"Miss Addie! Your neck!" Addison raised a hand to her throat, and it was most defiantly sore. She tried to swallow but the pain was worse than the night before. "Come down and we will take a better look at it. Does it hurt?" Susan asked concerned.

Addison tried to respond but it only came out as a croak, so she nodded her head instead. She followed Susan down the ladder and into the kitchen. The warm tea that Susan set in front of her relieved the throbbing in her throat.

"What are the plans for the day?" Addison whispered, trying not to irritate her throat too much, but still winced in pain.

"You are going to rest while I do some baking." Susan still had a worried expression on her face. "Should I send for the doctor, Miss Addie? Your neck looks terrible." Addison shook her head. If a doctor came, they would know she was there and she didn't want to put the Gracie family in danger. After several minutes of silence, Susan spoke again. "I think you should tell Lord Blackwell."

Addison pondered on it for a few minutes before giving a small nod. "I need to let him know I'm here without alerting those men." Addison whispered.

"We could send a coded message?" Susan suggested and a thought came to Addison.

"Susan, write Jack a letter telling him that you are still waiting for your roof to be repaired. Tell him it had been several years, and it leaks terribly." Addison smiled at Susan. Susan gave her a confused look. "Jack and Daniel were with me when we came to check on the repairs. He should know that your roof was just repaired, and he will come to see what is going on. And it is all in my records." Susan's eyes lit up and she raced into the other room to retrieve her writing supplies.

She wrote a simple letter and put it on the table. Hopefully, he would come before she left for her new position. Addison also hoped that Jack wouldn't drag her back to the house before those men were captured. She admitted to herself that she was terrified to even return home. She didn't know if she was brave enough. They were able to get into her home twice and she was not going to allow them a third chance to get her.

Just after their midday meal, servants from the manor house came again. Addison sat in the attic as she listened to them asking again if Susan had seen her. Susan again said she hadn't but asked if they could deliver her repair request to Lord Blackwell. They agreed and left.

Two more days passed without so much as a single word from Jack. Addison wondered if he ignored her letter again. Logically, she knew that he was probably busy with the search for her or that he hadn't understood the hidden message, but there was still a part of her that worried he didn't care.

Each day someone from the manor house would come to inquire if Susan had seen Addison. Every visit was done by two different men than the day before. On day four of her being there, a letter was delivered to Susan on the search party's visit. As soon as they left, Susan tore open the letter and read it to Addison.

Susan's cousin, Rose Laramey had procured a position for Addison under the name of Hannah Smith as a kitchen maid. Addison was so relieved to be leaving the Gracle's home. She had been feeling more and more horrible as she continued to put the family at risk with her presence.

The rest of the day was spent gathering supplies for Addison so she could leave that night after everyone was in bed. The plan was set for Addison to leave the cottage and travel to town to get a room at the local inn as Hannah Smith. First thing in the morning, Addison was to catch a travelling coach and head for Lakeview Park.

As Addison sat in the attic alone, she let her tears fall. She did not want to leave. She knew that Ashton was still at the estate, and she missed him terribly. She finally admitted to herself that she had feelings for him despite her resolve to not put her heart through that kind of pain.

Looking at the small watch Susan gave her; Addison wiped the tears from her cheeks. It was time. Silently slipping out the front door with her small bag of borrowed belongings, Addison hurried along the path that cut through the woods towards town.

It was a thirty-minute walk and the temperatures at night were getting cooler with the approach of fall. She pulled her borrowed cloak snuggly around herself and tried not to think about everything she was leaving behind. Spartan, her friends, Jack and Daniel, Ashton, Titan.

Susan had assured Addison that she would send a message to Jack letting him know that Addison was safe and hidden until the men could be found and caught. Blinking back tears, Addison trudged on. *No more tears, Addison. You have cried enough. It is now time to be brave and stay one step ahead of your attackers*. Addison told herself firmly. *And when all this is over, you can hopefully see Ashton again*.

She rolled her eyes at herself. Of course, Ashton wouldn't want to see her. She was just his friend's little sister that needed a shoulder to cry on and he obliged. She was most likely just a diversion for him since there were literally no other females at the house party.

Before she knew it, Addison was stepping into the inn. She was able to get a room easily. A benefit of being so isolated for three years and growing from a child to a woman, no one recognized her.

Once in her room, Addison felt so alone. She missed her brothers, Titan, Spartan, and Ashton. No matter how many times she scolded herself for missing him and wishing he were there, it didn't seem to matter. Addison let out a heavy sigh as she climbed into bed. Maybe the time she was in hiding would help her foolish heart forget all about Ashton Fenwick.

She lay on the uncomfortable bed, and she tried to relax. What if they came to the inn looking for her? What if the men found her here? Addison took a slow deep breath. She closed her eyes and pretended that Titan was lying with her. She could almost hear Ashton's quiet whisper, telling her everything was going to be okay.

Morning came slowly thanks to her mind conjuring up all sorts of scary thoughts. She was a bundle of nerves as she boarded the travelling coach. Luckily, she was able to board without any hassle and she was on her way in no time. Today marked the first day she would officially be Hannah Smith, the maid.

Chapter 13

Ashton was awakened by a blood curdling scream. He jumped out of bed and threw on his trousers as he stumbled towards the door. The scream sounded like it came from Addison's room. As he yanked open his door, he saw Daniel running past a very upset Mary who stood in the doorway of Addison's room with a hand over her mouth as she cried. A door down the hall opened and Ashton looked to see who it was. Mr. Blake stumbled out into the hallway as well.

"Get Lord Blackwell!" Ashton yelled at Mr. Blake who nodded before running in the opposite direction.

Ashton wasted no more time as he ran to Addison's room. He did not know what he expected to see, but he knew it wasn't this.

The bed was a mess of blankets that were hanging off the side. Daniel knelt on the ground next to an unmoving Titan who had a knife sticking out of his side. The fire poker was laying on the ground next to Titan and there was blood on the ground near the fireplace.

Daniel looked up at Ashton's entrance into the room, with a serious expression. "Titan is still alive but where is Addison?"

Ashton's jaw tightened as his heart constricted. Where was she? Was she hurt? What had happened? He couldn't see her leaving Titan in this condition unless...unless she was forced to.

Ashton turned to the weeping maid. "What happened?" He snapped out.

"I-I don't know, My Lord." Mary seemed to be coming out of her initial shock. "When I woke up and entered the kitchen, Miss Addie wasn't there like she usually is. I noticed that the kitchen door was open slightly. When I went to close it, I saw a small bloody handprint on the wall next to the door. I ran up here to check on Miss Addie. The door was open, and Titan was like that." Her chin was starting to tremble again.

"What's going on?" Lord Blackwell's voice yelled above the commotion in the hallway.

"Titan has been stabbed and Addie is gone." Daniel yelled back.

Silence filled the room. "You, call for the doctor. You and you, wake up the housekeeper and tell her that she needs to gather everyone in the entry hall immediately." Ashton listened as Jack snapped out orders as he pointed to various people. How could this have happened with him and Daniel so close to her room?

"Where's Miss Addie?" Joshua asked loudly in the hall. Ashton stepped from the room to see an anxious looking Joshua making his way quickly through the gathered men in the hallway.

"We do not know, Joshua. What is the matter?" Ashton asked as he studied the boy's worried face.

"There is a footman unconscious in front of Spartan's stall. Father sent me here to tell Miss Addie." Ashton barely waited for Joshua to finish speaking before sprinting down the hall towards the stairs. Maybe the footman could tell them who took Addison.

When Ashton arrived, James was examining the unconscious man's arm. The man was tall, probably close to Ashton's height, but he was also very thick with large muscles and broad shoulders. On the right side of his forehead, he had a large goose egg and a cut that ran through it. Dried blood was all over that side of his face. Someone had hit the man, hard. He had scratches on his hands and wrists that looked like they too had bled some. Ashton stepped up to James' side. The man's entire forearm had puncture wounds and tears all over it.

"What happened to him?" Ashton asked James.

"I'm not sure, My Lord. I came to feed the horses this morning and found him face down on the floor." James said with his brows knit together. "Is it just me or do these injuries look like dog bites?" Ashton narrowed his eyes as he studied the wounds.

"If those are dog bites then he is most likely the one who attacked Addison." Jack's angry voice sounded from right behind Ashton.

"Miss Addison was attacked?" James jumped to his feet as surprise was quickly followed by anger.

"I'm gonna get her this time." The man mumbled and he tried to push himself up. "Don't worry brother, she will pay."

Jack stormed over to the semiconscious man and grabbed him by his collar and shook him. "Where is she?" He yelled in the man's face. "Where is Addison?" The injured man's head lobbed to the side. He was definitely not in any shape to give them information. Letting out a growl, Jack dropped the man and paced away before looking at Ashton. "Help me get this low life back to the house. He needs a doctor, and we need to keep him locked up until the local authorities arrive."

Ashton would have loved to watch the man take his last breath, but Jack was right. They needed him treated by a doctor so that they could get answers from him regarding Addison's whereabouts.

Ashton and Jack dragged the unconscious man back to the house and up to an empty guest room. Jack called for someone to bring rope and they tied the man to the bed so he could not escape. Jack settled into a chair and sat glaring at the man.

"Lord Blackwell?" a young maid tentatively asked from the doorway. "Mrs. Jankins has everyone assembled in the entry hall, My Lord."

"Ashton, stay here. I need to address the servants and start the search for Addison." Jack stormed from the room followed by the worried-looking maid.

Jack was gone for an hour and the man continued to talk in his sleep. He mentioned how the mangy mutt ruined the plan and about making her pay. Ashton was near to breaking the man's nose when Jack returned. He gave Ashton a quick nod before he returned to his previous seat and sat down heavily. Ashton left and headed for Addison's room. He wanted to see if Titan was still alive.

"You do realize that I am a human doctor and not an animal doctor, correct?" An older man with a bald spot on the back of his head said. Ashton recognized him from the night Joshua had been injured.

"I will pay whatever the price if you save him." Ashton stepped into the room. The doctor looked up at him with a grim expression. "That dog was injured protecting Addison. I need you to do the best you can so when we find her, she can have her dog back. Heaven knows she is going to need him after this."

The doctor nodded his head before turning back to Titan. Ashton sat against the wall next to Daniel as they watched the doctor examine Titan carefully. Quietly, Ashton told Daniel about the man they found in the barn. Daniel's fists clenched as his jaw muscle ticked.

Titan whined and moved a little when the doctor finally pulled the knife out of him. Ashton quickly moved to the dog to help keep him still. At least Titan was still alive. Addison would be completely heartbroken if he died. The doctor, Mr. Thompson, told Ashton and Daniel what to do as the three of them worked to save Titan's life.

Hours later, Titan was laying on Addison's bed with a thick white bandage around his middle. The three men washed their hands in the water some maids brought up for them. Daniel hadn't said anything since Ashton told him about the man tied to the bed down the hall.

"Did I hear you say that there is a man injured somewhere?" Dr. Thompson asked as he continued to watch Titan.

"Yes, sir. We believe he is the one that attacked Addison. Jack is sitting with him now." Ashton said as he clenched his fist. He wanted nothing more than to pummel the man for what he did to Addison.

"I guess I have to treat him as well." Dr. Thompson did not sound like he wanted to, but he headed for the door anyway. "Titan shouldn't be left alone, and he needs to be watched carefully." He said over his shoulder.

"If you want, Daniel, I can stay with Titan for a while so you can go talk with Jack." Ashton offered.

"If Jack is with that man, then I better stay here." Daniel growled and Ashton looked over at him. "I would probably end up killing him." The look on Daniel's face told Ashton that Daniel was deadly serious. He couldn't blame him for wanting to kill the man. Ashton wanted to kill him as well.

They sat in silence for a long time as they watched Titan's chest rise and fall. A maid mentioned that the other gentlemen from the house party had taken their leave. Apparently, they all felt it best to allow the family the time they needed to face such a tragedy.

Daniel rolled his eyes after the maid left. "And they thought they were worthy of Addison. They left within a couple of hours of someone attacking her and her going missing. At least Mr. Blake left to take a note to a friend of Jack's who is a detective. But I doubt he will return to aid in the search."

"Not that it would matter anyway. I fully plan on begging her to be mine once we get her back." Ashton said glancing over to gauge Daniel's reaction.

"Beg? Wow Ashton, you really are hopeless." Daniel chuckled.

"Of course, I have to beg." Ashton's lips twitched. "It will take a miracle to convince Addison to give me a chance." He really hoped he didn't screw everything up by kissing her.

"Excuse me, Mr. Blackwell, Lord Fenwick. Lord Blackwell has asked you to meet him in the guest room. I am to stay with Miss Blackwell's dog." A maid stood at the door.

Ashton and Daniel looked at each other. Ashton could feel the tension returning to his shoulders at the thought of having to see the man again. He could tell that Daniel was just as thrilled to be going as he was.

They walked down the hallway in silence. When they got to the room, Jack was glaring down at the man as he thrashed against the ropes. Ashton stepped into the room first with Daniel right behind him.

"You have no right to be doing this!" The man yelled. "I have done nothing wrong!"

"What is your name?" Jack asked calmly. The man spit in Jack's direction as he strained against the rope.

Ashton stepped up to Jack's side. "What happened to you? We found you unconscious in the barn?" Ashton asked.

"That stupid girl attacked me along with that dumb mutt." The man growled out.

Ashton clenched his jaw. He needed to keep his temper under control. "Why would she attack you?"

The man's scowl turned to a smirk. "I refused her. She came on to me and I turned her down." Daniel lunged for the man, but Jack held him back.

"We all know that did not happen." Daniel growled out. "Where is she?"

"Where is she?" The man repeated as he smirked at them. "You want a piece of her too? Just so you know, you better get what you want from her quick because she isn't going to be around much longer."

"What do you mean by that?" Jack asked, obviously trying to keep himself calm.

The man laughed humorlessly. "That girl is the very reason we are in our current circumstances. She..."

"Lord Blackwell." A footman walked into the room with a tense expression. "The authorities are here to see you, sir."

Jack turned and walked out of the room quickly followed by Daniel. Both brothers were fuming. Ashton wasn't very happy with what this man had said about Addison throwing herself at him. She would never do such a thing.

If what the man said was to be believed about the reason for them targeting her, Addison put him and his accomplices in bad straights. Ashton watched as the man in the bed and the footman shared a look before the footman left. Ashton wanted to follow the footman, but someone had to stay with the prisoner so he couldn't get away.

"What's your name, sir?" Ashton asked. He was suddenly feeling completely exhausted. Seeing Addison collapse like she did, followed by a restless night, only to be awaken by screaming and Addison missing was taking its toll on him.

The man sent him a look as if to call Ashton an idiot before closing his eyes and settling back onto the pillow. Ashton asked the man a few more questions, but the man remained silent. It seemed that he was no longer talkative.

Ashton settled into a chair and watched the man closely. He wished he knew who this man was so he could find out what Addison had done to him to make him angry enough to kill.

Ashton was unsure how much time passed before Jack, Daniel and two other men walked into the room. He got to his feet as the men were introduced to him.

Mr. Cook and Mr. Stevens were the officers brought in to transport the prisoner so he could be questioned by some detectives. Upon hearing their introduction, the man on the bed began to thrash again. The officers looked over at him, but their serious expressions did not change after seeing the absurd behavior.

"Well, this is going to make for an enjoyable ride." Mr. Cook commented as he and Mr. Stevens untied the man and dragged him kicking and screaming from the house to a carriage with steel bars on the windows. Ashton stood on the steps and watched until the carriage was out of sight.

*   *   *

Jack, Daniel, and Ashton were in the study the next day. They were discussing search patterns and possible places Addison could be hiding. A knock on the door had Jack barking out the command to enter. A young footman came into the room and handed Jack a letter. Jack opened it and read it. His brow furrowed as he reread its contents.

"What is it?" Daniel asked.

"It is a letter from Mrs. Gracie." Jack tossed the letter off to the side of the desk so they could resume their planning. "Her roof is getting old and is starting to leak. I need to send someone to repair it."

Daniel and Ashton nodded their heads before turning back to the map of the estate. Ashton remembered another tenant having their roof repaired recently. Mrs. Gracie's home must have been built around the same time as the other tenant.

They all agreed that they needed to continue to search the house, barn, and grounds each day. They would assign different routes each day to the servants so that fresh eyes would see the areas. Hopefully, someone would spot some clue they could use to locate Addison.

Chapter 14

Addison was finally settling into her new life. It had been four weeks since she arrived at Lakeview Manor. The large house had been empty for a long time. Only a small staff was required to run the estate, but now that the family was coming back into residence, more were needed. The Earl of Fenton and his wife were arriving that week, which is the only reason she was hired.

Addison kept her head down and did as she was asked without complaint. She did not want to draw attention to herself. The bruising around her neck had drawn many looks and questions at first, but as the marks faded, so did the attention.

The cook, Mrs. Harper was kind and patient with Addison as she learned how Mrs. Harper ran her kitchen. It was not bad work and Addison liked staying busy.

She was grateful for all the time her father had allowed her to assist Mrs. Harvey in the kitchen over the years. Addison was learning a lot from Mrs. Harper, and she was also able to teach Mrs. Harper a few little things.

One of the best things about working in the kitchen was the fact that she rarely had to be around any of the male servants. She was able to keep her anxiety under control by thinking about a pair of ocean blue eyes and a dimpled smile.

Addison gave herself a mental shake as she continued to knead the bread dough. These last four weeks were supposed to rid her of her infatuation with Lord Ashton, but it only made her miss him more.

"Hannah." Dalia, a chamber maid, moved to her side. "How are you this morning?" she asked with a friendly smile.

"Good. And you?" Addison smiled back at her.

"I am doing great. So, I was thinking that maybe, if you are free tomorrow night, we could meet up with my brother. He works in the stables.

His name is Derek, and he has mentioned a few times about wanting to get to know you better."

Dalia was a sweet girl and Addison knew she meant no harm, but her stomach clenched at the thought of being near a strange man; let alone getting to know him.

"I'm sorry, Dalia. I mean no offense to you or your brother, but I am not really interested in getting to know any young men at the moment." Addison gave Dalia her most apologetic look.

"Oh." Dalia covered her mouth, trying to hide her wide grin. "So, who is he?" She whispered loudly.

"Who?" Addison focused on the dough.

"The man that has stolen your heart." Mrs. Harper laughed from the other side of the worktable.

Addison felt her cheeks flush as an image of Ashton came to mind. She shook her head. "I do not know what you two are talking about. My heart is firmly in my own chest." She said calmly, but she could not look either of them in the eye.

Both Dalia and Mrs. Harper laughed as they watched her. "I take it you haven't talked to this mystery man about how you feel yet." Dalia said as she bumped Addison's shoulder with her own. "Is he handsome?"

"Leave her alone, Dalia." Mrs. Harper laughed. "It seems that Hannah and her mystery man are still in the very early stages of their relationship."

"I am not in a relationship with him." Addison said firmly.

"So, there is a guy." Dalia giggled. Mrs. Harper shooed Dalia out of the kitchen while Addison fought the color that was burning her cheeks.

"Ignore Dalia's teasing, Hannah. You don't have to tell anyone about him if you don't want to." Mrs. Harper gave Addison a small smile as she got back to preparing the evening meal.

Addison didn't say much the rest of the day. She was lost in her thoughts as she cut carrots, baked bread, and peeled potatoes. Did Ashton have her heart? She had known him for three weeks before she fled from her home. She had been so adamant about not allowing anyone near her heart again. She did not think she would survive another person she loved abandoning her. But Ashton had somehow cracked the walls she had built around her heart. He had become a friend. A source of comfort.

Addison was still thinking about Ashton as she lay in her bed. It was late and she needed to get up early in the morning. She let out a heavy sigh as she closed her eyes.

Addison wondered why she felt so comfortable and protected whenever she was with Ashton. She felt safe with her brothers, and she knew they loved and cared for her. Daniel was her best friend for the longest time. But given the choice, Addison would much rather stand next to Ashton than Danny.

Addison's eyes shot open. She loved him. She loved Ashton Fenwick. She covered her mouth and squeezed her eyes shut. How could she allow herself to fall in love? She set herself up for another heartbreak. Addison curled up into a ball on her side and cried herself to sleep.

Morning came quickly and Addison felt depressed. How could she have allowed herself to fall in love with Lord Ashton? She dressed quickly and made her way to the kitchen. She helped make breakfast for Lord and Lady Fenton.

She had just finished cleaning up her workstation and was starting on lunch prep when Mrs. Arnold, the housekeeper, stepped into the kitchen.

"Miss Hannah." Mrs. Arnold said in her normal emotionless tone and Addison looked up from what she was doing. "Come with me."

Addison glanced over at Mrs. Harper who gave her an encouraging nod. Addison's nerves caused her hands to shake as she followed Mrs. Arnold. Why was she being pulled aside? Had she done something wrong?

As she stepped out into the hall, Mrs. Arnold began walking quickly. Addison fell into step just behind her. Once they reached the entry hall, Mrs. Arnold turned and began to climb the grand staircase. Addison's nervousness increased the higher they climbed.

She was led down a hall to their left. They finally stopped in front of a door and Mrs. Arnold gave a quick knock before opening it. She stepped aside and motioned for Addison to precede her into the room. Addison took a tentative step into the room.

Mrs. Arnold nudged her further in as she said. "Miss Hannah Smith, My Lady." Mrs. Arnold presented Addison to a beautiful woman who looked to be in her mid to late forties.

The woman, who Addison believed to be Lady Fenton, had brown hair with streaks of grey here and there. Her eyes were a beautiful deep blue.

Addison blinked a few times. Lady Fenton's eyes reminded her so much of Ashton's. *Great. Now you are seeing him everywhere. Stop thinking about him.* She scolded herself.

Lady Fenton's smile was warm and inviting. It took a moment for Addison to realize that Mrs. Arnold was no longer standing behind her and that the door was closed. Addison dipped into a belated curtsey before dropping her gaze to the floor.

"Please, Miss Smith. Have a seat." Lady Fenton's voice had a very comforting quality to it.

Addison moved to the chair opposite Lady Fenton's and sat. Without thinking about it, Addison sat as she had been schooled to do all her life. On the edge of her seat, back straight, ankles crossed, and hands gracefully in her lap.

"Do not be nervous child. I like to meet with each of my new staff members to get to know them. Have you been enjoying working here?" Lady Fenton asked with a smile.

Addison felt some of her tension releasing as she realized she was not in trouble. Lady Fenton seemed nice enough too. "Yes, My Lady."

Lady Fenton watched her carefully for a few minutes. Addison's nervousness started to return the longer Lady Fenton studied her.

"Mrs. Arnold told me of your unique start here." Addison flinched slightly. She knew when she first arrived that she looked a complete mess. "I was informed that you had bruising around your neck." Lady Fenton looked concerned as she softly inquired.

Addison's hands curled into fists as she tried to block the memories and resist the urge to touch her throat. "Yes, My Lady." She answered quietly.

"Do you ride, Miss Hannah?" Lady Fenton gave her another soft smile.

Addison was prepared for questions about the bruises not horseback riding. "Yes, My Lady." Addison finally answered. She was sure her confusion was written on her face.

"Good. You will be accompanying me on my ride this afternoon." Addison's head snapped up and she met Lady Fenton's gaze. "I believe I might have a riding habit that would fit you. As soon as you are changed, we will go." Lady Fenton stood and walked over to the rope and pulled it.

Addison knew that she was calling for her maid. Addison's room back home had one as well. A young woman entered the room and Lady Fenton asked her to get her old riding habit.

The maid was gone for only a few minutes before coming back into the room with a deep blue fabric in her arms. Addison was still unsure of what was going on. Why was Lady Fenton asking her to go riding with her when Addison was known as only a kitchen maid?

Addison was still puzzled as Lady Fenton's maid assisted her into the riding habit. Lady Fenton returned a few minutes later with a huge grin on her face.

"My Lady, why have you asked me, a kitchen maid, to ride with you?" Addison asked.

Lady Fenton laughed as she looked at Addison with a mischievous glint in her eye. "If I do not take a maid with me, my husband requires me to take a groomsman. I much prefer not to have a groomsman shadowing me and Rose does not ride." She gestured to her maid. "Now, Miss Hannah, follow me."

Lady Fenton led the way out to the stables. Addison hadn't been out here before. The familiar smell of hay, horses and leather hit her, causing a wave of homesickness.

Lady Fenton immediately started talking with the stable master that came up to them. Addison couldn't resist walking down the stalls as she studied the horses.

She paused at a large brown mare with a wide blaze down her face. Addison reached her hand out to stroke the mare's head, but she snorted loudly and shifted her hooves in agitation.

"You must be quite the spirited little thing." She murmured to the horse. "Will you at least allow me to touch your head?"

The mare snorted again but stepped up to the gate. This time when Addison lifted her hand to touch the horse's face, she stopped just shy of making contact. She held her hand there and waited for the horse to initiate contact.

It took a few seconds, but eventually the horse pressed her muzzle into Addison's hand. Addison blew gently into the mare's face, letting the mare get accustomed to her scent.

She smiled as she slowly stroked the mare's head. She felt eyes on her and turned to see the stable master, Lady Fenton and a stable hand watching her.

"How did you get Tana to let you touch her?" The stable master asked in shock.

"I didn't. She touched me." Addison kept her hand on Tana's head and lowered her gaze.

"Saddle Tana for Miss Hannah to ride, Noah." Lady Fenton said as she moved up to Addison's side.

"My Lady, only his lordship has been able to ride Tana and even than she has thrown him four times." Noah, the stable master, said anxiously.

"Do you think you can ride Tana, Miss Hannah?" Lady Fenton asked her. Addison looked back at the horse. She really wanted to ride the fiery beast. Tana reminded her so much of Spartan when she first got him.

Addison turned back to the three watching her. "If her ladyship believes this is a good mount for me to ride, then I shall ride her."

"There you have it, Noah. Saddle both Tana and Star. Miss Hannah and I wish to be on our way." Lady Fenton clapped her hands with a wide smile on her face. Tana jerked her head up at the sudden noise.

They silently waited outside the stables for the horses to be brought to them. Addison was beyond excited to ride Tana. Star was brought out first. She was a small chestnut mare with the same color mane and tail as her body. She had a small white star on the center of her forehead with one white sock.

The stable hand that brought out Star assisted Lady Fenton into the saddle. Several minutes later he returned with a skittish Tana. Without thinking about it, Addison took the lead rope from the man.

Tana reared up, but Addison held firm. She kept calm and her voice soft. "Easy girl. Do you remember me?" It took another minute for Tana to finally stop trying to yank the rope from Addison's hands. Addison stood still and waited for Tana to decide what she wanted to do.

If what she heard was correct, his lordship had not been in residence for well over a year and a half. If she was skittish back then and no one was able to ride her for the whole time he was gone, Tana was going to be nearly back to square one in her training.

Another several minutes passed with Addison and Tana watching each other with three feet separating them. Slowly, Tana lowered her head and stood in a more relaxed posture. Addison slowly turned her back to the mare and waited.

She met Lady Fenton's curious look, but both remained quiet. She saw the older woman's eyes widen just before she felt Tana's head press to her shoulder. Just as slowly as she had moved before, Addison turned around and scratched Tana's forehead. Taking a step to the side she led Tana to the fence and climbed on top before mounting.

Once Addison's weight was in the saddle, Tana jumped and began to try to toss Addison to the ground. She gripped Tana's mane tightly. The stable hand ran towards her, but she yelled at him to stop. Addison continued to cling to Tana. After what felt like hours, but was mere seconds, Tana finally settled down and Addison let out a tense breath.

She gave Lady Fenton a nod and the woman headed out into a large field. Addison gave a gentle squeeze with her heels and Tana sprang forward. It took fifteen minutes before Tana settled into a nice easy trot that suited both her and Addison.

"Now that Tana is not trying to kill you, may I continue to ask you some questions to get to know you better?" Lady Fenton asked. Her voice was full of curiosity as she smiled at Addison. She gave Lady Fenton a nod as she glanced over at her. "The bruising on your neck when you arrived here; Mrs. Arnold seemed worried that something drastic had happened to you. Would you be willing to tell me how you got them?"

Addison closed her eyes briefly before opening them. She was so tired of lying, so she decided to stick as close to the truth as possible. "A man attacked me a few days before I arrived. It is the main reason I left my previous home."

"You poor thing. Was the man caught?" Lady Fenton's worry nearly brought Addison to tears. She was still trying to process the event of that night, and her emotions were still raw even though it happened weeks ago.

"I don't know, My Lady." Addison's voice was quiet as she continued to fight to keep her emotions under control. "He grabbed my throat, but I was able to get away. I ran and did not stop. Now, I am here."

"You aren't a servant, are you?" Lady Fenton's question caused Addison's heart rate to pick up and she felt the blood drain from her face.

"What makes you think that?" Addison asked as normally as she could, but she could hear her voice shake.

"Your speech. Your manners. Your skill with horses. And you look just like your mother, Lady Blackwell." Addison pulled Tana to a stop and looked over at Lady Fenton in a panic. "Your mother was a good friend of mine. I remember meeting a very fiery little girl who could barely walk but was still as sassy as could be." A sad smile touched Lady Fenton's lips. "I will keep your secret, Miss Blackwell. I cannot even imagine the trauma you have endured."

"Thank you, My Lady." Addison breathed a sigh of relief as she nudged Tana back into a trot.

"I may not fully understand why you feel the need to hide as a servant, but may I ask one other thing?" Lady Fenton had a serious expression on her face.

"Of course, Lady Fenton." Addison looked at her.

"Instead of working in the kitchen, would you be willing to be my companion?"

Addison chewed on her bottom lip. How much longer would it take to hunt down the men that attacked her? Had Susan been able to deliver the information to Jack?

Lady Fenton had said she was friends with her mother, maybe Addison could learn more about her mother if she spent more time with Lady Fenton. "I think I would like that, Lady Fenton." Addison finally replied.

Chapter 15

"Four weeks!" Daniel slammed his hand down on the dining room table.

Jack, Daniel, and Ashton were looking down at a map of the area and discussing their options. They had been going through every area of the estate with no luck in finding any sign of Addison.

Ashton ran a hand through his hair in frustration. He was getting desperate to find her. All of them were. The whole household was completely thrown out of order by Addison's disappearance. The only good thing that had come from the last four weeks was Titan's recovery.

Miraculously, the dog had lived. He still wasn't his normal self, but he was able to walk around on his own. He stuck to Ashton's side like glue, and he whined often. He constantly laid in Addison's favorite spots. Ashton was glad to have Titan's constant presence nearby. It was like having a piece of Addison with him.

"No, I will see him now!" A female voice yelled down the hall and all of them looked at the door.

"Ma'am please. I will see if he is available to see you, but you need to wait at the door." A man said clearly irritated. Ashton recognized the voice that belonged to one of the footmen.

"I don't care if he is busy. I need to see him. Now!" The woman said again, this time her voice was much closer.

A woman holding a baby stomped into the room with a very angry footman right behind her. "I'm sorry, My Lord. I couldn't stop her." The footman glared at the woman and her child.

Jack waved his hand dismissively at the footman before he turned his attention to the woman. She looked familiar with her long blonde hair and brown eyes. Ashton wondered where he had seen her before.

Before he could place her, Jack spoke. "What can I help you with Mrs. Gracie? I am very busy at the moment." Jack's voice was tired.

"I have been waiting for your response, My Lord." She spat at him. Ashton smiled as he remembered the name. Mrs. Gracie was the young mother Addison visited frequently.

Ashton just happened to be standing between the irate woman and Jack. As she passed Ashton, she set the baby in his arms and continued advancing towards Jack.

Surprised, Ashton's eyes widened as he looked down at the baby girl and then up to Daniel, who looked like he was trying not to laugh, then back to Mrs. Gracie. She stood with her hands on her hips, glaring at Jack. Jack ran a hand down his face before responding to her.

"I have not been able to even look at the roof yet, Susan. Addison is still missing, and we are concentrating on locating her." Jack threw his hands up as Mrs. Gracie jammed her finger into his chest.

"You haven't even looked at Addison's books, have you?" Mrs. Gracie said accusingly.

"All my efforts have been in finding Addison. I am sorry for neglecting your roof. I will send someone to look at it first thing in the morning." Jack took a step back trying to put more distance between him and the angry woman.

The baby began to fuss a little and Ashton put the baby up to his shoulder and began patting her tiny back like he had seen Addison do weeks ago. Mrs. Gracie's fiery gaze snapped over to him quickly before returning to Jack.

"I expect the 'Lord' of the manor to personally see to the roof issue today, Lord Blackwell. I've been waiting for four weeks." She growled out before turning towards Ashton. She gently took the baby from him. "Thank you..." she said in a soft voice and looked at him expectantly.

"Lord Ashton Fenwick." Ashton gave a slight bow while keeping a wary eye on the woman in front of him.

"Oh yes. You came with Addison several weeks ago." Mrs. Gracie said kindly before heading for the door. Just as quickly as she had come, she was gone.

There was a stunned silence that followed Mrs. Gracie's departure. There was something about what she said that did not sit well with him. He was missing something.

"Well, motherhood has changed Susan." Daniel laughed lightly. "The only other time I saw her this angry was when Addison had to step in between you two so that she didn't tear off your head." Ashton smiled at the memory too.

Addison had been absolutely amazing that day. She had looked beautiful as she rode Spartan through the fields. And then her shooting. Ashton was hopelessly lost to her.

"Why don't we take a break from this and see what Addison's notes say about Mrs. Gracie's roof." Jack suggested as he headed for the door.

Ashton and Daniel followed him out of the dining room and into the study. Jack pulled out the ledger, Mrs. Gracie's note that she sent four weeks ago, and the book that was labeled as The Gracie's. He began to flip through the pages and Ashton picked up the letter. He read it and then read it again. His brows furrowed as he looked at the signature. It was signed, 'A. Gracie'.

"Am I right in assuming Mrs. Gracie's full name is Susan Gracie?" Ashton asked.

"Yes. She is Mary's older sister and married Ted Gracie a year or so ago." Daniel responded while flipping through Addison's notes while Jack looked through the ledger. "She was Addison's maid before that."

"Is there any reason she would sign this note as 'A. Gracie'?" Ashton stepped closer to the desk and laid it down, pointing to the signature.

Daniel glanced over at the letter with a puzzled expression. "A. Gracie? That doesn't make sense."

"Why would Susan be requesting a new roof when Addison's ledger shows she replaced the roof last month?" Jack turned the ledger so that Ashton and Daniel could see the expense documented.

Ashton's heart started hammering in his chest. Could Addison have been trying to send them a message four weeks ago? He swore as he ran from the study.

Could the A. Gracie be Addison's subtle way of signing the note? Could demanding a new roof for a roof that she had just replaced be her way of letting them know that she was there? He took the stairs two at a time. He was going to get his riding boots and then he was going to pay Mrs. Gracie a visit.

As he was tugging on his boots in his room, the door burst open. Jack and Daniel were coming in with confused looks on their faces. Jack closed the door behind him.

"Where are you going?" Daniel asked.

"The A in the signature. What if it stands for Addison?" He started tugging on his other boot. "The note and Mrs. Gracie were demanding Jack to personally look at her leaky roof, but Addison had just replaced it and it was fine. I think she is there." Ashton stood up and headed for the door. Jack and Daniel raced to their own rooms.

Ashton had just reached the entry way when there was a knock on the front door. Since he was right there, he pulled it open. Two gentlemen stood on the porch with grim expressions. They were shorter than Ashton and held themselves with an air of confidence.

"Is Lord Blackwell in?" The shorter man asked. His voice was much deeper than Ashton would have guessed given the man's smaller stature.

"What can I do for you gentlemen?" Jack's voice came from the stairs behind Ashton. Ashton didn't want to be delayed any more. All he wanted was to get to the Gracie's cottage and see Addison.

"I am Detective Moore, and this is my partner Detective Allen. We need a few moments of your time, Lord Blackwell." Detective Moore said as he took off his hat revealing short, straw-colored hair. Daniel came down the stairs and joined them all at the door.

"Do you detectives have horses?" Jack asked as he stepped out the front door with Daniel and Ashton right on his heels. He walked quickly as he headed for the stables and waited for their response.

"We do, but they are exhausted from our journey here." Detective Allen said.

"You can use a couple of our horses then. I cannot delay this business, so if you want to talk, you can talk along the way." Jack stepped into the barn. Somehow, for Ashton, the atmosphere of the building seemed much darker since Addison's disappeared. "James. Joshua. I need two of our extra horses saddled for the detectives."

Ashton was glad that Jack wasn't having James and Joshua saddling all five horses. It saved a large amount of time with Ashton, Jack, and Daniel saddling their own mounts.

In less than ten minutes, all five of them were trotting out of the stable yard and into the meadow, heading for the Gracie's cottage. Jack kept the pace slower than Ashton would have liked, but he knew the detectives needed to say what they came to say.

"We have been looking into the man that attacked Miss Blackwell. We found out his name." Detective Allen started off.

"His name is Samuel. He is almost always with his elder brother Silas. Both are extremely dangerous. If Samuel is the one that attacked your sister, she is extremely lucky to be alive." Detective Moore continued.

Jack pulled his horse to a stop. His face was pale as he looked over at the detectives. Ashton, too, felt sick to his stomach. What had Addison done to get two highly dangerous criminals hunting her down?

"What is that supposed to mean?" Jack asked through clenched teeth.

"The last man they killed was unrecognizable. They don't care who the person is: male, female, mother, father, the elderly, children. If they are paid, they will do whatever it is that is asked of them." Detective Allen answered. "We were hoping to get Miss Blackwell's first-hand statement and ask a few questions. Is she available?"

Jack kicked his horse into a faster gait. "No."

"No, as in she is unavailable or no, as in you won't let us speak with her." Detective Allen asked.

"No, as in we do not know where she is." Daniel snapped at them.

"She's missing?" Detective Moore sounded upset.

Ashton spotted the Gracie Cottage in the distance. As they stopped in front of the gate. Jack dismounted and faced the detectives with a straight face. "Addison has not been seen since the night before the attack. We found Samuel unconscious in the stables and Addison's dog stabbed in her room, but she was nowhere to be found." Jack pointed to Titan who stood by Ashton. The detectives' eyes widened with the information.

Jack turned and headed for the door. They were halfway down the walk when the door opened. Ashton was disappointed that it wasn't Addison standing in the open doorway. Mrs. Gracie glared at them as she crossed her arms over her chest.

"Who are they?" She jutted her chin toward the detectives.

"This is Detective Allen and Detective Moore. They are working to arrest the men that attacked Addison." Jack answered as he continued to walk towards her.

She studied the men carefully before stepping aside and allowing the five of them into her home. "Is she here?" Ashton couldn't stop himself from asking. He was the last one in, and he paused next to her.

"I am sorry, Lord Fenwick. Addison is no longer here." She gave him a sad smile, her eyes full of sympathy.

"But she was here? Is she okay?" Ashton reached out and grabbed her upper arms, desperate to know if she was okay.

"Ashton, let Susan go. She will tell us all where Addison is and how she is doing." Jack growled out.

Ashton slowly released Mrs. Gracie. He hung his head, but looked up when he felt a hand on his arm. "Don't worry Lord Fenwick, your lady love is safe for the time being." She said quietly and Ashton nearly sank to his knees in relief. "Lord Blackwell, I won't be telling you where Addison is. She is safe and that is all you need to know at the moment."

"Why did she not wake us up when she was attacked?" Daniel asked angrily.

"She was terrified when she pounded on my door. When I opened the door, she pushed her way inside and locked the door behind her. She was shaking and crying for at least an hour before she even attempted to talk." Mrs. Gracie had her eyes closed with a pained expression. "She could hardly speak and the bruising that was on her neck worried me. She refused to let me send for a doctor."

"So, she was strangled?" Detective Allen was jotting notes down in a small notebook.

"If you count being able to see ten fingers in bruises around her neck as being strangled, then yes, detective." Mrs. Gracie said dryly. He looked up from his note taking and gave her an apologetic look.

"Why didn't she come home?" Jack asked with sadness in his eyes.

"She was too scared to go back. The man that tried to kill her was one of the two men that attacked her during the break-in." Ashton's jaw clenched as he listened to Mrs. Gracie. "She didn't even want to stay in case they figured out she was here. She said it was too dangerous for me and Evelynn. So, she made plans to hide until both men are arrested. She had me write you that note, Lord Blackwell, so that I could tell you all this. She doesn't trust any of the new staff members that were hired for the house party." Mrs. Gracie walked over to a cabinet and opened it before pulling out two pieces of paper.

"What are those?" Detective Moore asked curiously.

"I was the only person Addison told everything about the break-in. She had me sketch two images the week after it happened. One of each of the men." Ashton moved to stand by Jack who now held the images.

Ashton felt the blood drain from his face. He looked at Jack and Daniel who were pale as well. The image on the left was the man they found in the stables. The other image was of another footman that had a scar on his face.

No wonder Addison had such a severe panic attack that night when she saw the footman that gave Jack a note. He was one of the men that had attacked her. Ashton ran his hand through his hair in agitation. The detectives moved closer to see the images.

Detective Moore let out a low whistle. "These two attacked Miss Blackwell before?"

"Yes. It was almost nine months ago. They broke into the manor house, went up to her room, and yanked her out of her bed. This one…" Mrs. Gracie pointed to the one with the scar. "…tried to kiss her, but she fought back. He ended up shoving her to the other man. She tripped by the fireplace and grabbed the fire poker. She used it to keep them away from her long enough that she was able to get out of her room. She fell down the stairs and she was in a lot of pain from her fall. She couldn't get up and they caught up to her. She said the first guy sat on her while the other held down her legs. They accused her of stealing money from them and they were going to extract it from her flesh."

"The man you pointed to, with the scar, is Silas and the other is his brother, Samuel." Detective Moore sounded impressed. "Miss Blackwell must have angels looking out for her if she survived more than one encounter with one of them, let alone both."

Daniel sniffed as he walked toward the window, turning his back to the room. Mrs. Gracie went back to the cabinet and pulled out a stack of papers. She wiped her cheeks as she set them on the table.

"I documented Addison's injuries and recovery. I also did one of the bruises on her neck." She wrapped her arms around her waist as she stepped back.

The detectives went immediately to the table and started looking through the drawings. Jack and Ashton held back for several minutes. Ashton wasn't sure he wanted to see them, but at the same time he needed to see what Addison had lived through.

As he looked through the pictures, Ashton's eyes teared up. His precious, fiery Addison had been totally broken. He moved to stand next to Daniel. His hands were shaking. How did she survive those attacks?

"Are they bad?" Daniel asked in a quiet voice as he turned to face Ashton. Ashton was sure Daniel could see the tears in his eyes and his pale face because Daniel swore before rushing to the table.

"Your drawing skills are phenomenal, Mrs. Gracie." Detective Allen commented. "But these three pictures seem to show different injuries."

"I did those after Mr. Drake beat Addison nearly to death the day after her father's funeral." Mrs. Gracie's voice was soft and full of pain. "She was mostly recovered from those injuries when she was attacked several weeks later."

The detectives asked a few more questions about Addison's encounter with Mr. Drake before they were ready to go. Mrs. Gracie gathered up all the pictures and put them away.

The five men rode back towards the stables in silence. Ashton was lost in his own thoughts. All he wanted to do was pull Addison into his arms and never let her go. Seeing what she had been through made her fear of men even more understandable. She had nearly been killed three times in the last year.

"I think Addison is correct." Jack's voice pulled Ashton from his thoughts. "She needs to stay hidden until Silas is arrested."

"That is another thing we wanted to speak to you about, Lord Blackwell." Detective Moore said uneasily. "Samuel never arrived at the prison. When we went along the path we knew the officers were taking, we found both men dead, an empty transport wagon, and no sign of Samuel."

"We can't suddenly stop looking for Addison or someone might get suspicious." Daniel said.

"Detective Moore and I will head back to London immediately. I want to investigate this, Mr. Drake. Something about the timing of all the attacks on Miss Blackwell seems off to me. In the meantime, I want you to continue 'searching' for her. I am pretty sure Samuel and Silas are watching to see if they can get a location on Miss Blackwell." Detective Allen said looking at all of them.

They arrived at the stables and allowed Joshua and James to take the horses. Ashton again noted that the normally chatty and smiling Joshua was quiet and walked with his shoulders hunched.

Addison brought life to this place and with her gone, all seemed bleak. At least Ashton knew that wherever Addison was, she was safe.

The only person who knew was Mrs. Gracie. That thought worried him. If Samuel and Silas were as dangerous as the detectives described them, Mrs. Gracie was in danger. He would need to speak to Jack about seeing if he could get Mrs. Gracie to go and visit family or send her and the baby somewhere until all this was over.

Chapter 16

Addison sat in her room across the hall from Lady Fenton's. She had moved her things up here two weeks ago. She closed her eyes and took a deep breath as she tried to shove her homesickness to the back of her mind.

She had been at Lakeview for six weeks now and she just wanted to be home. Not that she did not like Lady Fenton and the rest of the household, but she missed Spartan and her brothers and the freedom she had at home.

Ashton frequently invaded her thoughts and dreams. Addison had given up fighting her feelings for him. It had been six weeks since she saw him last and her feelings for him had only grown.

On her rides with Lady Fenton, Addison thought about her father a lot. Shortly after her father's death she had promised him that she would never allow another man close enough to hurt her. Since Ashton came into her life, Addison was forced to amend that promise.

A soft knock came at her door just before Lady Fenton stepped into the room. She had a concerned look on her face as she studied Addison.

Last night Addison had had another nightmare. Luckily, she hadn't screamed, but she had woken up to Lady Fenton shaking her awake. She had been sobbing and Lady Fenton had heard her. She stayed with Addison the rest of the night and well into the morning.

She had not asked any questions; only held her while singing lullabies. Eventually, Addison fell back to sleep, and Lady Fenton had stayed.

"How are you feeling, my dear?" Lady Fenton asked.

"I am doing better. Thank you, Lady Fenton." Addison couldn't bring herself to look up at the kind woman's face. "Thank you for staying with me. It helps not feeling alone."

"You are never alone, child." Lady Fenton pulled Addison into a hug. "I'm not sure what you have been through but judging by the housekeeper's description of the bruises you had when you arrived, I can't even begin to imagine the horrors."

"It is all right, My Lady. I just sometimes have nightmares. I will be fine." She gave Lady Fenton a big smile, trying to reassure the older woman.

"Are you feeling up to meeting some new people today?" Lady Fenton asked.

Addison swallowed hard. She had not told Lady Fenton about her fear of meeting new people, well more accurately men. She hadn't needed to.

Over the last two weeks, whenever Lady Fenton had visitors, Addison came up to her room to allow Lady Fenton time with her guests. That and Addison was able to avoid anxiety inducing situations. "You do not need to worry about me, My Lady. I will be fine staying in my room while your guests are here."

"My son and a couple of his friends have returned home for the day. Against all my pleas for him to stay a few days, he insists they need to leave first thing in the morning." Lady Fenton's smile fell from her lips. She loved her son dearly. She spoke of him often and told Addison all the cute and silly things he used to do as a child. She had never said his name, only called him her 'dear boy' or 'my son'. "I was hoping to introduce you to him. You do not have to stay long if you feel overwhelmed."

Addison chewed on her bottom lip. Did she feel up to meeting several new gentlemen? She didn't have Titan to help her this time, but Lady Fenton said she didn't have to stay after the introduction.

Addison let out a long breath. Meeting Lady Fenton's son was the least she could do for Lady Fenton staying up all night with her and for keeping her secret.

"Okay." Addison relented.

"Perfect, they just arrived and are down in the drawing room. We can introduce you to them. If you get overwhelmed, you can bring your dinner up here." It was close to dinnertime so at least Addison would not have to see the gentlemen for long, especially if they were leaving in the morning. "Get dressed and I will meet you downstairs." Lady Fenton leaned in and placed a motherly kiss on the crown of Addison's head before leaving.

Lady Fenton had done that several times over the past few weeks. Addison felt incredibly comfortable with the older woman. She had spent many hours listening to Lady Fenton tell stories about her mother. It helped Addison feel closer to her mother and Lady Fenton.

Addison's mother had fallen ill and died when Addison was three. Lady Fenton was quickly becoming a mother figure to her, and Addison knew she would miss her terribly when she finally left to head home. At least, she could write her letters and stay in contact with her.

Addison dressed in a cream-colored evening gown. Rose helped her with her hair. Addison wanted a simple twist, and it didn't take long. She slowly made her way down to the drawing room as she took deep breaths.

You can do this, Addie. Just a quick introduction and a short conversation and you can go back to your room. Addison told herself as she approached the door.

Her hands were beginning to sweat as she reached for the handle of the door. She hesitated for just a moment before stepping into the drawing room.

She kept her gaze on the ground as she took a few steps into the drawing room. All conversation stopped. There were several gasps and Addison looked up in time to see Jack before he pulled her into his arms. Addison's breath caught in her throat. Why was Jack here?

He looked just as shocked to see her as she was to see him. He held her tightly for several minutes before she was pulled away from him. Daniel crushed her to him, and her confusion increased.

No one had spoken since she entered the room, and she did not know what was happening. She glanced back at Jack, his eyes were red. When Daniel finally released her, he stepped back and wiped his eyes.

Addison looked between her brothers, who were both blinking back tears. She was still in shock as she watched them. A movement to her left drew her attention and she looked over.

Ashton stood there watching her with a look of shock and relief. He looked like he wanted to move to her but was holding himself back.

Tears stung her eyes as his gaze held hers. She took a step towards him and that seemed to be all he needed. He closed the gap between them in two long strides and she threw her arms around his neck. She buried her face in his neck and couldn't stop the tears that broke free.

"Ash." She breathed out in little more than a whisper and he tightened his hold on her.

He pulled back and cupped her face with one of his hands, using his thumb to wipe the tears off her cheek. She closed her eyes and leaned into his touch.

"Addison." He whispered before pressing his lips to hers.

A throat cleared and Ashton broke the kiss but kept his arms tightly around her. She laid her head on his shoulder as she glanced over at her brothers to gauge their reactions to her and Ashton.

Daniel gave her a wink while Jack raised an eyebrow at them, and she felt her cheeks heat. Addison closed her eyes and breathed in Ashton's unique smell of leather and mint. She leaned more heavily against him, and his arms again tightened around her.

"I am guessing you already know each other." Lord Fenton said with a light laugh.

Addison's eyes flew open, and she tried to step away from Ashton, but he didn't let her. He placed a quick kiss to her forehead before sitting on the couch with Addison still held tightly to his side.

"Son, what is going on?" Lord Fenton asked.

Addison had met Lord Fenton several times over the past few weeks. He often wore a serious expression like Ashton did, but his eyes were kind, and he had a remarkable sense of humor. Every time she was in the room with him, he had her laughing at something.

"It is a very long story, father." Ashton said as he began running his hand slowly up and down her arm.

"Not too long." Daniel laughed, and he sat down on Addison's other side. "Addison was attacked by a very dangerous criminal, got away, went into hiding, the man escaped, and we came looking for additional man power to look for the man and Addison, since we had no idea where she was, and to our great surprise and relief she walked through the door of Ashton's drawing room."

Addison sat up and turned to look at Ashton who looked down at her. "This is your house?" She asked in surprise.

He gave her his crooked smile that made his dimple appear. "Yes, my dear. This is my home." Addison pulled her eyes from his handsome face and looked over at Lady Fenton.

"Addison, may I introduce my son, Lord Ashton Fenwick the future Earl of Fenton." Lady Fenton smiled at her. Addison's eyes widened as she turned back to Ashton, who gave her a quick kiss before giving her a wink. "Ashton, how do you know Addison? After all, you seem rather close. And your friends seem to know her as well."

Addison's cheeks felt hot as she laid her head back down on Ashton's shoulder. "After Daniel and I got back from traveling, Jack invited us to a house party. While there, I met Addison." Ashton brought her hand to his lips and kissed the back of it. "She quickly became very important to me. She disappeared and I have been helping Jack and Daniel look for her. Finding Addison was our first priority." Ashton explained.

Lord Fenton looked between the four of them for a minute. "And how do you two know our Miss Blackwell?"

"She is our sister." Jack said as he moved to stand behind the couch Addison was sitting on. He touched her head softly and she craned her neck back to look up at him. "We talked with Susan." Addison immediately tensed and jumped from the couch.

She regretted the loss of Ashton's warmth. She studied all three men and by the look of deep sadness on their faces, she knew. Susan had told them everything and most likely showed them the pictures she had drawn.

Addison wrapped her arms around her middle as if that could protect her from the memories that started to surface. A hand touched her upper arms and Addison blinked. Ashton stood before her, concern in his blue eyes.

"Addison, breathe." he said calmly as he ran his hands up and down her arms. Addison stepped closer to him, and she wrapped her arms around his waist, then he put his arms around her. "Everything is okay, love." He whispered in her ear. Addison froze. Did he just call her love?

"Dinner is ready, My Lord." The monotone butler announced from the doorway.

"Thank you, Crawford." Lady Fenton said. "Miss Blackwell, will you be joining us for dinner?" Ashton released her and stepped back as Lady Fenton approached. "I know you had a rough night last night."

"You had another nightmare?" Ashton grabbed her hand as he looked at her with concern.

Addison smiled at him. "It was a milder one." Ashton watched her closely. Daniel, too, had moved closer to her.

"That was mild?" Lady Fenton asked in disbelief.

"I am fine." Addison said again. "I would love to have dinner with everyone." She tried to redirect the attention of everyone back to the meal that was waiting for them.

"Come on, my dear." Lord Fenton said as he grabbed his wife's hand and threaded it through his arm before heading for the door.

Ashton offered her his arm and she took it. Jack and Daniel followed them as they followed Lord and Lady Fenton. He slowed his steps slightly, so his parents were out of earshot. "We need to talk later this evening." He whispered loud enough that Jack and Daniel could hear him.

Addison glanced back at them, and they both nodded. "Not only about what happened to cause you to run away, but also about you and Ashton." Jack gave her a pointed look. Addison's cheeks flushed again, and she quickly turned back around.

Ashton pulled out Addison's chair for her before taking the seat to her left. As soon as everyone was seated and the food was placed in front of them, Ashton reached over and grabbed Addison's left hand that was resting in her lap. She glanced over at him, but he was eating with his left hand and acting like he was not doing anything out of the ordinary.

Addison took a small bite of her food just as Ashton rubbed his thumb over the back of her hand. Addison glanced over at him again and his dimple was showing, even though he had a neutral expression on his face. Addison could tell her own cheeks were, at the very least, pink if not red.

"When have you used your left hand for anything, Ashton?" Lord Fenton asked with a twinkle in his eye.

"It's a newly acquired preference." Ashton commented as he took a sip of his water. Daniel coughed as he tried to cover a laugh. "So mother, have you had the pleasure of riding with Addison yet?"

"I have. She has a gift with horses." Lady Fenton smiled at Addison.

"Which horse have you been riding, Addison?" Ashton turned and smiled at her.

"Tana." Addison replied. Ashton's hand tightened on hers and his smile dropped from his face.

"You've allowed Addison to ride Tana?" Ashton asked his mother. He was clearly upset by the news. "You know how dangerous Tana is mother, why would you allow anyone to ride her?"

"Addison and Tana have a connection and Addison is an excellent horsewoman." Lady Fenton defended herself.

"What makes Tana so dangerous?" Jack asked.

"She has thrown me many times, almost killed a stable hand when he tried to lead her to the pasture, and she kicks anyone who comes near her." Ashton voice was tense. "From now on, no one is allowed to ride Tana."

Addison pulled her hand from Ashton's and his head snapped over to her. She stood from the table and gave Lady Fenton her attention. "On second thought My Lady, I do feel a bit tired. I think I will retire early." Lady Fenton gave her a nod and Addison gave a quick curtsey before moving toward the door.

How could Ashton come in and start telling her what she could do? He was doing exactly what Jack and Daniel did when they finally came home. Addison knew that he was just worried for her safety, but at the same time, he had no faith in her.

She was good with horses. She and Tana had developed a relationship. Addison was beginning to trust that Tana would not attempt to throw her off randomly on their rides. She had yet to be thrown by the mare.

She did not want to be mad at Ashton. She had finally gotten him and her brothers back and she did not want to ruin the evening by getting angry.

She stopped in the entryway and looked back down the hall. She was debating if she should return and apologize for her rash behavior or if she should just talk with Ashton in the morning. The sound of the front door opening behind her caused her to turn around to see who was entering.

She froze in fear as the two men from her nightmares smiled at her. "Perfect." The scarred one sneered as he grabbed her arm and pulled her towards the door.

As they reached the bottom step, Addison finally found her voice. "Ash!" She screamed at the top of her lungs as she was dragged toward the waiting carriage.

The one that had strangled her a few weeks ago slapped her across her face. "Keep quiet or we will hurt that woman and baby that helped you get away." He growled out before shoving her roughly into the carriage and climbing in after her. Almost immediately, the carriage began to race down the drive, and away from Lakeview Manor and Ashton.

Chapter 17

"Ash!" Addison's scream sounded far away but Ashton still heard it.

"Was that Miss Blackwell?" Lord Fenton jumped to his feet as he looked at the door. Ashton was already running for the door, and he knew that Jack and Daniel weren't far behind him.

"Addison!" He called loudly. He turned towards the stairs as he called her name again. They were halfway up the stairs when a door creaked behind them. Ashton turned to see the front door slowly swinging open with the breeze from outside.

He raced back downstairs and out the door. There was a carriage moving fast as it disappeared over the top of a hill. "Addison!" Ashton yelled again as he ran out onto the gravel drive.

He dropped to his knees. He just got her back and now she was gone again. This time was probably with the men determined to kill her.

"Come on, Ashton." Daniel called as he and Jack ran for the stables. Ashton was right behind them.

Ashton bridled Leo but didn't bother with putting on a saddle before leading him out and jumping on his back. He kicked him into a run and headed in the direction he saw the carriage disappear. Ashton pushed Leonidas fast as he reached the road.

After several miles, Ashton pulled his horse to a halt. His heart dropped from his chest as he jumped from Leonidas' back and stumbled towards the tipped carriage.

He made it to its side just as three more horses pulled to a stop nearby. He glanced over and saw his father, Jack, and Daniel as they all rushed over to him. Ashton climbed on top and pulled open the door.

He was both relieved and disappointed that Addison was not inside. Daniel quickly climbed up next to him and looked in. There was blood on the bottom door and broken glass all over the interior of the carriage.

"Is she in there?" Ashton's father called up.

"No. Its empty." Ashton answered as he ran a hand through his hair before climbing back down to the ground.

"The horses are missing." Jack was walking around the overturned carriage.

"Where would they take her?" Ashton asked anxiously.

"We will find her, son." Ashton's father placed a hand on his shoulder. "Since they unhooked the horses, they could have gone in any direction. We should head back to the estate and send word to the authorities. We could use their help in finding Miss Blackwell."

Returning to the estate was the last thing Ashton wanted to do. He wanted to find her. Daniel stepped up beside him and placed a hand on his shoulder.

"Lord Fenton, why don't you and Jack head back and get more help. Ashton and I will continue looking around. Maybe we can find a clue as to which direction they went. The longer Addison is with her captors the more dangerous it is for her." Ashton and Daniel watched as Jack and Lord Fenton rode away. "Come on Ashton, let's look around."

It didn't take long for Ashton to find hoof prints that led away from the tipped carriage. Ashton and Daniel followed them on foot as they led their horses behind them. They did not want to be surprised by running into a trap of some sort.

They kept quiet as they moved, but Ashton could tell that Daniel was just as desperate to find Addison as he was. Ashton was terrified that they would not find her in time.

She had evaded Samuel and Silas twice before. There was no telling how angry they were or what they planned to do to her. Ashton and Daniel still had no idea why they attacked her in the first place.

The sun had dipped below the horizon over an hour ago and the uneasy feeling that filled Ashton only grew. They were now in a forested area and with the sun no longer providing light, it was impossible to see the tracks they had been following.

Daniel let out a frustrated growl before tying his horse to a branch. Ashton did the same. They sat on a fallen log and Ashton looked up at the star filled sky. He silently prayed that Addison was safe and that they could find her.

Daniel ran a hand down his face. "I think we should stay here for the night. We do not want to lose the tracks and I feel like the faster we find her the better."

"I agree. It's going to be a cold one though. Should we build a small fire?" Ashton kept his voice low as he began looking for dry wood.

It could be a risk lighting a fire. If Samuel and Silas were close, they could see the fire, but if Ashton and Daniel did not have a fire, they could become too cold. It was a gamble, but Daniel agreed that they needed the fire.

It was well after dark, and the fire was going strong. Ashton sat quietly as he stared into the flames. Daniel had pulled his saddle off his horse and was using it as a pillow. He wasn't sure if his friend was asleep or not, but Ashton couldn't bring himself to even try to sleep.

His mind kept playing through all the possible scenarios that Addison could be experiencing at that moment. It was driving him crazy. He kept hearing her scream his name. The terror in her voice was clear and he felt like he had failed her. He was not quick enough to save her from being taken.

Ashton ran his hand through his hair in frustration. How did Samuel and Silas find her?

The lightening of the sky was a blessed sight. While Daniel saddled his horse, Ashton put out the fire. He could tell by the dark circles under Daniel's eyes that he did not sleep either. They didn't talk much as they continued to follow the hoof prints in the soft earth. This time on horseback.

"Where do you think they are taking her?" Daniel asked.

"I wish I knew." Ashton said as they galloped through a clearing. Again, they fell into silence as they rode. It was nearly midday when Ashton looked around. The area was starting to look familiar. "Is this the clearing that Addison does her shooting?"

Daniel whipped his head from side to side. "Yes." He said as his mouth pulled down in a frown.

Why would her captors bring her back here? They picked up their pace as the trail became clearer. Ashton pulled Leonidas to a stop as they drew closer to some of the tenant cottages. He slid off his horse's back and tied him out of sight of the home in front of them.

He slowly moved closer to the structure. The Gracie's cottage? Ashton never felt more grateful for Jack sending the Gracie family away until Samuel and Silas were caught. Two horses were tied at the side of the house and Ashton knew that both men and Addison were inside.

"They are in the Gracie's cottage." Ashton whispered as Daniel crouched next to him.

"One of us should ride back to the house for more manpower and some weapons." Daniel suggested. Ashton was so close to Addison now; he did not want to leave. He looked over at Daniel, but before he could say anything Daniel gave him a quick nod. "You stay here. I will go. But Ashton, stay out of sight. Do not approach them. They have Addison and we don't want them to feel threatened and hurt her." Ashton understood and nodded.

Daniel quietly left and Ashton settled in to wait. He found a good spot to watch the front of the house and the horses while keeping well hidden.

Time seemed to tick by at a snail's pace and Ashton was getting anxious to make a move. He kept reminding himself that if he moved before the right time, he would be putting Addison in more danger than she already was. It was torture not being able to run in there and get her.

Ashton kept his mind occupied by thinking about what happened the night before. His utter shock of seeing Addison step into the room had quickly turned to relief. It took every ounce of self-control not to run to her immediately.

She had seemed just as shocked as they were to see her, but when she stepped towards him, he gave in. She had wrapped her arms around his neck while calling him the nickname she alone called him, and it undid him.

He could not bring himself to let her go all night. He felt that if he couldn't feel her, that she would disappear again. He had been terrified when he found out she had been riding Tana. That horse was dangerous. She had broken several of his bones by throwing him off and nearly ran over one of the stable hands. The thought of Addison riding her... he squeezed his eyes closed briefly.

He had definitely messed up by telling her she could no longer ride the mare. He knew it the moment the words fell from his mouth. She had pulled her hand from his and he flinched. He knew he had made her angry. He was just about to excuse himself to go after her when she screamed his name.

He let out a tense breath. He would do anything to have her back at his estate angry with him over horses instead of being trapped in a small cottage with two murderers.

Time continued to tick by slowly. The sun was starting to set when he heard a stick snap behind him. He turned and saw Daniel, Allen, and Moore approaching slowly.

"Look who I found at the house." Daniel whispered as he passed Ashton a gun and an overcoat. "I also sent a message to Lakeview. There are also seven footman and James spreading out behind us and through the meadow."

"Not that I am complaining, but what are you two doing here?" Ashton asked the detectives.

"We have found some information about the case that we felt we needed to bring to Lord Blackwell's attention." Allen said quietly. "What has been going on in the cottage?"

"There has been some movement in the windows, but no one has left. All has been quiet." Ashton glanced at the man before returning his attention to the cottage.

"What should we do?" Daniel asked.

"Since it is getting dark, I think we should wait until early morning to make our move. They aren't going to do anything during the night. It will be difficult for us as well." Detective Allen whispered.

"You mean they will not leave with her during the night. They could easily hurt her while she is locked in there with them." Ashton managed to keep his voice low, even though he felt like yelling.

"As difficult as it is, attacking the house at night will be more dangerous for everyone involved. Waiting for morning will give us time to watch and take note of their behavior as well as possible weapons they might have and Miss Blackwell's location. Until we know where she is being kept, we cannot go in. We could accidently kill her in the crossfire." Detective Moore stated.

Ashton swallowed hard and Daniel put a hand on his shoulder. When he turned to look at his friend, Daniel gave him a small nod. It looked like he would have to wait one more night to rescue Addison. Another long night.

At least this time he knew where she was. He just had to be patient. Ashton saw Daniel's jaw clench as a large shadow passed by the window that overlooked the front of the house. Allen and Moore settled back against a tree as they watched the house closely.

It was fully dark with a sliver of moon to provide the tiniest of light. Ashton noticed a small movement near the house, and he turned to point it out to the detectives and Daniel. Allen wasn't sitting near his tree anymore and Moore was staring intently at the shadow.

The shadow crept up to the window and very slowly peeked into the cottage. The figure quickly ducked back down and then held still. It took another ten minutes for Allen to make it back to the small group after peaking in the window a few more times.

"It's Samuel and Silas all right." He whispered. "I didn't see any sign of Miss Blackwell, but the brothers have multiple guns and knives laid out on the table. They are taking turns sleeping." Allen reported.

Where was Addison? Ashton guessed they could have locked her in a different room for the time being. The temperature continued to drop, and he could start to see his own breath as they waited in the tense silence.

Ashton was aware of Allen and Moore quietly discussing various options they could do once it was light enough. Ashton half listened to the conversation and half willed Addison to walk out the front door completely unharmed.

Chapter 18

Addison sat quietly holding her cheek and was thrown against the side of the carriage as it tipped dangerously around a corner. The man that tried to strangle her, sat opposite of her, and didn't seem bothered with the insane speed they were travelling.

Addison's heart was beating nearly as fast as the horses' hooves as they raced away from Lakeview Manor. They made several more curves and each one tossed her around. She gripped the seat to try to keep herself in one spot, but to no avail. The man who sat opposite of her glared at her the whole time and Addison knew that she needed to find a way to escape.

The carriage tipped up on two wheels again and Addison began to slide across the seat. There was a second that Addison thought they might stay upright, but the carriage continued to tip. She let out a scream as she was slammed against the side of the carriage and glass shattered all around her. A heavy weight fell on top of her, pressing her more into all the broken glass. For a moment everything went still.

Addison tried to take a few deep breaths but the weight on her was making it hard for her to fully fill her lungs. She was beginning to feel pain in her arms and head. She tried pushing the weight off of her, but it wouldn't budge. She was about to try again when it began to shift off her. The man that attacked her groaned in pain as he moved to stand.

"Sam!" A gruff male voice called from outside the carriage.

"Yeah." Sam replied still a bit dazed.

"What about the girl?" The man asked.

Addison lay there too afraid to move. She was sure she had glass imbedded in her skin. Sam looked down at her and seemed to be looking her over for injuries without touching her.

"She's alive, but there is quite a bit of blood." There was no sympathy in his voice. No movement to stop any bleeding. Just a hard look that made Addison shiver.

"Pass her up." Addison pulled her eyes away from Sam's cold dark brown one's to see the man with the scar leaning into the carriage through the door that was directly above them. "I've already unhitched the horses so we can continue on."

Sam grabbed Addison's arm and pulled. She let out a cry as pain shot up her shoulder. Sam quickly let her go and she fell back onto the glass causing her to hiss as more glass cut into her. Sam leaned down and scooped her up in his arms before passing her up to the other man.

The scarred man grabbed under her arms and lifted her easily out. He helped her down and set her on the dirt. Her shoulder was still hurting, and she wasn't able to use her arm. Addison could also feel blood running down her face. She must have hit her head on something.

The man with the scar knelt beside her and grabbed her shoulder as she tried to scoot away from him. He laughed as he watched her. "If you want to keep that shoulder dislocated all you had to do was say so." He watched her for a minute before saying. "Would you like me to reset it?" Addison felt tears burn her eyes. She did not want this man touching her. But she knew she couldn't escape with a dislocated shoulder, so she gave a small nod. "Good girl." He smirked at her, and Addison wanted to spit in the man's face.

He moved closer to her and again grabbed her shoulder. She bit her lip to keep from crying out as he felt it. He squeezed her shoulder as he gave her arm a hard jerk. A scream tore from her lips as tears coursed down her cheeks. The man stood up and helped her to her feet. He guided her towards where Sam was already sitting on one of the horses. It gave her a little pleasure seeing his face scratched and bleeding.

"Pass her up, Silas." Sam said as he reached for her.

Addison shook her head and tried to back away. "Please, no." She begged, but both men ignored her protests. "If you are going to kill me just do it already." She spat out.

"Sorry, Sweetheart. We have plans for you." Silas said as he grabbed her around her waist and lifted her easily onto the horse in front of Sam.

She was sitting astride, and her dress rode up to her knees, exposing her lower legs. Sam's arm came around her waist, pinning her to him. She desperately wanted to get away but didn't see any way to do it at the moment.

"Play nice, my pet, and maybe I will be nice to you." Sam said into her ear and a shiver ran down her spine. Tears continued to fall as her disgust for the men grew.

"Leave her alone for now, Sam. Uncle needs her for his plan, and he doesn't want damaged goods. She looks a mess as it is." Silas said as he mounted the other horse.

Sam and Silas pushed the horses into a fast gait. Addison's head began to pound with each step the horse took. Her whole right side radiated with fire and her right shoulder ached from being dislocated. She didn't say anything; too afraid that they would hurt her if she delayed them in anyway.

As darkness descended around them, Addison was sure they would stop to rest the horses, but they did not. The only thing they did was slow the horses to a walk. The pain in her head became unbearable and she thought she might actually throw up.

Another wave of nausea hit, and Addison pushed Sam's arm away from her and she fell to the ground. He started yelling at her and just as Addison felt strong hands grab her arms, she began throwing up.

Immediately, the hands let go of her and she fell to her knees. Several minutes passed and she finally had no more left in her stomach. She managed to move a little away from that spot before collapsing into darkness.

* * *

Addison blinked her eyes open. Everything around her was dark. She groaned as she sat up. She looked around her. There was something familiar about the room, but at the same time, she had no idea where she was. Her head was still pounding and her shoulder ached. The right side of her face, neck, and arm stung and burned.

A small light grew brighter just before a man's head popped up out of a hole in the floor. The candle was placed next to him, as he continued to climb into the room.

Once the man moved closer, she recognized him. Silas. "How are you feeling?" He asked. Addison remained silent as she glared at her captor. A smile spread on his lips. "Do you know where your friend and the baby are?"

He asked as if they were having a completely normal conversation. Addison continued to not say anything, and she saw a muscle tick in his jaw. "Since they are not here, I am guessing they are visiting family or something. So, do you know where they are?" He asked again. This time less friendly.

They were at Susan's cottage? Addison shook her head no. At least she could be honest answering the question; she really didn't know where Susan and Evelynn were. Silas continued to watch her. He seemed satisfied with her answer and climbed back down the ladder, leaving the candle behind.

She heard voices from downstairs as Addison looked around the room. She needed to think. If this really was Susan's attic, she was so close to home. All she needed to do was find a way to escape and run for the manor house.

There were several things being stored up in the attic. Crates were stacked in multiple spots. If she could somehow lock Sam and Silas downstairs, she would at least be safe from them until she could figure out how to escape.

Addison moved as quickly as she could, with her pounding head, over to the opening. She grabbed the hatch door and quietly lowered it into place. Next, she moved to the boxes and other items and stacked the heaviest things she could find on top of the hatch door. Her shoulder was protesting every move she made.

She prayed that it was enough to keep them from coming up into the attic. Addison had no idea how much time she was going to have before they tried to come up the stairs again. She moved to the window and cracked it open. The cool night air was a welcome relief to her aching body. All she wanted to do was go back to sleep, but she couldn't allow herself to do that. If she slept, she would be as good as dead.

Closing her eyes, Addison pictured the terrain around the Gracie's cottage and the routes back to the manor house. She knew that there was a small trail that was at the back of the cottage that looped around near the lake before turning toward the stables and manor house. That was Addison's best chance. It would take longer, but it would also keep her hidden from the front of the house the longest. That way if either Silas or Sam looked out the windows, she would not be spotted.

With it being so cold outside and dressed in her thin cream-colored evening gown, Addison decided to wait for the sun to start to rise before she attempted to leave. Sitting on the ground she winced. Her hip was extremely sore.

She looked down and blinked back tears. The cream-colored gown was covered in blood, mostly on the bodice. She shook her head and immediately regretted it, the action making the pain in her head worse. To help pass the time, Addison began picking glass out of her numerous cuts and scrapes on her hand.

Addison had a nice pile of glass shards when she heard a cock crow in the distance. She got to her feet and looked out the window. The first rays of sunlight were just peaking over the horizon.

She pushed the window open all the way and stuck her foot through. This was going to be more difficult in a dress and without Spartan to land on, but she was determined to get away.

She found herself hanging from the ledge in no time, despite her dress catching a few times and her shoulder screaming in protest. Taking a deep breath, Addison let go. She was airborne for a second before her feet hit the ground and she fell backwards onto her back. She looked up at the window, but a movement in a lower window caught her eye.

Silas was watching her through the glass with an amused smile on his face. Addison did not wait to see what would happen next before taking off running for the woods. She reached the trail she knew was there and raced along it.

Her lungs were burning, but she refused to stop. The trees finally opened to the steep hill that sat just above the far side of the lake farthest from the house. Addison continued to run along the top of it. Something hard hit her back, sending her flying over the edge. She screamed as she rolled down the embankment.

When she finally came to a stop, she was face down and gasping for air. Someone rolled her onto her back before jumping on her. Sam's angry face appeared above her, and she screamed again.

He reached behind him and pulled out a gun. Addison tried to grab for it, causing Sam to lose his grip and the gun started to fall. They both tried to get it as Sam kept her pinned with his weight. Both of them struggling to gain control over the weapon had brought it in between them. Addison kicked and wiggled, trying to distract him so she could get the gun.

A gunshot rang out and Sam stopped moving for a second before he fell forward. Warmth spread across Addison's abdomen. She froze. Sam wasn't moving either. Had she been shot? It took her a moment to process that she had no pain where the warm liquid continued to soak her.

She tried to move, but both her hands were trapped between her and Sam's body. Tears stung her eyes, and she gave up struggling. There was no use. His body was too heavy for her to move on her own, especially with her injured shoulder.

Addison heard voices yelling in the distance. Fear took over. Was Silas coming? She closed her eyes and held as still as she could. Maybe Silas would think she was dead too, and leave her be.

It was only a few minutes later that she felt the weight of Sam's body being rolled off of her. She fought with her need to take in a deep breath now that she could fill her lungs all the way without Sam's weight on her. A hand touched her face and she couldn't stop herself from flinching.

"Addison?" A familiar voice choked out.

Addison opened her eyes to see Ashton looking down at her. Fear was all over his pale face. "Ash." She half laughed; half cried.

Ashton leaned down and pressed his lips to her forehead. When he sat back up, tears were in his eyes. Addison tried to sit up, but Daniel's voice stopped her. "Do not move, Addie. We need to make sure you aren't seriously hurt." His voice was thick with emotion.

Addison looked down at herself. Her abdomen was covered in blood. She shivered. The blood wasn't hers. Suddenly, all she wanted to do was change and get Sam's blood off her. She started to have a panic attack. She needed to get the blood off of her. Now. She again started to sit up as her breathing became more erratic.

"Addison, it's okay. Look at me." Ashton cupped her face to try to get her to look at him.

Addison shook her head. "It's not mine." She whimpered. Once she was in a sitting position, Addison looked at Ashton. "Please, Ash. Take me home. I can't. I need." Her tears were flowing again.

Ashton quickly scooped her up, not needing her to fully explain. "How do we get her back to the house?" Ashton asked.

"We can follow the hill. It will take us to a trail that will lead us back." Daniel answered and Ashton began to walk quickly.

"What about...?" Ashton asked in a quieter voice.

"He's not going anywhere. We can send Allen and Moore for him when everyone gets back to the house." Daniel replied quickly.

Addison rested her aching head on Ashton's shoulder and closed her eyes. She tried to calm her racing heart and regulate her breathing as they walked back to the house.

Before she knew it, Ashton was climbing the grand staircase while Daniel yelled for Mary to bring water for a bath, and he sent someone for a doctor. Ashton smoothly opened the door to her room while continuing to hold her. Once inside, he set her feet down gently, but Addison continued to lean on him.

"Addison where are you hurt?" he asked softly.

Addison shook her head. "Most of my injuries are from the carriage accident." She whispered.

"That doesn't answer my question, love." Ashton took a small step back, keeping her at arm's length.

Daniel came rushing in with Mary and several other servants as they prepared a bath for her. "Please, Ash. My head hurts too much to think." Addison closed her eyes, and she felt Ashton step close to her again. He guided her head to his shoulder and she let out a sigh.

Ashton once again took a step back from her. Addison let out a small growl of frustration as she opened her eyes. Ashton's worried eyes flashed with amusement as he gave her a smile.

"Your bath is ready." He nodded towards the steaming tub full of water. Addison looked at it in surprise. How long had she been standing there with Ashton? "Take your time. Daniel and I will be in the drawing room when you are done. Hopefully, the doctor arrives soon." Addison looked from the tub back to Ashton. She wasn't sure she wanted a bath right then. Ashton's smile widened and he pressed a kiss to her forehead. "You need to get cleaned up, Addison. If you need anything, Mary will let us know and Daniel and I will be right here."

"Promise?" Addison asked as she looked up into his eyes.

"We promise, Addie." Daniel said as he pressed a light kiss to her left cheek. Just as they were leaving, Ashton turned back to her and gave her a wink.

Mary closed and locked the door before turning back to face Addison. She wiped tears from her face. "Miss Addie, we have been so worried about you."

"I have missed you all so much." Addison said with a watery smile. "Mary, I need to get this blood-soaked dress off."

Mary nodded and they made quick work of it. Addison flinched and gasped as she sunk her battered body into the water. Mary took great care in helping get Addison as clean as possible. Addison discovered her whole right side was covered in bruises.

Once she was dressed in a dark blue dress, Mary began to help Addison pick all the glass out of her body. It was a slow, painful process. Two hours later, they felt like they got most, if not all the glass out.

Addison left Mary to dispose of the ruined dress as she slowly made her way down to the drawing room. It took her more than twice the normal time, but she finally made it. She stepped into the room and found Ashton asleep sitting on one of the couches and Daniel asleep lying on the other.

Addison quietly sat on the couch next to Ashton. She was beginning to feel stiff and sore all over. She leaned back against the couch and closed her eyes.

Addison was just starting to relax when there was a large crash and raised voices. She jumped and her heart started to race. Both Ashton and Daniel were on their feet in an instant. They positioned themselves between her and the drawing room door.

She stood and grabbed onto the back of Ashton's shirt. He glanced at her quickly before turning his attention back to the door. It slammed open a minute later and Addison jumped again. She rested her head on Ashton's back as she began to shake.

"Where is she?" A voice boomed through the room. It took Addison a moment to recognize it as Jack's. She tentatively peeked around Ashton; still worried Silas would be there too. The second Jack saw her, he rushed to her. "Addison." He pulled her into a tight embrace that caused a cry of pain to escape her lips.

Jack immediately let her go and she stumbled back a few steps. She squeezed her eyes closed as she took several deep breaths. When she opened them, she was met with six men's worried expressions. Besides Jack, Ashton and Daniel, there was Lord Fenton and two men she didn't recognize. Ashton took a step towards her, but she held up her hand to stop him.

"Just give me a minute. It will pass." She said through the pain. The moment Jack squeezed her there was a sharp pain that stabbed her shoulder.

"What's wrong, Addie?" Daniel asked anxiously.

Before Addison could respond, Dr. Thompson rushed into the room. He stopped as he scanned the room. His gaze stopped when it settled on her. His eyes widened before he made his way over to Addison. "This isn't exactly what I was expecting, Miss Addie." he said with a forced smile.

Addison tried to smile, but she was sure it looked more like a grimace. Her shoulder was still spasming and she did not feel like she could move or speak. Her breathing was a little ragged as she fought the rising nausea. She was losing the battle and before she lost the contents of her stomach in the house, Addison ran from the room.

She barely made it off the front porch before her stomach started to heave. She could feel eyes on her, but she ignored them. When she finished, she felt a gentle hand on her back. She looked up into Dr. Thompson's kind, worried eyes.

"Miss Addie, where does it hurt?" Dr. Thompson asked.

Addison took a step to the side before sitting down on the bottom step. Someone sat down next to her, and she knew it was Ashton without having to look at him. She leaned against him, and he gently put his arm around her. She drew strength from his presence as she looked back at Dr. Thompson who was studying her closely. She shifted to try to get more comfortable and winced. Where did she hurt? Her head, her shoulder, her whole right side, her hlp. What didn't hurt?

"Everywhere." She finally answered and she felt Ashton press a kiss to her head.

"Why don't we get you up to your room and you can tell me what happened so we can get you feeling better." Dr. Thompson said as he continued to watch her.

Addison nodded but did not make a move to head inside. Ashton shifted away from her slightly, and she was just about to protest, when she was lifted into his arms. He was careful as he carried her up the stairs and laid her gently on her bed.

Addison looked around as everyone squeezed into her room. The tub was gone but her dress was still on the floor. Dr. Thompson picked it up and looked at her.

"I don't know how much of that is mine." she said quietly looking away from it. She normally wasn't squeamish about blood, but it was also a reminder of all she had been through.

"What do you mean, Addison? The dress is more red than anything now." Jack sounded upset.

"Why don't you start from the beginning, Miss Blackwell. What happened after you left the dining room?" One of the unknown men asked as he stepped closer to her.

"I'm sorry, who are you?" She asked as she winced again.

"These are the detectives who were helping us locate you and apprehend Silas and Samuel. They came to deliver some break in the case." Daniel said.

"Why don't we hold off on the interrogation until Miss Addie's injuries are looked at, detective." Dr. Thompson stepped between her and the men in the room. "I will need Mary and two other maids in here with me, but you gentlemen need to leave. Now." he said sternly. As the men filed out, Dr. Thompson spoke again. "Lord Blackwell, I need you to send for my wife. The quicker she is here; the quicker we can get Miss Addie fully treated." Jack nodded before leaving.

Ashton looked back at her as Dr. Thompson closed the door in his face. The doctor turned to her and raised a brow in question. She knew that look. He wanted her to explain what happened. Addison had learned through the years that Dr. Thompson liked to know how the injuries occurred. In his opinion, knowing how the injury happened was just as important as treating the injury.

Addison looked over at Mary and the two maids, Maggie and Marissa, before looking back at Dr. Thompson. "My abductor slapped me as he shoved me into a carriage. The carriage tipped over. I landed hard on the downside and got cut up by the broken window. One of the men that took me landed on me. My shoulder was in a lot of pain, and I could not use it. The other man that took me, grabbed my shoulder and yanked on my arm. There was a pop before the pain dulled to an ache. My head was hurting really bad. I started throwing up just before I lost consciousness."

"Is that all?" Dr. Thompson asked as he began looking into Addison's eyes and the cuts on her face and head.

"I was tackled and fell down a hill." Addison looked at the bloody dress the doctor had dropped on a chair. "That's it."

Mr. Thompson nodded his head as he continued to look at all the cuts and abrasions on Addison's arms, neck, and face. He put a couple stitches in the cut on her head and cleaned all the cuts he could see. A soft knock came at the door and Mary answered it.

Mrs. Thompson quickly stepped in. She was a petite woman with dark blue eyes and white hair that she wore in a tight bun on the back of her head. Dr. and Mrs. Thompson talked quietly for several minutes before Dr. Thompson slipped from the room.

The couple worked as a team to treat those in the area. Mrs. Thompson spent most of her time acting as a midwife, but she was just as knowledgeable as Dr. Thompson about treating illnesses and injuries. Mrs. Thompson was a wonderful woman. Addison had helped her deliver Evelynn.

Mrs. Thompson helped Addison undress and took a closer look at the injuries that Dr. Thompson could not see. She wore a grim expression as she felt along Addison's ribs and hips. Both were bruised and tender. When the older woman was done, she helped Addison get dressed again. Addison insisted on going downstairs and Mrs. Thompson reluctantly followed her from the room.

Chapter 19

Dr. Thompson walked into the drawing room and Ashton stopped pacing. The doctor's wife just arrived, and he had not expected to see the doctor so soon. Jack walked up to the man and Ashton saw the doctor shake his head. Ashton felt like he couldn't breathe. What was wrong with Addison?

"Gentlemen, why don't you all have a seat. I would rather just say this once." Dr. Thompson moved further into the room. No one moved to sit, but all the attention was on the doctor. "Miss Addie has been through a lot and is lucky to be alive. She said she was in a carriage accident. I believe most of her injuries are from that. I only checked her injuries on her head, neck and arms. She had a dislocated shoulder that was reset by one of her captors. My wife is checking her for other injuries as we speak. This exam will probably take longer."

Ashton ran a hand down his face. He wished he could be up there with her. He had decided during the long night that as soon as Addison was safe, he would ask her to marry him. He didn't think he could go another day without her. Daniel walked up and leaned against the wall next to Ashton.

"The detectives said they were here to tell us something about the case, but they want to wait until they hear what happened with Addison before saying anything." Daniel said quietly.

"They might have found the reason why Silas and Samuel were targeting Addison." Ashton glanced over at the detectives who were speaking quietly in a corner. "What happened with the other man?" He asked.

"After you chased after the first guy that ran from the cottage, the second one came out and saw you. He ran back inside and came out with a gun. Allen and Moore both opened fire on him and he went down. He didn't survive." Daniel shrugged. "What happened with the first guy?" Daniel asked.

"I ran after him and just as the trees gave way, I saw Addison not far ahead of the man. He dove for her, and she went flying over the top of the hill. She screamed as she fell. I ran for the spot where they disappeared as a gun went off. I looked down and the man was lying face down and not moving. I could not see Addison anywhere. I called for her, but she still did not respond. I made my way down the hill and caught sight of her dress under the man. I rolled him off her and that is when you showed up." Ashton could not get the image of her covered in blood and lying motionless. He had thought she was dead.

Silence fell between them as they waited for Mrs. Thompson to come down and bring word about Addison's condition. An hour passed, and Ashton took up his pacing again. His father had tried to get him to sit down, but Ashton could not sit still. He was too anxious; he needed to know how she was doing.

A noise at the door drew his attention. An elderly woman with white hair walked in followed by Addison. Addison moved slowly and her arm was in a sling. When she met Ashton's gaze, she immediately started to move towards him.

Ashton closed the distance quickly and he gently put his arms around her. He did not want to cause her anymore pain. She let out a sigh as she leaned heavier against him. "Let's get you sitting down." He whispered into her ear, and she nodded.

Ashton guided Addison to the couch and as soon as he sat beside her, she scooted closer to him. "They are like magnets, aren't they?" Ashton heard his father remark.

"You should have seen them before Addison disappeared the first time. They did not even realize they would gravitate towards one another no matter where we were." Daniel commented back.

"Mrs. Thompson, how is Addison?" Jack asked.

Mrs. Thompson looked over at Addison and Ashton felt her nod her head as she rested against his shoulder. "Miss Addie has a concussion, cuts from glass, a massive amount of bruising, a dislocated shoulder and..." the woman paused, and Ashton tensed. "...she is in need of lots of rest. She will be extremely sore for the next several days. Her leg is also hurting a bit."

"You didn't mention anything about your leg before." Dr. Thompson moved in Addison's direction.

"I forgot I dropped from the Gracie's attic window." Addison spoke softly.

Ashton closed his eyes. He could easily picture her climbing out the window and dropping onto Spartan's back. But this time she had fallen all the way to the ground. It's a miracle she didn't severely break her leg. "That's why we didn't see you leave the house." Ashton said to himself.

Addison shifted and he looked down at her. Her eyes were wide. "You were there?" She sounded surprised.

"Of course, I was there. Daniel and I followed the hoofprints from the carriage to the cottage. Daniel rode back here to gather more men while I stayed and watched the cottage." Ashton pressed a kiss to her forehead. "He sent a message to Jack and my father who had returned to Lakeview to get men to help search for you after we found the overturned carriage. Daniel also brought back the detectives. We were planning on attacking once the sun came up, but one of the men ran out of the cottage and circled around back."

"Miss Blackwell, could you tell us about the events leading up to the kidnapping and what happened during?" Allen asked as he pulled his notebook from his jacket pocket.

"No." Addison sat up. She glared at the detective. "I will not tell you anything until you tell me why you are here." Allen's eyes widened in surprise.

"Miss Blackwell, Detective Moore and I like to have all the information we can before we share our information." Allen gave her a tight smile.

"I see. Very wise of you gentlemen but since you were already planning on giving my brothers and Ashton the information before I was kidnapped, I see no reason why my experience would have any bearing on what you have to say." Addison fired back.

Detective Moore laughed. "Touche, Miss Blackwell. You will have your hands full with her, Lord Fenwick." Moore winked before clearing his throat. His smile dropped from his face as he stood and looked at everyone in the room. "Do you know a Mr. Simon Drake?" He asked Addison

"He was our father's solicitor." Addison answered.

"You, Miss Blackwell, discovered he was stealing money from your father." Addison nodded. "From talking with many of your staff, it sounds like he nearly killed you." Addison again nodded but didn't say anything. "Samuel and Silas Drake, Mr. Simon Drake's nephews, visited him in prison. We had several conversations with Mr. Simon Drake, and he finally told us that he sent his nephews to capture you. They were to use you for ransom. Once your brothers paid the price for your release, Samuel and Silas were to kill you." Moore explained what they had discovered.

"That explains their somewhat concern for me after the carriage tipped over." Addison mumbled. "Where are Samuel and Silas now?" She asked.

"Both men are dead, Miss Blackwell." Detective Allen said quickly. Addison sat in silence for several minutes before blinking a few times. Ashton watched her carefully. Would she be upset? Would she go into shock? "Now, what happened when you were with them." Allen said curtly.

Addison gave Detective Allen a long, hard look before taking a deep breath. "I was angry, so I left dinner early. I was standing in the entry hall of Lakeview Manor debating whether I wanted to go to my room or return to dinner. I heard the door behind me open and when I turned, Samuel and Silas were stepping into the house. They saw me and pulled me quickly through the door. I screamed, was slapped, and then shoved into a carriage. Samuel was in the carriage with me while Silas drove. The carriage tipped over and we rode on horseback until I threw myself off the horse. I got sick and then blacked out."

"You fell off a horse too?" Dr. Thompson asked.

"I would describe it as throwing myself from the horse." Addison shrugged with her good shoulder causing the doctor to pinch the bridge of his nose. "I woke up in the Gracie's attic. Silas heard me moving around and came up. He asked me a few questions and then left. I closed the hatch door and piled everything I could on top of it to keep them downstairs." Addison looked up at Ashton. "Once I saw the sun rise, I climbed through the window and ran. I was hit from behind and I fell down a hill. Samuel rolled me to my back before sitting on me and pulling out a gun. I tried to grab it and we fought for it. The gun went off and Samuel fell forward. I wasn't sure if I was shot or if he was. Then Ashton came."

"Addison." Jack knelt in front of her and grabbed the hand that wasn't in a sling and squeezed it. "I am so sorry."

Addison gave her brother's hand a squeeze in return. People started to pair off into groups as they continued to talk about different things. Dr. and Mrs. Thompson were speaking with Jack while the detectives were talking with Daniel. Ashton couldn't believe everything Addison had gone through and the pain she must be in. She settled back against him again. She gasped softly and sucked in a quick breath.

"Addison?" He whispered, concerned she was causing herself more pain.

"I'm okay, Ash." Came her quiet response.

Ashton smiled as she used her nickname for him again. She was the only person who had ever called him that and he loved it. "What are your plans for the rest of the day?" he asked softly.

"Staying right here and taking a nap." She yawned. Ashton chuckled before placing a kiss to her head again. He would not mind staying here and taking a nap as well. Being able to feel her close, he felt like he could actually relax.

"I think we need to have a talk with the two of you." Ashton's father said and Ashton turned to him. His father had a stern expression on his face, but there was a twinkle in his eye.

"I agree." Jack said as he and the Thompsons walked closer.

"Before you do, Miss Addie, I gave Mary the instructions for the poultice for the bruises and the recipe for the tea that will help with the pain." Mrs. Thompson said as she smiled at Addison.

Dr. and Mrs. Thompson said their good-byes, and they left. Ten minutes after the Thompson's departure, the detectives left to check up on the progress at the cottage and the field. Ashton barely registered Jack's invitation for them to stay the night and their acceptance of it.

Ashton dozed with his cheek resting against the top of Addison's head. Her breathing had deepened not long after the Thompsons left, and he was sure she had fallen asleep.

A throat cleared and Ashton slowly opened his eyes to see his father, Jack and Daniel sitting across from him and Addison on their couch. He blinked a few times to clear his head and shifted into a more upright position. When he moved, Addison let out a groan before jumping slightly. She sat up more as she continued to keep her eyes on the three men watching her.

"Is everything okay?" she asked nervously as she glanced at Ashton. He must have had an equally confused look on his face because she turned her attention back to the occupants on the other couch.

"You tell me?" Jack asked calmly. Daniel looked like he was trying to fight a smile from surfacing.

"Considering you are the ones who woke me up and are staring at me like you expect me to say something specific; I think you should explain to me what you are wanting." Addison did her best to cross her arms, but her injured arm made it impossible.

Daniel lost his battle and began laughing. Ashton's father's eyes crinkled at the corners as he too fought against a smile. Ashton watched Jack, curious as to what all of this was about. His sleep deprived brain wasn't working very fast. Addison seemed put out and it made his own smile fight for release.

"Do you remember what I said when Daniel and I first got home?" Jack asked as he crossed his arms over his chest. Addison's brows furrowed in confusion. "I said you could not just jump into some man's arms. The same goes for cuddling on the couch with a man." Jack's voice was stern.

Addison scoffed. "Ash, isn't just some man." She said as she glared at her brother.

"If he isn't just a man, then who is he to you?" Jack asked curiously. Ashton too was very curious to hear her answer. What was he to her?

"That is a very broad question, Jack." Addison said with a lift of her eyebrow. When Jack remained silent, Addison continued. "To me he is Lord Ashton Fenwick. A man I mistook for my brother. He is the son of Lord and Lady Fenton and apparently a future earl. He is Daniel's best friend. Do I need to go on?" Ashton's father started laughing.

"Addison this is serious." Jack said with a scowl, even though Ashton could see the glint of humor in his eyes.

"If it is so serious Jack, why am I the only one getting asked these kinds of questions?" Addison shifted slightly further from Ashton, and he didn't like the distance she was creating.

"Daniel and I have already discussed this with Ashton." Jack smirked.

"Have you?" Addison asked in surprise. "Well, Lord Fenton and I weren't at such a meeting. Plus, I have already had a thorough discussion about this already with someone else." That got everyone's attention. Ashton wasn't sure that he liked the sound of her having this conversation with someone else. "I will ask again, Jack, what is all this about?"

Jack remained silent as he watched his sister through narrowed eyes. Ashton's own nervousness was rising. Did she not care for him like he cared for her? Who had she talked to and what was said?

"Joshua! Control him!" A woman shrieked from down the hall.

There was a loud bark and Joshua's grunt before a large black dog barreled into the room. Titan jumped on Addison, and she cried out. Ashton jumped off the couch and tried to pull Titan off of her, but her arm came around Titan's neck, keeping him there.

She started sobbing as she pressed her face into his side. Titan was whining and whimpering with his rearend wagging. Ashton sat back down. After several minutes before Titan laid down with his head in Addison's lap as he continued to whine.

Addison wiped her cheeks and sniffed. "I thought he killed him." She said as she stroked Titan's large head.

"He almost did. Dr. Thompson was able to remove the knife and get Titan back on his feet." Daniel said smiling at her. Addison ran her hand over the dog's side before tracing the scar with her finger. "He hasn't really been the same since, though. After Titan was able to move around more, he became Ashton's shadow while we were inside. He only goes outside to use the bathroom, but other than that he stays close by."

"Have you been good?" Addison asked Titan. The room fell silent except for Titan's occasional whine. Addison kept her attention on the dog while Ashton watched her. He was so glad that Titan was able to survive the stabbing.

Jack cleared his throat again, but Addison didn't look up at him. "Addison, how do you see your future?" He asked.

"Honestly, I do not know. My life has been nothing but lessons, then taking care of father, then running the estate and teaching the servants to read and write. I have not thought about my future in a very long time." Addison looked at Jack. "I have had to concentrate on surviving one day at a time."

"Have you never thought about getting married?" Daniel asked Addison with his brows furrowed.

"I did when I was young. Then father became ill." She took a deep breath. "Danny, my faith in the males of our species was shattered the week the three men that I loved most in the world left me. A day after that, my trust in men was broken when a man that I had trusted for years almost killed me. I was seventeen when I swore on father's grave that I would never allow another man to hurt me the way I was hurt before."

Ashton felt his heart breaking with each one of Addison's words. He didn't blame her for feeling the way she did, but it still hurt knowing the woman he loved could not love him back.

Chapter 20

"Addison." Jack said in a pained voice, but Addison cut him off.

"It is okay, Jack. Really it is." Addison said with a smile that did not reach her eyes. She felt Ashton stiffen beside her, but she kept her eyes on the guilty faces of Jack and Daniel. "Over the many weeks I was at Lakeview, I had a lot of time to think. I realized my eldest brother has terrible taste in friends. All of them were jerks and I secretly hoped someone would punch one of them or Titan would bite all of them. I also quickly realized that all I wanted to do was go home because I missed you all, despite Jack and Daniel being complete knuckleheads. It was hard knowing I could not go home because I was too terrified of those men finding me. I was heartbroken."

"Addie, we are so sorry. I should ha..." Daniel rushed on to say, but again Addison cut him off.

"When Lord and Lady Fenton arrived at Lakeview and Lady Fenton recognized me, I was scared she would contact you. I didn't want you to take me back home, not when the Drakes were still out there. She promised to keep my secret considering the state the housekeeper said I arrived in. We started riding every day. Tana was at first a handful, but she is learning quickly. I discovered she had been abused in the past. That is when I realized Tana and I were the same. We understand one another. We both had lost our trust in men.

"On our rides, I did a lot of self-reflection. When I made that promise on father's grave, I was very broken. I was barely walking around again after the break-in. Titan had just arrived, and Joshua accompanied me to the church because they did not think I could stay mounted the whole way. It was a very dark time for me. Working with Tana had me thinking back on my promise and I decided to amend it." Ashton shifted beside her. "I will never allow a man to break me like that again. I just need to find a man that will not break my heart, but protect it instead."

"Miss Addie, sorry for the interruption," Mary stepped into the drawing room. "But if you are feeling up to it, cook wishes to speak with you."

"Thank you, I will be right there." Addison tapped Titan's head and he got off her lap. She stood up and winced. She hated feeling so battered and bruised. "Fuss." She said, and Titan moved to her side.

Just before she walked from the room Daniel called after her. "What would a man have to do to prove to you that he would protect your heart?"

Addison paused in the doorway. "Hmm. That would be something he would have to figure out. Maybe outshoot me?" She smiled as she looked over her shoulder.

Daniel and Jack laughed. "Is there a man alive that has that ability?" Jack smiled. Addison glanced over at Ashton. He looked like he was in pain as he watched her. When Daniel and Jack turned back around, she winked at Ashton before stepping out into the hall.

Addison knew she made Ashton think that she did not see him as a potential husband. She didn't want to be the first to say how she felt. Sure, he had shown her that he cared for her by comforting her. He had even called her 'love' a few times, but he had never said he loved her or that he even wanted to marry her. She had heard many men in town, when she was younger, call women 'love' all the time without it meaning anything.

Titan licked her hand as they slowly walked down the hallway to the kitchen. Before she bared her heart, she needed him to make the first move.

She finally made it into the kitchen, her muscles stiffening more and more as time passed. Everyone was there. James and Joshua, Mrs. Harvey and Mary, Mrs. Jankins and all the maids.

"We wanted to welcome you home, Miss Addie." Mrs. Harvey beamed at her. Addison smiled and accepted the cook's gentle hug. "Now, what would you like me to make for dinner?"

"You don't have to go through all the trouble of doing that, Mrs. Harvey." Addison waved her off. She didn't want to make her do more work than she needed to.

"Nonsense, child. Those men have hardly eaten a thing since you disappeared. I was lucky if they ate more than once a day." Mrs. Harvey's frustration over that fact made Addison smile.

"In that case, why don't we have roasted chicken, carrots, potatoes, rolls, and a custard and scones." Addison said thoughtfully. "They really haven't been eating?" She asked. Daniel usually lived for food.

"No, Miss." Mary answered.

"Cover your ears." Once everyone had done so, Addison yelled. "Jack!" She smiled as four panicked men came running into the kitchen moments later. They looked around and their alarm changed to confusion. "Have you really not been eating?" Addison asked, placing her good hand on her hip as she glared at them.

"Geez, Addison. You gave us a heart attack." Jack snapped at her.

"Mrs. Harvey said you three haven't been eating." Addison persisted.

"So, you thought it was a good idea to give us all a panic attack?" Jack growled through clenched teeth.

"Mrs. Thompson said to not walk around much for a few days. Should I have walked back to the drawing room to yell at you there for not eating?" Addison bit the inside of her cheek to keep from smiling and scowled at her brother.

"I like her." Lord Fenton laughed as he moved to her and gave her a hug. "Be nice to him." He whispered before heading back to the door. "I think I am going to find the library." He called over his shoulder as he disappeared.

"Addie, none of us felt much like eating. We were worried about you. For weeks we weren't sure if you were even alive or not." Daniel said in their defense.

"Well mister, you are eating tonight. That is absolutely ridiculous for you to starve yourself because of me." Addison shook her head. "And did you not talk with Susan?"

"Well, we did, but only after she came storming into the dining hall and scolded us for not responding to her request." Daniel admitted, looking a bit embarrassed.

"How long did you wait?" Addison asked in surprise.

"We talked with her two weeks ago." Jack said quietly.

No wonder they were beside themselves with worry. Addison let out a tired sigh. "I'm going to go rest for a little bit until it is dinner time."

She slowly made her way past them and out into the hall. She planned on going to see Spartan but wanted to change into her riding pants first. She stopped at the base of the stairs and looked up. There were so many stairs.

Titan nudged her hand, and she looked down at him before looking back up the stairs. Her leg was hurting, and she was not sure she could make it up the stairs on her own.

"Addison?" Ashton asked as he walked up to her. Addison turned to him, and he looked at the stairs before looking back to her. His eyes held uncertainty in them. "Would you like some help?" he finally asked.

"Yes, please." Addison sighed in relief. He gave her a crooked grin as he stepped close to her.

Her heart rate picked up as she stared into his eyes. Ashton moved slowly as he carefully lifted her into his arms. She winced slightly as she tried to lift her injured arm to put it around Ashton's neck. She let out a frustrated sigh.

At the top of the stairs, Ashton set her down. "Thank you." She whispered.

"Anytime, Addison." Ashton said softly as he kept one arm around her back. Addison was tempted to raise up on her toes and kiss him, but she didn't think her leg would agree to that plan. Ashton reached up and tucked a strand of hair behind her ear. "I need to go talk with my father. I will see you later?"

Addison was disappointed but nodded her head. He hesitated as his gaze dropped to her lips. Addison held her breath, but Ashton took a step back, gave her a nod, and then walked away.

Addison's heart was racing as she turned in the opposite direction and headed for her room. It took much longer to get dressed than she thought it would. Her bruises were darkening by the minute and her sore muscles protested every move.

Mary had brought up some of the tea the doctor had left for her to help with the pain, but she declined. Mary did not look happy as she left the room. Addison headed for the servant's stairs with Titan. At least those stairs were closer to the back door.

It took twice the time it normally did to walk across the yard to the stables. Joshua came running up to her but stopped before reaching her. He moved slowly as he hugged her. They chatted for several minutes as Addison stroked Spartan's head.

Joshua seemed skeptical when she led Spartan from his stall. She told Joshua she would be fine and tapped Spartan's front leg. The large stallion laid down and she climbed on.

She gasped as her sore hip twinged, but she grabbed hold of his mane with her one hand, determined to ride. She had missed Spartan. Addison clicked her tongue and he got to his feet. She fought the tears that stung her eyes. Her body was screaming at her, not liking the abrupt movement.

"Miss Addie? Maybe you should give it a few days." Joshua's voice was full of worry.

"I am not planning on doing anything crazy. I am only planning on walking a little." Addison smiled down at Joshua before letting Spartan walk from the stables.

Addison closed her eyes and concentrated on breathing. Spartan was moving slow, but her body didn't like the uneven movement. After thirty minutes, Spartan came to a stop. Addison looked around. They were in the middle of the closest field to the house. She could still see the house and stables.

Spartan laid down and Addison slid off his back and settled on the ground with her back resting against Spartan's side. Titan laid down next to her with his head in her lap. Addison closed her eyes and breathed in the familiar scent of grass, Spartan, and Titan.

She didn't know how long she was there before Titan let out a happy bark. Addison opened her eyes and saw Ashton walking towards her.

"You weren't lying about Titan taking a liking to you." Addison said once he was close enough to hear her without her yelling.

Ashton gave her a smile as he crouched down and gave Titan a pat on his head. "He is a good dog. But he much prefers you." Ashton stood back up and put his hands behind his back. Addison didn't think she had ever seen him so unsure of himself. He was always so confident, and he always seemed to know what to do.

"If you are planning on staying, please have a seat. It hurts my neck to look up." Addison smiled at him, and he took a seat quickly next to her. They fell into silence and Ashton started tapping his leg with his fingers. Was he nervous? "Was your conversation with my brothers as awkward as mine was?" she asked as she glanced at him.

He laughed but did not look at her. "Mine was very different from yours." Addison turned to fully look at him. He glanced at her before he looked back out over the field. "Mary said you refused to drink the tea to help with your pain."

Addison rolled her eyes. "I know what that tea does to me. I had it after my encounter with Mr. Drake. It makes me tired, and I do not want to fall asleep right now." Addison said. "And the pain isn't that bad."

"Joshua seemed to think it was." His voice had softened.

Addison sighed. "Compared to a stubbed toe, yes, it's bad. But compared to last time, it is not bad at all." Addison glanced over and he was studying her. "How was your conversation different? They didn't ask about your future or thoughts on marriage?"

"You're not going to drop this, are you?" Ashton wiped his hands on his pants. Addison shook her head with a smile. "No, they didn't ask me about my future or thoughts on marriage."

"That seems a bit unfair." Addison mumbled under her breath.

"Daniel already knew the answers and pretty much told Jack my views." Ashton said evasively. Addison wanted to know the answers. Was he intentionally frustrating her? "What caused you to amend your promise to your father?" Ashton asked.

"I don't plan on revealing all my secrets today, my Lord." Addison smirked at him.

"What happened to calling me 'Ash'?" Ashton asked her while turning to face her.

"Do I?" Addison asked, pretending to not know what he was talking about.

"Never mind." He cleared his throat.

Addison let out a frustrated sigh. She just wanted to know how he truly felt about her. He was always kind and comforting to her. He held her and kissed her. He came after her when she was kidnapped, but she needed to hear how he felt about her.

Addison turned her attention to the field of long grass. The blades danced in the light breeze that blew around them. She took a deep breath and let it out on a sigh. "It's beautiful out here, isn't it?" she asked quietly.

"It sure is." Ashton said and she turned to look at him. He was watching her, and her cheeks heated.

Addison quickly turned her gaze back to the field. They lapsed back into silence for several minutes. "What does your future look like?" she finally asked.

Ashton was quiet for so long that Addison wasn't sure he was going to answer. She was too nervous to even look at him. She still could not believe she had actually asked him that question. It was not a very smart thing to do. If she could move normally, she would get up and leave, but he would easily catch her if she tried in her current state.

Titan got up and ran off after some birds and the quiet between them was broken by his barking and the calls from the birds. Addison finally mustered the courage to turn and look at Ashton.

Ashton was watching her with an intensity in his eyes that she had often seen, and her heart rate increased. "I'm looking at it." he said softly. Addison sucked in her breath and held it as she searched his face. "I love you, Addison. And I will do whatever it takes to prove to you that I will never break your heart." He swallowed hard. Addison rotated onto her knees and winced as pain shot up her hip. Ashton looked alarmed as he reached for her. "Addison don't move. Please, I do not want you hurting yourself."

"Are you serious?" Addison asked, ignoring him grabbing her arms.

"Of course, I'm serious, I don't want you to hurt yourself more." He was looking at her with a hurt expression on his face.

"No, the other part." Addison continued to watch his face carefully. She desperately wanted it to be true but was worried she had misheard him.

His expression softened and his dimple appeared as a small smile tugged at his lips. "Every word, Addison. I love you and I want you to be my future." A tear slipped from Addison's eye. He reached up and cupped her face as he used his thumb to wipe it away. Addison closed her eyes and leaned into his touch. "Am I to assume you aren't scared of me now?"

Addison laughed and looked at him. "Not even close." She said and Ashton pulled her head towards his. His lips pressed against hers in a sweet kiss. Addison went to put her arms around his neck but gasped as pain shot through her shoulder. Ashton pulled back with a concerned look. "It was just my shoulder. I forgot it was hurt."

"You forgot your shoulder was hurt?" Ashton shook his head in disbelief. "Maybe we should get you back to the house so you can have some of the tea the doctor left."

"Do we have to?" Addison asked. She was disappointed they couldn't stay out longer. She just learned Ashton loved her and all she wanted to do was stay in this happy bubble.

Ashton chuckled. "Yes, love. We have to head back." Ashton got to his feet and helped Addison get to hers. "I think we should walk back. Riding takes more muscles than walking does." He grabbed Addison's hand as he began walking towards the house.

"What about Titan? He took off after the birds." Addison stopped walking. She did not want to go back yet and would use any excuse to delay their return. "We should go look for him."

Ashton let out a whistle and Titan came running towards them. He gave her hand a squeeze as he continued to walk. Addison gave up on delaying their return. She stayed quiet and just enjoyed Ashton's hand in hers.

By the time they got to the stables to return Spartan, Addison was limping. Joshua gave her a look as he led Spartan into the stall. As they left the stables, she knew the moment Ashton noticed her limp because he started glancing at her more frequently as they walked back to the house.

"Ash, wait." Addison said as she stopped. She was breathing hard. Walking had been more difficult than she had thought it would be. Her leg was throbbing with pain.

"I'll carry you the rest of the way." Ashton let go of her hand as he picked her up.

This time she was able to put her good arm around the back of his neck as he carried her inside. He was climbing the stairs when Addison started to run her fingers through the hair at the base of his neck.

"If you keep doing that, I'm going to trip." Ashton whispered in her ear.

Addison bit her lip to keep herself from laughing. They reached the top of the stairs, but Ashton didn't put her down. He continued to carry her towards her room. He stopped several feet from it and set her down.

As soon as her feet were on the ground, his lips were on hers. The sound of a door opening had him pulling back. Mary stepped into the hall from Addison's room and stopped when she saw them.

"Mary, I think I am ready for that tea now." Addison said with a smile.

"Yes, Miss." Mary said, and she hurried away.

"Did you only say that to get her to leave?" Ashton asked softly.

Addison turned back to Ashton who was smiling at her. "Partly." Addison admitted as she felt herself blush. "And I really am ready for it."

"Are you in a lot of pain then?" Ashton's teasing expression turned serious.

"Ash, I am going to be hurting for several weeks. It is part of the healing process and the sooner you stop worrying over every wince or gasp of pain, the easier the next few weeks will be." Addison gave him a hard look.

"What can I do to make it easier for you?" Ashton asked while searching her face.

Addison reached up and brushed some of his hair off his forehead. She took a deep breath and held it. She knew it was going to hurt, but she did it anyway. Addison rose up on her toes and gave Ashton a quick kiss on the lips. "You've been doing it. Just keep me from overtaxing myself."

Addison took a step back and towards her door. Just before she walked in, she turned back around. Ashton was still standing where she had left him. He was watching her. She smiled at him. "Thank you for carrying me up the stairs, love." Addison stepped into her room, closed the door, and locked it.

The handle jiggled and Addison laughed quietly. "Addison, open the door." Ashton called through the wood. He tried the handle again, but the door remained closed. "You can't say something like that and walk away."

Addison unlocked the door and opened it slowly. Ashton stood there with both hands braced on either side of the door. "I can't say you are doing a good job at keeping me from overdoing it?" Addison asked.

"I thought you called me 'love'." Ashton said as his eyes bore into her.

"I did, what?" Addison asked as she furrowed her brows.

Ashton squeezed his eyes closed. "Please don't toy with me, Addison." He whispered.

Addison pushed on his chest gently and his eyes flew open as he took a step back. She followed him into the hall as she continued to push him farther back. He kept his eyes on her the whole time. Once they were in the center of the hallway, Addison stopped. She glanced down the hallway quickly.

"You asked me a question in the field that I refused to answer." Ashton nodded his head slowly, but a look of confusion crossed his face. "You asked me what caused me to amend my promise to my father." Addison said.

"As much as I would love to hear why you amended your promise, I need to know if I heard you correctly." Ashton said as he clenched his jaw.

Addison studied Ashton's face as they stood silently. His gaze seemed to be searching her face for the answers he sought. A throat cleared and Addison jumped. She glanced to the side to see Mary standing nearby with a tea tray. Mary looked unsure if she should continue into the room or wait.

"Thank you, Mary. You can take that into the room. I will be there in a minute." Mary quickly entered Addison's room. She closed the door enough to give them some privacy, but left it cracked open for propriety.

When Addison turned back to Ashton, he was still watching her. Addison carefully took her sling off. Her shoulder felt tight and a little sore, but not too bad at the moment. "I don't think you should be doing that." Ashton protested.

Addison placed her hands on Ashton's chest, stopping his protests. She slipped her hands up until her arms were around his neck. He swallowed hard as he continued to watch her.

She ran her fingers through the hair on the back of his neck and he dipped his head. Right before his lips touched hers, Addison pulled back slightly, and Ashton froze. There were so many questions in his eyes.

"Ash?" She barely spoke above a whisper.

She watched him swallow again. "Yes?" His voice was equally soft.

Addison moved one hand from the back of his neck so she could run her fingers along his jawline. He hadn't shaved in several days and she was amazed at the roughness of the scruff there. When she returned her gaze to Ashton's eyes, his ocean blues were a tempest of emotions.

"*You* caused me to amend my promise." Addison said before pressing her lips to his. She felt him smile against her lips as he put his arms around her and gently pulled her to him. Addison leaned back slightly. "I should probably go; Mary is…" Ashton pressed his lips to hers, cutting off whatever she was going to say.

Ashton finally pulled back enough to rest his forehead against hers. "You are going to be the death of me, you know that?" He muttered.

"I think you mean to say that I keep you on your toes." Addison corrected with a smile.

Ashton gave her a quick kiss before putting more distance between them. "I think we need to talk about the future."

"How so?" Addison asked.

"I already told you that I see you as my future. I am hoping to make that future happen as quickly as possible."

"Are you asking me to marry you?" Addison asked with a raise of her eyebrow. She tried to keep a calm demeanor even though her heart was nearly beating out of her chest.

"I am asking you to marry me, hopefully in the next couple days, if Jack and I can procure a special license." Ashton clarified.

"I guess that's quick enough." Addison took a step back and her hip caused her to stumble.

Ashton caught her and gave her a stern look. "You go drink that tea the doctor left for you and get some rest. I will go talk with Jack and Daniel." He pressed a kiss to her cheek before he turned and headed down the hallway.

Addison entered her room to find Mary grinning ear to ear. She handed Addison a cup of tea as Addison sat carefully on the bed.

Chapter 21

Addison woke a little disoriented. Her mind felt consumed by a thick fog as she looked around the room. She blinked several more times trying to clear her mind. After a few minutes, the fog began to lift.

Titan lay on the bed next to her and she lifted her arm to run a hand over his head, but a twinge of pain in her shoulder stopped her. Titan lifted his head off her chest and looked at her.

"I'm okay, boy." Addison smiled at her faithful companion. She had missed him so much over the last several weeks and could not express how grateful she was that he was still alive. "Shall we let you outside?" She asked and Titan stood and stretched.

Addison groaned as she sat up. Her body protested every movement. She knew she should probably stay in bed for a little while longer, but she didn't feel comfortable in this room.

She slowly got dressed while Titan lay on the bed and watched her every move. Her shoulder was even more sore and stiff today than before, so she left her hair down, settling for just brushing the tangles out. Letting out a sigh, Addison slowly stood from her vanity.

She stiffly walked to the door and Titan moved to her side. It took her longer than the day before to move down the servants' stairs, but she made it without having to rest. She opened the door and Titan hesitantly moved outside. She closed the door and faced Mrs. Harvey.

"Can you let Titan back in when he is ready?" Addison asked.

"Of course, Miss. But shouldn't you be up in bed?" Mrs. Harvey watched her with a worried expression. "You look like you need some more rest."

"Thank you for your concern, Mrs. Harvey, but I am well." Addison gave the cook a smile. "I am going to the drawing room, and I will rest there."

Mrs. Harvey grudgingly nodded her head as Addison headed for the door. Addison saw the look of concern on the older woman's face as Addison slowly and gingerly made her way out of the kitchen.

By the time she made it to the drawing room, Addison was exhausted. She carefully lowered herself down on the couch that sat nearest the fire. A groan escaped her lips as she settled back, her hip protesting the movement.

Titan came trotting into the room not long after she finally found a comfortable position. He settled at her feet on the other end of the couch, and she let out a sigh of contentment. Addison closed her eyes and she felt herself relax as she drew closer to sleep.

A knock at the front door caused Addison's eyes to fly open. Her heart rate picked up as thoughts of Silas and Samuel coming after her slammed into her. She knew they were both dead, but the fear was still there.

A loud commotion in the entryway sounded and Addison was sure something was dreadfully wrong. She moved to a sitting position.

"Pass auf." Addison whispered as she heard raised voices through the open drawing room door. Titan stood in front of her, alert for any danger. Addison strained to hear what was being said as the voices moved closer.

"Please, My Lady. Wait here and I will get Lord Blackwell for you." A male voice said.

"I will see Miss Blackwell immediately." A female voice snapped back.

"What is going on here?" Jack's voice entered the fray. His voice was loud and commanding. Addison wished she could go see for herself who was there to see her and why.

"My Lord, her ladyship is demanding..." The first male voice started to say, but he was interrupted.

"I will see Miss Blackwell immediately." The woman demanded again.

"Mother?" Ashton's surprised voice reached her ears. The angry woman was Lady Fenton? Addison had never heard the woman so much as raise her voice, let alone angrily demanding things.

"We can set you up in your husband's room with him, but as for seeing Addison, that is impossible at the moment." Jack said sternly. "She has been through a lot and has been asleep for two days. The doctor has said she needs the rest, so no one will be disturbing her."

"I need to see my girl." Lady Fenton pressed. "I won't wake her. I just need to know she is all right."

"Mother, please. Jack hasn't allowed anyone but Addison's maid into the room. Dr. Thompson has assured us that Addison should be waking soon." Ashton sounded tired.

Addison attempted to stand, but immediately regretted it. A spasm of pain shot through her hip, and she let out a soft gasp. Titan let out a bark as he turned to look at her. Addison closed her eyes and breathed through the pain.

She vaguely heard the sound of people running into the room. Hands cupped her face, and she opened her eyes. Bright blue eyes full of worry looked back at her.

"Addie? Where does it hurt?" Ashton asked, studying her face.

The pain had finally dulled to just an ache, and she let out the breath she didn't realize she had been holding. "I'm all right." Addison breathed. Ashton's hands dropped to hers as he bowed his head, resting his forehead on their hands. Titan watched everyone closely. "Platz." She commanded, and he laid down at her feet next to where Ashton was kneeling.

"Addie, how did you get down here? When did you wake up? How are you feeling?" Danny asked as he moved to her side.

"I have been awake for hours. It took me a while to make my way down here, but as you can see, I am just fine." Addison smiled at her brother. Ashton moved to sit on the seat beside her and she gave him a smile as well.

"My dear, I have been so worried." Lady Fenton moved to the couch across from Addison, since Ashton sat on one side of her and Danny sat on the other. "I have been beside myself with worry since my husband and son have neglected to inform me of your condition."

"I am as well as I can be, Lady Fenton. I am sorry that they have neglected to keep you informed." Addison gave the woman a big smile.

"You look dreadful, Addie." Danny said beside her. "Are you sure you should be up?" Addison turned to see her brother watching her closely.

"If I stay in bed all day, my body will become stiff with disuse." Addison reached over to pat Daniel's leg, but winced as her shoulder protested the movement.

"Your body needs to heal, Addison." Jack said. "Dr. Thompson said you should be in bed for at least a few weeks."

"A few weeks?" Addison said loudly. "I will not stay in bed for weeks, Jack. I have the estate to take care of and Spartan..."

"No, Addison." Jack interrupted her. "I have the estate to run, and Ashton has been exercising Spartan daily. Your job is to rest and recover." Jack had crossed his arms over his chest as he glared at her.

Just then a footman entered the room and crossed to Jack. "My Lord." The footman bowed as he offered Jack several letters.

Jack glanced through them before stopping at one. He quickly opened it and scanned its contents. After a minute of silence, he looked up at Ashton and Daniel as a smile spread across his lips. "The correspondence that we have been waiting for has just arrived."

Ashton smiled as Daniel jumped to his feet. "I will send for..." Danny stopped speaking before he finished his sentence as he moved to the door. "I need to send a quick note." He quickly disappeared and Addison furrowed her brow.

She looked between Ashton and Jack as she waited for them to explain. They remain silent. "What is going on?" she finally asked.

"There is nothing for you to worry about, Addison. We have it all taken care of." Jack said. "Lady Fenton, I will inform the housekeeper that you will be staying." He bowed and left the room.

"Are you truly well, my dear? Last I heard you were in a tenant cottage with the men that stole you from our home." Lady Fenton asked in concern.

Addison nodded as she sagged back against the couch. Her side spasmed and she hissed in pain. A moment later her body began to relax again, and she let out a tense breath. Ashton began filling his mother in on all that had happened. Addison laid her head on Ashton's shoulder and closed her eyes as she listened to the conversation between mother and son.

"I am so glad she is all right." Lady Fenton said in a quiet voice. "But she looks quite pale, and she seems to be in pain."

"Unfortunately, Addison's injuries will require quite a bit of time to fully heal. This morning was the first time she has been awake in two days. She is quite lucky to be alive." Ashton responded just as quietly.

"I like her very much, Ashton." Lady Fenton stated.

"I gathered as much from your sudden arrival and concern for her." Ashton said lightly.

"I have half a mind to insist you marry her after kissing her in our drawing room. That kind of behavior can ruin a woman's reputation, Ashton." Lady Fenton didn't sound like she was teasing.

Addison blinked her eyes open, but neither Lady Fenton nor Ashton noticed she was awake. "You would force me to marry her?" Ashton asked with a bit of a laugh in his voice. "Since only you, father and Addison's brothers were witness to the kiss, it should be easy enough to keep quiet. Plus, Jack and Daniel forgave me for such a display of relief in finding Addison safe." Ashton said indifferently.

"Yes, but I can insist on the marriage. I admit I wanted to introduce you two in hopes that you would form an attachment."

"Leave the boy alone, dear." Lord Fenton said. Addison glanced to the door as Lord Fenton and Jack entered the room. "No one will be forcing a marriage. Miss Blackwell is engaged already."

Lady Fenton gasped. "Engaged? To whom?"

"I am sorry, Lady Fenton, but that is something that is not going to be discussed at this time. It does not matter anyway; my sister will be marrying the man she is already promised to." Jack said as he gave her a wink before taking a seat.

Addison sat up with a groan and everyone turned to her. After several moments of silence, Jack pulled the Fentons into conversation. Addison felt Ashton lean close to her. "Do you need more tea?" Ashton whispered close to her ear. Addison shook her head and he scowled at her. "You are in pain and need it."

Addison turned her head to look at him. In doing so their faces were mere inches apart. "I don't wish to go back to sleep just yet."

Ashton's expression softened. "Addie..."

"He will be here within the hour." Daniel announced as he came into the room with a wide grin.

Addison leaned back away from him with a furrowed brow. "Who is?" Addison asked, turning her attention to her brother.

"Just a dinner guest, Addie. Not to worry." Danny waved a hand in the air as if to say it didn't matter. But it did matter to her. She still felt out of sorts around strange men, and they were going to have another one over for dinner. "Ashton why don't you help me get Addison and Titan up to bed so they can rest for a little bit before dinner."

Before Addison could protest, Ashton had swept her up into his arms. As they headed for the stairs, Ashton rubbed the tip of his nose along her cheek and back to the sensitive skin behind her ear. He pressed his lips to her neck, and she bit her lip to keep from giggling.

"Oh, how I have missed you these past days. Jack would not let me in to see you." Ashton whispered into her ear.

A throat cleared behind them and Addison realized they had stopped at the bottom of the stairs. Ashton leaned back with a smile before continuing to her room.

Instead of putting Addison on the bed, like she thought he would, Ashton set her on her feet. He kept his arms around her to support her while she found her balance. Once she was no longer swaying, Ashton pressed his lips to hers and Addison sighed.

"Can you please stop." Daniel's voice sounded near the bedroom door. "As happy as I am that you two are happy, I would prefer not to see my best friend kissing my sister like that." Addison laughed and Ashton smiled as he helped her lay down on the bed.

After the spasm of pain subsided and she was able to relax, she looked back at her brother and Ashton. Daniel hovered by the door while Ashton looked torn between leaving and staying. Danny let out a dramatic sigh. "I guess I will stay as chaperone so that Ashton can stay with you, Addie."

Addison sent her brother a grateful smile as Ashton settled into a chair next to her bed. She closed her eyes and let out a long breath. She was so tired. Addison allowed herself to relax. It felt like no time had passed when she heard footsteps near her door.

"How is she?" Jack asked quietly.

"She seems to be resting peacefully with Ashton close. And Ashton seems to finally be sleeping as well." Danny's voice was equally quiet.

"Well, it's time to go downstairs. Wake them up and I will let everyone know you all will be down in ten minutes." Jack said as he left the room.

A hand gently touched her shoulder and Addison slowly opened her eyes. Danny stood above her, and she gave him a small smile. "It's time to get up. Jack is sending Mary up to help you dress for dinner."

"Is there a reason I must be there for dinner? I thought you said I needed to rest?" Addison yawned as she looked over at Ashton. He was asleep in the chair with his hand holding hers.

"Trust me, you are needed downstairs for dinner. Now, let's wake up Ashton." Danny moved to Ashton's side.

He shook his friend's shoulder and Ashton jolted awake. Ashton's hand tightened around hers before he registered where he was. His grip relaxed.

"Come on, Ashton. Jack just let me know that our guest has arrived, and it is time for you two to get dressed and head downstairs." Daniel started heading for the door but paused just before stepping into the hall and looking back at Ashton expectantly.

Ashton looked over to her with a crooked smile. He stood and leaned over her. He pressed a lingering kiss to her forehead before following Danny to the door. He glanced back one more time before disappearing into the hallway. Mary came rushing in with a big smile on her face.

* * *

It took more than twenty minutes for Addison to get dressed into the ivory evening gown that Mary set out. It was an empire waist gown and Mary was just tying a sage green ribbon around Addison's waist when a knock came at the door.

Mary opened the door, letting in Jack and Daniel. They both wore smiles and Addison's suspicions grew. "Are you ready, Addison?" Jack asked.

"Ready for what?" Addison asked, moving slowly towards them. Her body felt stiff and sore as she walked.

"Dinner, of course." Daniel had a mischievous glint in his eyes that Addison had learned a long time ago, not to trust. Something was happening and she had no idea what it could be.

"And I need two escorts because...?" Addison let her question hang in the air hoping to get an answer.

Instead of answering, Jack stepped to her side and lifted his arm for her to take. She let out a resigned sigh and placed her hand on her brother's arm. As they stepped out into the hall, Daniel fell in step on Addison's other side.

They moved slowly for Addison's sake, and the stairs took a huge amount of her stamina. When they reached the bottom of the stairs, Jack's hand covered hers on his arm and gave it a gentle squeeze.

Addison was confused when they stepped towards the sitting room instead of the dining hall, but she did not question her brothers. When they stepped through the door, her breath caught in her lungs.

Standing across the room near the fireplace was Ashton. On Ashton's right stood the vicar and on his other side stood his father. All three men watched her enter with smiles on their faces. Lady Fenton stood from her spot on the couch, at their entrance.

Addison started to smile as she thought that the scene in front of her resembled a wedding. Her smile and steps froze as realization dawned. This was a wedding. Her wedding.

Addison started to laugh as tears filled her eyes. Danny leaned down to her ear and whispered. "Are you ready?"

Addison looked up at her brother, who was beaming down at her. She turned to look at Jack, who wore a matching expression and she nodded. They walked her slowly across the room before they took turns pressing a kiss to her cheek. Jack passed her hand over to Ashton before her brothers stepped back, leaving her standing with Ashton in front of the vicar.

The ceremony went by quickly and before Addison knew it, Ashton pressed a chaste kiss to her lips and Lady Fenton clapped excitedly. They moved their celebration into the dining room for dinner.

Halfway through the meal, Addison's smile began to slip. Her hip was throbbing and all she wanted to do was lie on her bed. She was pushing her food around her plate when Ashton covered her hand with his.

"Let's get you upstairs so you can rest." He whispered in her ear. Addison nodded and Ashton got to his feet. He pulled her chair back from the table and helped her stand. "Addison needs to rest. We will see you in the morning." Ashton addressed the room as he grabbed Addison's hand.

Addison slowly followed Ashton from the room and down the hallway. As soon as they made it to the stairs, Ashton swept Addison into his arms. She sucked in a quick breath as pain shot up her hip. Addison put her arms around Ashton's neck and took several deep breaths.

"I'm sorry, love." Ashton pressed a kiss to her cheek before heading up the stairs. Once in Addison's room, Ashton set Addison down on the bench next to the vanity.

A soft knock sounded at the door before Mary entered. Ashton stepped out into the hall so Mary could help Addison change into her night dress. When Mary left and Ashton reentered, Addison gave a tired smile. Ashton walked over to her side and helped her stand.

Once she got to her feet, she turned to face him. Ashton smiled down at Addison as he cupped her face. He leaned down and kissed her slowly. When Ashton finally pulled back, he leaned his forehead down to rest against hers. "I love you, Addison Fenwick."

"And I love you, Ash." Addison whispered just before Ashton's lips reclaimed hers.

THE END

www.ingramcontent.com/pod-product-compliance
Lightning Source LLC
LaVergne TN
LVHW010323070526
838199LV00065B/5644